The Guns of Dallas

The Guns of Dallas

Douglas Herman

Aventine Press

© May 2005, Douglas Herman
First Edition

Without limiting the rights under copyright reserved above, no part of this publication may be reproduced, stored in or introduced into a retrieval system, or transmitted, in any form or by any means (electronic, mechanical, photocopying, recording, or otherwise), without the prior written permission of both the copyright owner and the publisher of this book.

Published by Aventine Press
1023 4th Ave #204
San Diego CA, 92101
www.aventinepress.com

ISBN: 1-59330-276-2

Printed in the United States of America

ALL RIGHTS RESERVED

For my sisters, who believed in me,
and helped see this project through.
Kate, Lisa, Sheila, Trish & Laurie

"In an age of universal deceit, telling the truth is a revolutionary act."

---George Orwell

"1963 marked a major turning point in this century because the power elite moved that year to remove John F. Kennedy from the White House and to take the course of the Ship of State into their own hands."

---CIA liaison, Colonel Fletcher Prouty
JFK: The CIA, Vietnam and the Plot to Assassinate John F. Kennedy

"The Central Intelligence Agency owns everyone of any significance in the major media."

----William Colby, former Director, CIA

Chapter 1

Daniel Pilgrim sat at his desk and stared at the monitor. Wordless, the screen resembled a snow swept Minnesota field in December and seemed to stretch forever, sweeping over his mind, likewise blank, an appearance altogether without hope or horizon.

"Congratulations, Mr. Pilgrim," said an intern in passing.

Pilgrim neither turned nor responded. What were prizes or accolades, fame or acclaim, but vanity, stumbling blocks actually? Yesterday's accomplishments accounted for nothing, he decided. He stared at the screen and strained to see a story, better than any he had ever written before.

"You shoulda won," said Bobby Smith, ambling into Pilgrim's cubicle. "Goddamn Pulitzer committee musta had their collective heads up their collegiate asses."

Fifteen years ago Bobby Smith spun out of Liberty City and shifted into high gear at the University of Miami as a running back before destroying his knee and dropping out of school. Bobby still retained an edginess that appealed to Pilgrim and, besides, created some fine photographs for the South Florida Sun Satellite akin to Weegee's best work. Not that anyone knew who Weegee was anymore. That was the problem with fame; it was too damn fleeting and undervalued in direct relation to its merit.

"My brother thinks it would make a decent book," said Pilgrim, not entirely convinced.

"Maybe it would, if you padded it out." Bobby sipped a cup of coffee the same color as his skin: walnut brown from the heartwood. "But then again, one feather in your cap don't make a headdress and one three-part series on police corruption in South Florida, however good enough to get nominated for a Pulitzer, might not make a bestseller. I believe you still got better stuff in you yet, chief."

"Thanks, but it still sounds like envy to me," said Pilgrim.

The intern returned. "You have a visitor, sir, maybe your father, I don't know and he wouldn't say."

The two newsmen exchanged a look.

"Unless your father rose from the dead, it probably ain't him," said Smith. "But damn if it wouldn't make a fine story."

"Maybe even a decent book," deadpanned Pilgrim.

As a reporter, Pilgrim met a wide range of men. Most had a story to tell; few had anything newsworthy to say. Still, with a weekly column to write for the Sun Satellite and the occasional longer piece, he met everyone and discounted no one. The stripper who initiated, *Broward's Finest Fleece Fallen Angels*, which led to the three-part series and a Pulitzer nod, met him by chance at a Laundromat. As a reporter, you just never knew who- or what-- your next story looked like.

The man who slipped around the corner of his cubicle resembled a ghost attired in Salvation Army garb: gray sport jacket patched at the elbows over a shabby black shirt and stained khaki trousers suitable for an Irish, inner-city minister on a tight budget. Pilgrim half expected to see a clerical collar.

"Daniel Pilgrim?" he said, his hair a grizzled gray, his handshake firm yet veins visible like game trails on the back of each palm. The reporter noticed a gaze that seemed to sweep his entire cubicle without once leaving his face.

Pilgrim shifted uneasily and wondered if his guest might be a retired cop. After his investigative series he had received several, thinly veiled death threats but that was months ago.

"I'm Dan Pilgrim and you are?"

"I'll get to that soon enough, but first, let me tell you how much I admire your work."

"Thanks."

"I apologize for busting in like this--May I sit down?" He took a seat and stared at the reporter. "I'm not used to talking about myself but you seem able to, well, get to the meat of a story. I've been reading your stuff for years. I enjoyed that expose' you did a while back about the shakedown of strip clubs by that posse of local cops. Probably you got a lot more stories like it already lined up."

Pilgrim glanced at the blank screen. Maybe a story idea would come to him at lunchtime. His editor always seemed to have a surplus of leads.

"Well, I am kind of busy at the moment."

"I don't doubt that; like I said I really enjoy reading your work. Not just your newspaper columns but your other stuff."

Pilgrim stiffened. Few knew about the "other stuff", not that he was ashamed. Was he a cop?

"I read your stories on the Internet, that weird historical stuff the newspapers don't seem to print, the harder more interesting stuff."

"Like what?" he looked at his watch.

"You got some things figured out. Like that piece you wrote entitled, 'The Short Life and Sudden Death of the World Trade Towers.' My daughter pointed that out to me. She writes art reviews for that same website you do and that's why I decided to look you up."

"I'm flattered."

"You also did a piece on the CIA, very entertaining and readable."

"I didn't catch your name?" Pilgrim caught the eye of Smith sauntering past and Bobby did a quick turn and posted himself in the doorway.

"Jeremiah," he glanced once at the imposing photographer. "You can call me Jimmy Jeremiah. Not my real name but more like a cryptonym, which you might want to use if you do my story."

Pilgrim tried not to look skeptical. "And just what is your story?"

"I once worked for the government long ago."

Smith looked bored, turning away at the sound of his telephone.

"Lots of people worked for the government." Pilgrim feigned interest. "What makes your work so different or newsworthy?"

"Forty years ago I shot a man--an important man--while working for the government and lately I been thinking about it more and more."

The reporter straightened but said nothing for a moment, expecting more.

"Then you, uh, got away with it, or did you get caught and do time?"

Pilgrim, more than a little grateful he faced a former felon rather than a former cop, wondered if the old fellow's reticence concealed shame or mistrust.

"O sure we got away with it."

"We?"

"We--Us--." Flustered, the words issued out and Pilgrim wondered if he should be taping them. "Us--Me--What difference does that make? I'm the one doing the talking here not them."

"So you, Mr. Jeremiah, shot an 'important man', as you called him, forty years ago--that's a long time ago—"

"Not so long ago it doesn't seem like century of yesterdays."

"Shot and killed?"

"DOA."

Pilgrim met murderers and men who talked of murder but most of the ones he met were young. Maybe murder, the physical act, was a young man's work while remorse was reserved for old age.

"How old are you, Mr. Jeremiah?"

"Call me Jimmy. I'm 65."

Eligible long ago for senior discounts and social security checks, he hardly resembled a murderer, thought Pilgrim, fingers resting on his keyboard. More like a retired clerk, cleric or cop come to Florida for the sun and since bored with shuffleboard and now here with a story fabricated from too many long hours alone.

"You know there's no statute of limitations on murder?"

"I know." A glimmer of a smile brightened the gaunt blackbird's face. "According to the VA I have no more than maybe a year to live, maybe less."

"So who was he--this important man?"

"John F. Kennedy."

Chapter 2

Remember the dead.

The memory of incense permeated the air and somewhere in the distant eaves, above him in the loft over the sanctuary and confessional boxes of the Catholic Church, a men's choir practiced. The church was empty, the way he liked it. The way he remembered it. Jimmy stood before a statue of a saint to the left of the altar, not sure any more whether he stood before an apostle or martyr. He lit a succession of devotional candles and lingered, watching the light dapple his hands. The timelessness of sanctified dead; every religion or culture shared in the adoration of worthy souls spanning not centuries but millennia; fallen heroes. They were what most men aspired to be but would never become.

Remember the dead.

Daniel Pilgrim scrolled down the names of "convenient deaths" listed on a website devoted to the JFK assassination. Jimmy Jeremiah had shown him the website before he left. Pilgrim stared at the screen, slowly scrolling past the name of each person and the date of their death. He counted over six pages, almost a hundred people linked to the assassination, who were murdered or died suspiciously from 1963 to 1977. From strippers and cops to

CIA operatives. He read their brief bios and wondered about their lives, wondering even more about their deaths. Pilgrim wondered too whether he should waste his time on something that happened forty years ago but his lingering feeling of depression and self pity—the blow to his sense of self worth, his wounded vanity—left him prone to moments of morbidity.

Remember the dead.

Every man owes death a debt of one life. Jimmy Jeremiah inhaled the aroma of beeswax and incense and spoke the name of someone he knew long ago but was now deceased. The thought of his own demise did not bother him so much, or the thought of pain. Wasn't everyone given a choice of a sudden death coupled with a brief, intense pain or a lingering death together with increasing psychic or physical pain? Life didn't seem to offer too many third choices. The candles lent a warm glow to the plaster feet of the saint, feet incised and tinted red with the stigmata. St. Francis, Jimmy wondered? As for himself, he was no saint but maybe he had come close to sanctity once long ago. He didn't know. For some reason Jimmy thought of Archbishop Romero, murdered like Thomas a Beckett by political assassins, in a sacristy or chapel much like this one. Wasn't that about the time--in 1980 when Romero was murdered--that he lost faith in one religion and regained it in another?

Remember the dead.

A person's life reduced to a single line, like an inscription on an eroded tombstone. Pilgrim stared at the names on the screen and finally found one he recognized. Abraham Zapruder.

Abe Zapruder filmed the most famous frames in American political history, the footage of president John F. Kennedy being hit by bullets at Dealey Plaza that November day in 1963. Captured by a home movie camera, the grainy, 8 millimeter color film remained the ultimate "reality" footage, in a nation lately obsessed with reality television. Yet why hadn't the Zapruder film gotten more scrutiny by the intelligence agencies and news media he wondered? Where was the public outcry when the famous film remained hidden away in Life magazine vaults for years, unseen by the public? Was reality only of interest to the American public when it entertained rather than enlightened?

And yet what difference did a political assassination that happened forty years ago have now, he wondered? Pilgrim scrolled down the list; whatever happened that day happened ten years before he was born.

The skeptical side of his nature, the natural attribute of a good newsman, wondered also whether the list simply encompassed people related by nothing more than happenstance to an unlucky event. He noticed the names of several reporters and felt his interest growing. "Accidental shooting", he read, and "Blow to neck" describing the sudden deaths of reporters Bill Hunter and Jim Koethe. A person's life now reduced to a single, clinical phrase. How much did they know? Did some sinister group eliminate them because they knew too much, because they had been in Jack Ruby's apartment two days after the assassination? Pilgrim distrusted conspiracy theories; usually they had little basis in fact, buttressed by the paranoid for the benefit of the gullible. Yet public perception of JFK's death had definitely changed over the decades. According to the New York Times, a majority of Americans now believed Oswald had accomplices in the assassination. What was Jimmy Jeremiah's connection?

Remember the dead.

The screen slid open and in the darkness of the confessional booth Jimmy Jeremiah felt the familiar warmth and concealment, like being alone in a gazebo bowered by a shady grove of trees on a warm summer day.

"Bless me father for I have sinned. It has been six weeks since my last confession."

"Yes, please go on."

The act of confession used to terrify him as a small boy. Now Jimmy found the figure on the other side of the booth almost an equal, an equally troubled soul possibly tormented by the guilt of his own horrible, secret sins, yet useful for the dialogues Jimmy practiced in the dark. Nowhere else could he engage in discourse with another intelligent human so freely yet remain so faceless, so hidden.

"Suppose a man kills another man and regrets the deed and begs forgiveness—can God forgive this sinner?"

"Yes, the forgiveness of sins, even for such a crime, is possible."

"Suppose Judas had begged God for forgiveness rather than hanging himself; would God have forgiven him?"

"How do we know that God didn't forgive him? In the gospels the death of Judas Iscariot is reported twice, yet each time differently—the faithful reader is not told, however, what was Judas's final thought."

"Suppose an assassin kills for an idealistic purpose, the so-called greater good, like the German army officers who tried to kill Hitler in 1944 to shorten the war?"

"I'm unfamiliar with that bit of history."

"In 1944 a plot, by German officers, attempted to blow up Adolf Hitler with a bomb planted in an attaché case below a heavy wooden table during a conference. They failed; the table absorbed the blast. But if they had succeeded, however, maybe a couple million people who died in the last year of the war would have survived instead. The conspirators would have been heroes but because they failed—the bomb went off but Hitler miraculously survived--they were all shot or hung."

"I see what you're getting at. Every assassin, however idealistic, has to look deep into his heart and determine what are the true reasons behind his act. However, 'Thou shalt not kill' is the commandment. Now whether God allows extenuating circumstances is debatable, as in the case of soldiers, or submariners who must torpedo enemy ships or bombardiers who level entire cities."

"Or snipers in wartime?"

"Or snipers. Yes, God, unlike men, knows exactly what is in the human heart moments before the trigger is pulled. Possibly the sniper's bullet kills two persons—the one who delivers the bullet and the victim who receives the deathblow. Unlike in our law courts, God's justice is uncorrupted but, for all we know, maybe God's judgement is more merciful than our own. As you know, evidence is prone to tampering here on earth but not in the hereafter because, as the scripture says, 'For men look upon the surface of things but God looks at the human heart'. Depending on the motives, men are judged by God's examining the individual heart."

Jimmy sighed, thinking of Count Stauffenberg and the failed conspiracy to kill Hitler. He, however, had succeeded with his own hands, the hands of a man bathed in blood yet devoid of stigmata.

"Yeah father," he responded listlessly, "As you said, 'God only knows'. We the living won't find out definitely until we're dead."

Remember the dead.

Jack Zangretti, Gunshot victim.
Eddie Benavides, Gunshot to head.
Betty MacDonald, Suicide by hanging in Dallas jail.
Hank Killam, Throat cut.
Bill Hunter, Accidental shooting.

> Gary Underhill, Gunshot to head ruled suicide.
> Teresa Norton, Fatally shot.
> Rose Cheramie, Hit-and-run.
> Jim Koethe, Blow to neck.
> Lee Bowers, Car Crash.
> David Ferrie, Suicide by overdose.

Pilgrim tried to read between the lines, awed by the brevity of life now reduced to police blotter terminology. The list of so-called "suspicious deaths", remotely related to the JFK assassination. proved nothing whatsoever but made for interesting conjecture. Two names stood out and he read the briefest of bios, his imagination struggling to supply the sordid details of the deaths of the women. Betty MacDonald and Teresa Norton were strippers or otherwise employed by nightclub owner Jack Ruby, the killer of Lee Harvey Oswald and Pilgrim felt a brief kinship with strippers as subjects of his Pulitzer-nominated series.

How many stories of shortened lives were staring him in the face; how many missing chapters, how many mysterious characters remained hidden in all of these tragedies? And how exactly did Jimmy Jeremiah factor in these events, but more importantly why?

Chapter 3

"I sure hope you didn't believe that list I gave you the other day contained all the suspicious deaths related to the JFK murder--or that maybe some of those on the list are anything more than circumstantial."

Jimmy Jeremiah toppled a half dozen books on to a table covered with back issues of the Sun Satellite newspaper.

Surprised more than annoyed, the reporter shrugged.

Jimmy flopped onto the only other chair in the cubicle, a worn leather armchair, a chair that groaned like an arthritic old dog attempting to rise whenever anyone sat in it.

"Interesting reading but I had my doubts about some of the people listed," Pilgrim said, without looking up from the computer screen. "Life is violent sometimes, and one car crashes are more common than you might think."

"And gunshots to the back of the head that are ruled suicides. Those are more common than you might think too."

The reporter looked up with a bit more interest.

Jimmy stifled a cough with a handkerchief slowly drawn from the pocket of his sport jacket before he began to speak again.

"Life is violent and not much reported except in details that don't really matter, Dan. But the Internet, the Internet you and I know, speaks of stories that are too uncomfortable for regular newspapers to print, stories like 'Inconvenient Deaths'. Life and death is like a vast, uncharted literary territory and the Internet is overgrown and tough to navigate, where disinformation is as common as in any intelligence agency, yet where 'The truth shall set you free'--to paraphrase the blasphemous slogan over at CIA headquarters--can actually be found and the dead can be exhumed time and time again."

Daniel Pilgrim nodded. "Maybe the Web is the last bastion of free speech, somewhat given to demagogues and dime store orators but with a wide range of information and creativity tossed in—undiluted truth too discomforting for our so-called free press to acknowledge or print."

The old man smiled liked a gremlin with a terrible secret to gleefully share. "At least it is until the government decides to shut it down by patriotic decree."

"Ah yes, 'The present state of America is truly alarming to every man who is capable of reflection'—Tom Paine."

Jeremiah looked amused. "An Internet columnist?"

"A pamphleteer ahead of his time, circa 1776. He also said, with an eye to this age perhaps, 'Our present condition is legislation without law; wisdom without a plan; a constitution without a name.' Paine wrote pamphlets that became how-to books for the founding fathers."

"I tend to read only contemporary histories. If it hasn't happened in my lifetime—the last sixty five years--has it really happened at all?'

Pilgrim waved his hand. "Are you mentioned in any of those books?"

"No--that's why I'm still alive."

Pilgrim suppressed a smile. The skeptical glance he gave the old man returned to him with a look of guarded amusement. "So you're prepared to unburden everything now, Mr. Jeremiah; why is that?"

"History only got it half right."

"That's the description of history, isn't it?"

"Some history books are more honest than others. Some of the books I loaned you about JFK have more of, uh, more of a political agenda, but I wanted you to read various, different angles before I tell you my own story of what really happened that day. History always seems to be subjective."

"I thought history was always objective."

"Supposed to be but it ain't."

"You mean one historical event might have more than one history?"

"Depends on whose doing the telling. Okay. I'll give you an example. You can tell a lot about a guy if you asked him about the battle of Little Big Horn. You can tell a lot about the way he thinks. If he thinks Custer was a hero and goddamn right to subdue or slaughter Indians, he's probably blue collar or upper management, probably votes Republican if he bothers to vote at all, and maybe he owns a gun and was raised Christian but might not practice it. Now those who think Sitting Bull was right are probably environmentalist, liberal or college educated, white collar or craftsmen and believe in gun control."

"Sounds simplistic."

"So who was right, Custer or Sitting Bull?"

"Sitting Bull."

"Own any guns?"

"No."

"Proves my point."

Pilgrim picked up a book from the stack and began leafing through it, stopping only at the pictures.

"Why should people care about what happened in Dallas forty years ago?"

"People don't know how the country changed after Dealey Plaza"

"Yeah, that's what my parents said about Vietnam."

"Both related, by the way."

"So by telling your story, Mr. Jeremiah, you're culpable in some way for both events?"

"Some of us carry more of the blame than others. We pulled the trigger but others carried a helluva lot more responsibility."

"We? You keep saying 'we pulled the trigger'. How many more were there?"

"Bone up on the written account before you flood me with questions."

"Okay—but if 'We' work together I'll have to record most of what you and I say. What happens if the others, whom you refuse to mention, have any objection to your confession?"

"Most of them are dead."

Pilgrim pulled open a drawer and placed a small tape recorder before Jeremiah. "Think about it: If I tape your story and your words become public, whatever you say can and will be used against you—maybe not in a court of law, but certainly that too--but in the court of public opinion. Still want to record your confession, of one of the unsolved crimes of the century?"

"Better get lots of tape then."

"No holding back?"

"Better be prepared to be shocked."

Pilgrim stared at the old man who leveled a steely look in return. The guarded amusement was gone entirely. The truth was rarely plain and seldom simple, Pilgrim knew, rather shades of truth contained vivid hues, all tinted with bits of gray. What fresh perspectives or falsehoods, what surprises or tired conspiracies, would Jeremiah reveal or concoct?

"Cops met me in secret to talk about police corruption," said the reporter. "When I was writing my three part series for the paper we'd meet elsewhere but I've never collaborated on a book. Should we meet in various, out-of-the-way locations?"

"You mean like spies?"

"Well, you're talking about sensitive issues, aren't you?"

"Sure we can meet elsewhere; my doctor thinks I should get out of my apartment more often anyway. I got a sport fish boat parked at the marina, and it's almost bigger than my apartment."

"Good. I'll compile a list of other places. My editor might not understand if you hang around here and I use company time for something the newspaper would never deign to print."

"And you Mr. Pilgrim; are you prepared to put it all down, start to finish, no matter how horrible the story might be, or have you got too many--whatdya call them--too many prior commitments?"

"If you keep the story flowing and plausible I have time to listen."

"It may not be plausible but by God it'll be true. At least what details I can remember." Jimmy smothered a laugh. "My Alzheimer's is catching up on my recollective powers."

"So why'd you do it, first of all?"

"Various reasons, few of which seem valid now."

"Was it for money?"

"Money was the least of the reasons. Most of the guys in the group actually hated Kennedy for what we felt were good reasons then. I was one of them; I had my hates all neatly arranged then."

Pilgrim shuffled through the stack of books. "I'll read some of the details of the JFK assassination over the weekend, but before we get to the when, where and how of what happened in Dallas, I'd like to know more about the why?"

Jeremiah sat silent for a moment. "Like I said, I had my reasons. Just like everybody involved did. Those of us who did the deed, fired the guns, felt Jack Kennedy betrayed the country or was in the process of betraying the country but, now that I look back, those who most benefited by the killing of Kennedy, those wielding power, profited pretty well by the murder. They remained in the shadows and increased their wealth and power, where they remain even today."

"You ever meet Oswald, Mr. Jeremiah?"

"Three or four times. He once gave me a photo he developed—he was an amateur photographer, you know—of himself and his daughter June. I still have it."

"I'd like to see it some time."

"I remember he loved to read spy novels, Oswald did. He read James Bond, that sort of thing. Oswald even owned a certain book—practically memorized it—called 'How To Be A Spy'. I think he was an informant for the FBI and the CIA--not entirely loyal--who cloaked his true intentions in ambiguity; unsure of who or what he really served. An emotional double agent but way out of his depth. We all live in a dream world that parallels reality but Lee was an enigma wrapped in layers of denial and fantasy."

"What denial?"

"How hard do you think it was for someone who may have been gay to survive undetected in the US marines in 1959? How painful?"

"Oswald was gay?"

"Consider this, Dan: How hard do you think it was for someone who was sensitive and undersized, to survive in a squad full of macho leathernecks? I recall seeing a picture of Oswald, years later, smiling like a schoolgirl in his Marine Corps fatigues and jungle helmet. In every photo of Oswald you see in books about his life, Oswald seems to be smiling yet he's portrayed as an unhappy and violent loner. Why is that?"

"I didn't know Oswald was in the marines; I thought he was just a lonely and angry young Communist."

"Flying the red flag of convenience for our very own government."

"But this sensitive Oswald you describe pulled the trigger, didn't he? Even John Dillinger was sensitive to some people, even Al Capone."

"Funny you should mention the Mafia. I'm gonna tell you about the connection between the Mafia and the CIA. What I know, that is."

"And what do you know?"

"One is called The Family and the other is called The Company, but if you look at both organizations very closely they both share a whole lot of similarities. Loyalty, secrecy, brotherhood and, especially, cruelty for profit: a shadowy yet pragmatic self-interest.

The only difference between, say, Al Capone and Allen Dulles is that Dulles probably had a helluva lot more people murdered indirectly than Al Capone."

"But Allen Dulles got the airport named after him."

"Because the city of Washington was wise enough to realize where the real power lay. Anyway, the Mafia and the CIA are both businessmen's groups when you get down to it and strip away the secret rites—", Jimmy chuckled and then choked back a cough. "-But of course the CIA is a lot more bloodthirsty and unethical than the local, smalltown chamber of commerce. The CIA is like the Fraternal Order of Elks but without the ethics and with a helluva lot more firepower."

Pilgrim smiled but said nothing, reassessing the lively old fellow sprawling in the leather chair, seated below a large, laminated map of Florida, the Gulf of Mexico and the islands of the Caribbean. The reporter typed a few words more before he paused. A story he had been working on, of marijuana bricks drifting ashore on Big Pine Key, needed only a final edit before he finished. He rarely had visitors at the newspaper and none so quixotic or talkative as geriatric Jimmy Jeremiah and so the story could wait. An assassin? Not likely, but he might be an entertaining way to pass the time until he thought of a book idea. Perhaps, in the meantime, he could write a feature story on the secret fantasy lives of retired gentlemen like Jimmy Jeremiah, a sort of Walter Mitty Goes To Florida.

"You mentioned, uh, a limited amount of time left before you, uh, before you-"

"You mean before I die?"

"Yeah."

"Why not just say it then, Dan?"

"Okay. If you only have weeks or months to live, Mr. Jeremiah, then I want to get as much down as possible. Every incredible facet of your amazing tale."

"Call me Jimmy. See how easy that was. I got time; I got nothing now but daylight and eternity and not much filling either one."

Jimmy studied the reporter from the comfort of the armchair. A fellow of angles instead of curves, Pilgrim seemed, in the eyes of the former intelligence man, hewn from the white oak of wrecked ships Jimmy had seen on the Outer Banks of the Atlantic shore. A patient man not easily distracted or annoyed, the reporter worked deliberately; this unannounced visit might have vexed a nervous fellow, thought Jimmy. Corded wrists of a clean up hitter, square jaw with a curious gleam in his eye, the neck of an athlete rather than scholar. And yet the intelligent forehead and pensive look of someone used to abstract thought. A good choice, perhaps, although he would take convincing.

Pilgrim filed his news story for the Sun Satellite onto a disc and then minimized the page.

"So you knew Oswald?" he remarked.

"Slightly,"

"I've often wondered what sort of family man he was. I'd love to see that picture of him and his daughter. Bring it in the next time you come. Somehow, though, I can't imagine Oswald outside the scope of the Texas Book Depository and Dealey Plaza. I remember seeing that old film of him, I think it was black-and-white, where Oswald was shot and killed on national TV. He was walking toward the camera and then, suddenly, he was doubled over in pain, holding his gut. And then he was dead."

"One thing I've always wondered," replied Jimmy; "Was he already dead on the way to the hospital?"

"You mean did Oswald die in the ambulance while they took their own sweet time about getting him there?"

Jimmy nodded. "I mean he gets shot about 11:30 AM in the basement parking garage of the police station but instead of rushing him to the hospital in a police car they wait for an ambulance to come all that way from Parkland while he continues to bleed. Then he dies about 2 PM. Wasn't that the most convenient of convenient deaths?"

"Yeah."

Curious, Pilgrim leafed through the pages of one of the books Jimmy had given him until he found a picture of Oswald on a stretcher. "Says here he was taken to Parkland hospital in Dallas after Jack Ruby gunned him down, going to the very same hospital Kennedy went to after Oswald shot him. Makes sense if Oswald bled to death at the police station. After all, he'd killed a cop and a president and to most Americans he got what he deserved."

"Exactly. And if you demonize a man it becomes easier to erase him from humanity. Remember, nothing Lee Harvey Oswald said, for almost two days while in custody at the Dallas police station, was ever written down or recorded. How convenient was that? And he asked repeatedly for a lawyer, never varying from the claim that he was innocent. But then if Oswald had been allowed to speak on record to a lawyer, it would have revealed the whole conspiracy. To this day, I feel he informed the Dallas police he was an FBI undercover agent also working for the CIA and that, more than anything else, is why he didn't come out shooting when trapped in the Texas theatre. He could have put six slugs in a handful of cops but Oswald trusted the system right up to the end."

"So was Oswald completely innocent?"

"No way. But if you humanize a villain—even for one minute--and hear his side of the story, his villainy becomes just a little less evil."

"Like Custer?"

Jimmy chuckled. "I was thinking of Sitting Bull."

"So you think Oswald had any good qualities?"

"Yeah, he probably did."

"To his country? A spy and convicted murderer? To his family? What good qualities or lasting memories do they likely have of that oddball?"

"To understand Oswald you have to understand he was a chameleon; his favorite TV show while growing up was 'I Led Three Lives', the story of an FBI agent who pretended to be a Communist so he could infiltrate that group. In a way I think Oswald was a product of his times, a product of suspicion, a product of the

Cold War. Listen: Lee Harvey Oswald was not the oddest family man who ever lived but he may have been the most misunderstood Cold War spy in history."

"I don't know anything about Oswald the spy."

"From here on out the story's gonna get a lot stranger, and Oswald remains just one small piece of it."

Jimmy paused a moment as if remembering something. "Listen, in his strange fantasy game of spy or secret agent, Oswald got in way over his head, as most double agents do."

Chapter 4

"I'm convinced Oswald acted alone," Pilgrim declared. The reporter nodded twice, ever so slightly, certain of his conviction but open to argument.

Bobby Smith snapped another picture, tongue firmly pressed against his cheek in concentration. He knelt in the sand above the surfline on Big Pine Key, kneeling before a half-buried block of marijuana encased in plastic, vacuum-sealed against moisture.

"When a man sets out to find anything," said the photographer, wholly intent on his subject, "whether motives or marijuana bricks, the first thing he likely does is draw some hasty conclusions."

"So? You're saying I'm wrong, Bobby?"

"No, Dan, I ain't saying you're wrong. But are you done now, drawing all your conclusions about Oswald? Are you done making the pieces of the puzzle fit all the standard theories?"

"I spent the whole weekend reading about the assassination; I read five books; read the official reports—"

"Since when do you give 'official reports' blanket approval?"

"I already heard both sides of the argument, and now I have to agree that Oswald probably acted alone."

A plainclothes detective hovered over Smith, his shadow loping over the hills and hollows of the crouching photographer.

"Soon as you guys are done making pictures I gotta collect this for evidence," he said.

Smith stood and brushed the sand from his knees but not before methodically screwing the lens cap on his camera. The day was warm; the water shimmered a pale green and Smith scanned the horizon for images.

"People living along this beach say they didn't see or hear any boats last night, nor see anything suspicious all of yesterday," said the photographer. "So I guess--now that we got the 'official reports'—these here marijuana bricks got here all by themselves."

"Witnesses are rarely reliable; you know that."

"I know what witnesses saw in the Rodney King beating—and the videotape backed 'em up too. Same as in Dallas, I figure, with all the witnesses and that Zapruder film backing 'em up."

"But the eyewitnesses in Dallas saw and heard a lot of different things."

"Not the ones along the fenceline on the grassy area; they were ducking like homeboys caught in a shootout in the 'hood. And the videotape backs 'em all up. Turns out the witnesses all told the truth, I believe, and the government lied. Not that it would be the first time."

Pilgrim turned to the detective. "We have a dispute about the reliability of witnesses, detective. What do you think about the origin of this brick?"

"Probably drifted up with the tide, like the other ones we found two days ago."

"There you go, " said Pilgrim. He handed the detective his card. "I'm Daniel Pilgrim, reporter, Sun Satellite. How many pounds of grass altogether have been recovered?'

"So you're Pilgrim?" The detective gazed over the card with a distinct coolness, and then dropped the card in the sand. "I read your stuff, that series you wrote, and think you were out of line."

"Other people thought otherwise."

"Well, I don't think I have too much to say to you."

The detective motioned to a pair of uniforms standing near a strand of yellow plastic tape, restraining a dozen beachcombers.

Silent and seething, Pilgrim folded his notebook. The point of his pen clicked and retracted but there seemed to be no other sound than the soft hissing of the surf. He picked up his card.

"Let's go, Dan," said Smith. "Maybe those bystanders over there saw or heard something. We can at least get their unreliable opinions."

They walked along the beach. Mangrove thickets tufted the tidal mudflats and fossils shells poked from the limestone boulders higher on the shore. A pair of buzzards hovered aloft, indifferent to the living clustered below.

"I wrote a damn good series based on truthful testimony! I wrote the whole fucking story of police corruption in South Florida as objectively as I could!"

Smith shouldered his camera case, hitching the strap higher across his chest.

"Some folks saw it different. Many folks think you victimized the cops."

"Victimized!"

"See, Daniel, you saw it one way, and that cop over there saw it another, while somebody else saw it altogether different. When a person gets the facts, how does he know there ain't a few facts he overlooked?"

"You think I was wrong?"

"I think you wrote a Pulitzer Prize-winning piece but that don't mean people won't look at you cross-eyed—cops mostly--and think you got your story wrong."

"Oswald acted alone. All the facts concur."

Pilgrim deposited his notes beside the computer and checked his phone messages. There were none.

"Good, I'm glad you've drawn that conclusion, Dan."

"You are?"

"Sure. If I state my case to you beforehand, I'd prefer you be so damn sure that I'm wrong, than happily convinced that I'm right without ever hearing my evidence."

Seated in the leather chair in the reporter's alcove, Jimmy munched a donut while sipping a cup of coffee from a styrofoam cup, yesterday's newspaper serving as a napkin on his lap.

The reporter snorted, "Wouldn't you prefer someone who believed in you, just a little?"

"If I can't convince you, then how-the-hell are you gonna convince your own readers?"

Pilgrim stared at his laminated map. The Gulf Stream drifted past the Keys but did those bricks just wash ashore and how many were picked up already? Retirees had reported the few they found.

"What'd you learn about the marijuana out on Big Pine Key?"

Pilgrim turned and stared for a moment, wondering if the old fellow could read his thoughts.

"I asked your editor, Gonzales. Cuban guy. He's kind of a hard ass, ain't he?"

"He probably thought you were lost on the way to the public library."

"I've dozed off there a few times. While information gathering."

"Tell me something, old man: what do you hope to gain by your likely fabrication?"

Surprised by the anger spilling over, unsure of its source, Jimmy sipped the remaining coffee, flipped the cup into the trash, folded the paper from his lap and brushed the few crumbs from his trousers. Then, carefully drawing a folder from a soiled backpack he handed it to the reporter.

"I brought you something few people have ever seen."

Pilgrim studied what appeared to be a training manual. Although a slender volume of 22 pages, the title—"*A Study of Assassination*"-- struck Pilgrim as particularly sinister despite its obvious appearance as a government publication from another era.

"Where'd you get this? You buy it on the Internet?"

Jimmy chuckled. "Wonder what it'd be worth if I tried to sell it online—and included its history?"

"Tell me about it: Where'd it come from; how'd it get in your possession?"

"A fellow by the name of Bill Harvey gave it to me. Someone should write his biography; one of the more colorful Americans to have ever spooked in the deep dark shadows of our government. I worked for Bill in the early 'Sixties and we both worked for The Company."

"What do you mean 'spooked'?"

"Covert operations."

"You mean like agents for the CIA?"

"Now you're catching on."

Pilgrim slipped behind his desk and retrieved the tape recorder from the top drawer. Turning on the recorder, he placed it on the edge of his desk closest to his guest. Then Pilgrim resumed leafing through the manual.

"Mr. Jeremiah, you say your name is a cryptogram, is that correct?"

Jimmy chuckled. "I believe the word is Cryptonym. I was known simply as Jeremiah then."

"Were you an assassin for the CIA?"

"I worked for people within the company who wanted other people removed."

"By removed you mean assassinated; so you were an assassin?"

"I preferred to think of myself as an operative who worked for Bill Harvey and ZR-Rifle, a sub-agency within the agency."

"And what did ZR-Rifle do; what was its prime purpose?"

"Eliminate people, or assassinate them, to put it bluntly."

"And who authorized you to eliminate or kill people?"

Jeremiah paused, choosing his words with some difficulty.

"Remember, the directives came from the top man down but each guy only knew a limited amount of information and the rest was left to speculation or rumor."

"Top man? You mean the head of the CIA?"
"Yes, of course but even higher up."
"You mean the president?"
"Yes, Kennedy."
Pilgrim closed the manual and placed it on the desk.
"So a president who knew about and may have approved of a secret sub-agency for assassination ended up getting assassinated?"
"Now you're seeing the big picture."

Chapter 5

Bobby Smith's apartment on Atlantic Avenue wasn't much to look at from the outside but the inside resembled a shrine to photographic excellence. Aside from numerous framed silver-type and tin-type portraits of unknown people from the nineteenth century, Bobby had amassed a collection of black & white photographs of jazz musicians--Coltrane, Baker, Brubeck, Davis, Hubbard—from an earlier era matted and framed in a contemporary style. The showpiece of his collection, hanging in the living room, was a huge, colorful shot of Jimi Hendrix at Woodstock, taken by an unknown photographer, a picture that Bobby had bought at a garage sale in nearby Ft. Lauderdale. Bobby's own photographs—of the destructive forces of man or nature—decorated the entryway, hallway and bathroom walls.

The doorbell rang and Bobby swung it open to Daniel Pilgrim who wandered into the kitchen with a six pack of Coronas in one hand and a book in another.

"So where'd you find the film?" The reporter uncapped two beers.

"On the Internet; you can buy most anything there."

"I think I've seen it," said Pilgrim, listlessly, "I know I have."

"But not a tape like this one. It moves frame by frame; I can stop or go one frame, or fraction of a second, at a time. And maybe this Zapruder film might give you a convenient jumping off place to start a serious interrogation of the old guy."

"Yeah."

"Speaking of film, there's an event happening at a Ft. Lauderdale gallery tonight. Far as I know it's related to what we're about to watch." Bobby fast-forwarded until he got to the slow moving motorcade. Then he paused the video while he sought a printed invitation. "It's called 'All Along The Watchtower: Music and imagery from the Vietnam War'. I'm taking Teresa and maybe you'd like to come."

"Where's it at?"

"At the Virden Gallery. Some chick named Joyce Virden owns it and they've been showing mostly cutting-edge stuff."

Pilgrim nodded vaguely.

The VCR clicked to life again and then paused after the dark blue presidential Lincoln swung onto Elm. "Maybe if we look hard at all the windows on the upper floors of this video," said the photographer, "we can get a glimpse of old Jimmy as a young man."

Pilgrim sipped his beer and then spoke: "You don't really believe the old fool is plausible, do you? I mean, c'mon: he's just an affable old man with an over-active imagination."

"I ain't saying I believe him, but that training manual for assassins he gave you—I'm done reading it by the way." Bobby stretched for the shelf beside the big screen TV but couldn't reach the manual. "It does give a person pause to reflect."

"Yeah, but I'll bet anyone can buy the very same manual somewhere on the Internet."

"Maybe, but his booklet just looks genuine."

"Does he look genuine?"

"He sort of reminds me of your dad; he's got the same gleam of inner intensity."

"Said he worked for something called ZR-rifle. Remind me to look that up on the Internet."

Outside the apartment a mockingbird peppered the morning with a repetitious medley of songs and Pilgrim wondered why he didn't just tell the old fellow to forget the whole thing. Later that afternoon he intended to meet Jeremiah at a gym where the retiree said he kept in shape. That might be the best time to tell him that he had changed his mind.

"I think my belief in Jimmy Jeremiah is diminishing daily," Pilgrim confessed. "Where's the proof?"

"What do you expect from him—the sniper rifle with Kennedy's blood somehow splattered on it? Photographs of himself taken from above Dealey Plaza with the motorcade going by below him?"

Pilgrim snorted and took another pull on his beer. Bobby was right. What exactly did he expect? Tangible evidence would be difficult--if not nearly impossible--for Jeremiah to arrange. Did the old fellow even keep a scrapbook?

Smith finally stood up and retrieved the CIA manual. "I wonder if the old guy would like to sell this?"

"You thinking of assassinating someone, Bobby?"

"Might be."

Smith aimed the remote at the television and pressed Play.

"Much of the case turns on this here film; the argument for a second gunman and thus a conspiracy."

"He said there was more than one guy. More than one gunman."

"Jimmy said that?"

Pilgrim leaned forward. A picture's worth a thousand words but the grainy film, even when slowed to a single frame per second, seemed as treacherous to interpret as modern CGI, computer generated images. No wonder so many people saw so many different things after viewing the brief 18 seconds of Zapruder film.

"There goes Kennedy," Bobby announced, "going behind the trees and sign."

"He seems okay there," replied the reporter.

They looked close while the film snailed past frame by frame. A slight movement by the president caught their eyes and Smith paused the film. Pilgrim remembered reading that Kennedy had worn a full back brace that day in Dallas--because of an old back injury that had recurred--causing him to sit unusually erect. Normally a man struck once from behind by a bullet might have toppled forward or to the side.

"He looks like he got stung by a bee there," said Bobby. "That's the reaction I'd make if I was stung by something on my back."

"One scientist said it was a spinal reaction to being shot; the arms going upward and out like that."

"Still looks like a man reacting to a bee sting down his collar to me—or a minor bullet wound."

A few more frames slipped slowly past, the most famous seconds-to-death of a man ever recorded, the film as much a puzzle and an enigma as the man himself. The FBI had initially removed a couple frames to make their story more plausible but the convenient subterfuge had been discovered, only stoking the conspiracy theories. Pilgrim found himself wondering where Jimmy fit into the picture and his natural curiosity and instincts for unraveling a good story heightened.

"Looks like a second shot—or maybe even two-- either hit Kennedy and then Connelly right there." Smith said. "I gotta back up a few frames."

"I notice his arms are down," said Pilgrim. "Maybe you were right about that bee sting reaction."

Bobby nodded. "What do scientists know? Scientists used to think the world was flat and the sun went around the earth."

Kennedy slumped to the side but the back brace prevented him from falling altogether over Jackie Kennedy's lap--as the wounded Connelly had fallen and now lay across the lap of his wife in the seat ahead. So a device designed to alleviate pain now conspired to cause the president's death.

"He looks like he might have survived those shots," said Pilgrim quietly.

"Jackie can't get him over in time," said the photographer softly. "Get down, man."

They watched the still figures, staring at the whole composition on the screen. Not often history can be paused and rewound.

The frames slipped by and the motorcade rolled into a timeless place of myth and legend and muzzy facts. For a moment the famous tousled hair hung down and then the entire head exploded back and to the side, a dragon's breath of vermilion mist hissing from the wound.

"That's a frontal shot from close range," said the photographer. "Don't need no brain scientist to tell me otherwise."

"Maybe, maybe not."

"Ah c'mon man. You watching the same movie as me?"

The frames reversed and then replayed. How much collective psychic pain the country must have felt that day, Pilgrim thought.

To most people, whether they voted for President Kennedy or not, the assassination must have been like a sudden blow to the stomach.

The Warren Commission might have known something was not exactly right with the "lone gunman" theory but perhaps they felt the nation would be better off not knowing. To know your government was capable of removing a popular leader by a violent, well-coordinated conspiracy might have left the country cynical and resistant to authority. Their authority.

"I seen enough real life deaths from war zone footage," Bobby continued, "and even seen some Liberty City gunshots, to know the head goes where the bullet blows. JFK got smacked from the back by one or two shots—and then whacked for good from the front."

"That's not what the Warren Commission saw."

"And what did you just see, my man?"

The mockingbird paused abruptly and in the silence Pilgrim expected a secondary sound. "I don't know."

"Well, do your homework! There were credible witnesses on that there grassy knoll who saw and heard something. I wonder if your man, Jimmy Jeremiah, can add to your limited knowledge."

Pilgrim wondered that too.

The squalid gym in Lake Worth neither added nor detracted from the seediness of the area. Pilgrim peered around the space and heard, before he saw, the presence of Jimmy Jeremiah.

The heavy bag swung under the blows and the reporter wondered if the labored breath or the punches moved the bag more.

"Glad to see you, kid, " said the fighter, extending a glove.

Pilgrim pushed a fist against the firm glove.

"And I thought you were just a pussycat," he said.

"Just an old Tom, nearly defanged."

"I can come back if you're not finished."

Postpone the inevitable leave-taking, Pilgrim decided. He studied the shirtless figure of a man thirty years his senior, like appraising a weatherworn old house not yet entirely gone to ruin. Gravity swung the wrecking ball at us all, reflected the reporter, toppling sturdier forms than human flesh yet Jimmy Jeremiah did not appear months away from the inevitable final wreckage awaiting every man.

"No, I'm done—or done in," said Jimmy.

The familiar choking laughter a welcome yet foreboding sign, thought Pilgrim.

"You bring your tape recorder?"

Pilgrim patted his pocket.

"Good. I feel confessional."

"You boxed in your younger days?"

"What do you mean, 'younger days'? These are my younger days—the onliest days I got left."

Pilgrim searched the face of the old man for a sign of mirth and then saw a glimmer.

Jimmy patted his face with a towel. "I was good, but maybe not as good as I thought I was. I was Golden Gloves material out of Brockton, Mass. Known as the 'Brockton Bomber'. Brockton was tough then, when I grew up there in the 'Fifties but maybe tougher now. I fought welterweight then. Amateur all the way; a Navy recruiter sponsored me."

Jimmy thrust the gloves at Pilgrim and the reporter untied them.

"Out of loyalty I chose the Navy. I went in at seventeen and got out in 1959. Before I got my release my commanding officer suggested a career in intelligence. Said it had a future."

The reporter nodded.

"I enjoyed it. Enjoyed the rigorous discipline at the Farm. Camp Peary, CIA training base. Years before, before the Navy, I had been thinking of the priesthood—I was Catholic—and the Jesuits taught at the school I went to growing up. The Farm was like a militant strain of Jesuit monks teaching us that life was tough but we were tougher, and God was on our side in the Cold War; that's how I saw it anyway."

"So then you went to ZR-rifle?"

"Along the way I did. Part of Task Force W, if I remember right."

"What was the purpose of Task Force W?"

"To kill or harass and eventually overthrow Castro. After the Bay of Pigs failed—which anybody in their right mind could have foreseen—Kennedy got this grudge thing going against Castro, to get revenge."

"You mean a vendetta?"

"Yeah, vendetta; a good word for a bad deed."

Jimmy tossed the towel into a hamper, slipped a dry sweatshirt over his torso and zipped his gym bag, before moving toward the door.

"It's raining outside, Mr. Jeremiah; can I offer you a lift?"

"Seeing as how I walked here and seeing as how you showed up, I accept your offer."

Once inside the car, Pilgrim fumbled with his keys.

"I saw that Zapruder tape this morning; you know the one?"

"How could I not?"

"Pretty gruesome."

"I said at the beginning, Daniel, that you were gonna be shocked and you said to me, the last time I saw you, something about 'fabrications'.

You can back out now—I get the feeling that's what you want to do, isn't it--?"

"No- "

"Or you can get to the meat of this story and get it down. What you find out about your fellow countrymen, what you find out about me, will sure-as-hell shock you and maybe make you cynical. I promise you it ain't very pretty, it's gruesome, and you are probably gonna hate my guts before you're through writing it all down. Providing you have the balls to write it all down, which I'm beginning to doubt."

The reporter seethed but said nothing for a moment.

"Okay," said Pilgrim finally, "I see your game. But maybe you haven't got the guts or--what did you call them? the balls?-- to speak freely and openly about what you claim to know."

"Try me."

"Was the JFK assassination somehow related to Castro? Did Castro set that up? Was he behind Oswald?"

Jimmy chuckled, and then took a deep breath, releasing it slowly.

"Related might be putting it mildly. Do you believe in karma?"

"That the consequences of our actions, whether good or bad, spawn equal results—something like that?"

"I never believed in karma---but now, now that I'm dying I finally see the big picture."

"Why did Kennedy want to get Castro?"

"Kennedy promised the voters in 1960 he would get Castro, and he won the election because Nixon couldn't say a damn thing about a plan already in the works to do just that. Kennedy knew before hand there was a CIA plan in the works for assassination. Fidel Castro, you see, nationalized all those mob casinos and sweatshop sugar plantations and tobacco farms, and one huge nickel mine probably, worth a quarter billion Yankee dollars, nationalized 'em all after verified rumors of his impending assassination got back to him, and after US armed counter-insurgency guerillas began landing on his shore.

"Remember how I told you—that tape recorder on?--how the CIA is a businessmen's organization and they didn't like it when foreign governments nationalize US businesses, or when foreigners overthrow their puppet governments--even if they are corrupt or repressive as hell? Bill Harvey, my boss, he knew there wasn't much we could do about Castro except invade Cuba--which the Pentagon brass wanted to do--and that would cost a whole helluva lot of American casualties on both sides—a sort of Caribbean Vietnam."

"But what about the Bay of Pigs?"

"Get real. You think 1,400 civilian soldiers, no matter how well trained and equipped, could conquer a well-dug in, well-motivated and prepared, superior force on its home territory? Think what happened to Custer against Sitting Bull."

Pilgrim nodded in agreement.

"What I've never understood," Jimmy continued, " was how-in-hell Eisenhower approved an invasion plan—the Bay of Pigs—that was the exact opposite of the successful invasion force he himself lead, the invasion of Normandy on D Day?"

"Maybe they figured a few thousand US Marines could conquer Cuba?"

"But how could American military officers, recent veterans of the European campaign, sign on to a scheme that had little likelihood of victory? Easy to understand how younger men, impassioned Cubans and impressionable youths, could be persuaded by their leaders but how could intelligent, college-educated men in the Pentagon be so muddled about an invasion—unless, in their hubris, they wanted massive American involvement against a popular peasant uprising."

Pilgrim listened to the rain pelting the metal of his car and, while fascinated, he wondered how exactly Castro was connected to the death of JFK.

"There was air support at the Bay of Pigs wasn't there?" inquired Pilgrim. "I read that Kennedy sent air support."

The old man chuckled, more in disgust than anything else. "Not enough. And never would be. How much air support was needed to conquer Vietnam? We lost 10,000 helicopters in 'Nam providing air support and ain't Cuba about the same size and just as junglely as Vietnam? Listen, the Pentagon and CIA—hardass Cold Warriors, most of 'em--thought wrong at the Bay of Pigs, just like they thought wrong in Goddamn Vietnam. Maybe a five-sided building ain't conducive to rational thought."

Pilgrim checked his tape recorder, surprised at the old man's sudden burst of anger.

"So the Pentagon was upset with Kennedy?"

"Hell yes! They thought we should have sailed right up and shelled and strafed Havana and then sent the US Marines ashore. They were hoping for Teddy Roosevelt but they figured they got Mother Teresa instead."

"And how did you feel at the time, Mr. Jeremiah?"

"I felt the same. I felt we missed an opportunity. But I was young and gung-ho."

"What were the repercussions at the CIA?"

"A whole bunch of people got their walking papers."

"And so there was resentment toward JFK inside the CIA and the Pentagon?"

"I'm sure there was. I don't think Allen Dulles was any too happy."

"Dulles was on the Warren Commission, that looked into CIA involvement, after the JFK assassination, wasn't he?"

"Sure was," the old man snorted. "And wasn't that convenient?"

"So after the Bay of Pigs, what happened in your department?"

"A whole lot more exiled Cuban troops started training all over the Gulf coast, especially in Florida, Mississippi and Louisiana. I helped train some of them in weaponry. Anyway, Kennedy, especially Robert Kennedy, wanted more covert operations against Cuba and that's how Operation Mongoose got started."

"What was the purpose of Operation Mongoose?"

"To wreck the economy of Cuba and cause unrest, and maybe get people so angry they would revolt."

"How wreck?"

"We flew night flights—David Ferrie was one of our best pilots--and dropped pesticides, landed guerillas for black ops, wrecked harvests, introduced swine fever and killed 500,000 pigs. That sort of thing."

"What about health dangers to Cuban workers? What about food shortages and the spread of toxins? What about the health of old people like yourself and kids; did anyone think about them?"

The old man sat silent for a long time, recounting deeds done in the guise of patriotism. Pilgrim watched him brush the fog of condensation from his window. He looked suddenly tired to the reporter, diminished, as if the roof of his building sagged under the weight of memories. Outside the car, school children were wending their way home in the dwindling rain.

"I—I think I'm gonna walk home after all, Dan. I'll see you later."

Chapter 6

The sad song wafted from the storefront speakers into the street and the warm, humid evening lent the tune an additional air of poignancy.

"Soldier boy, oh my little soldier boy—I'll be true to you."

Teresa Delgado sang softly along with the Shirelles, accompanying Bobby and Daniel toward the gallery. Inside the door a crowd already packed the converted carpet showroom, many people seated along the unadorned walls. In the center of the room, surrounded by devotional candles and personal mementoes, a cluster of projectors angled at the three walls. A middle-aged man attired in camouflage fatigues wearing captain bars addressed the considerable crowd and Daniel hung back, lingering in the open door, and listened to fragments of song and speech.

"-Many of you were too young to remember or not even born then. But those days were not unlike these. For example, the Pentagon and the presidency hawked an unpopular war then and now, and a complaisant media served as an accessory after the fact to a war crime whose victims now lie in unmarked graves or who, if they were American soldiers, are inscribed on an infamous black wall in Washington.

"Alas the war criminals all got away, then and now. Later in the evening, after we enshrine or illuminate the soldiers and civilians on the walls--the images of the fallen--we will shed some light on a few of the rogues gallery accompanied by the music of, who else but Hendrix, his songs certainly representative of the Vietnam era. The remainder of the evening is dedicated to the unsung...the unknown 58,000 throwaways of our culture and the culture we tried to destroy.

"So allow your eyes to rest on the faces of those 'long time passing', as Pete Seeger would say. And allow your ears to follow. Maybe the faces of the dead shining on the walls, even for a few seconds, and the songs of the era will conjure some memories, painful and cathartic and yet again beautiful. That was our intentions with the show, to refresh our memories."

An old fellow in faded green fatigues slipped outside and stood alongside Pilgrim. He whipped out a cigarette and offered one to the reporter. Before he had finished shaking his head, Pilgrim heard the antique clasp of a Zippo lighter and the flare burnished the leathery face of the veteran with the chiaroscuro of certain Spanish paintings.

Seeger began as a slow lament over the outdoor speaker and the old soldier hummed along. Inside the gallery, the crowd began to sing and the lights dimmed. A series of projectors slowly burnished a trio of faces upon the walls, where they lingered for a few seconds before others briefly shone. Pilgrim found himself softly singing the lines, surprised he could follow them.

> Where have all the soldiers gone
>   Long time passing,
> Where have all the soldiers gone
>   Long time ago,
> Where have all the soldiers gone
> They've gone to graveyards every one,
>   Oh, when will they ever learn?
>   Oh, when will they ever learn?

People smiled or glanced quickly, quizzical, in passing. Pilgrim didn't mind. He thought of his father who served in Korea and died two years ago. Sons seldom know the wartime exploits or secret sorrows of their fathers and Pilgrim was no exception. Whatever heroic deeds or demons that lurked within his father had gone to the grave.

"If Kennedy hadn't gotten killed we wouldn't have had the whole goddamn war," sighed the veteran.

Pilgrim nodded, not knowing otherwise. Then he pushed inside the door into semi-darkness.

"I hadn't realized how young some of these cats were," said Bobby Smith from the back of the room. He sipped on a glass of wine. Teresa peered at the three walls, at the youthful faces of the fallen, drying her eyes with the corner of a napkin.

"Maybe if Kennedy hadn't gotten killed the war might not have happened," replied Pilgrim.

"God only knows. Maybe if Martin Luther King hadn't got shot we would have had more racial harmony. Who knows?"

A ring of flames in devotional candles on the floor circled the slide projectors and viewers wandered around the otherwise unadorned room. Half the crowd came attired in vintage clothes: buckskin vests and bellbottoms, headbands and tie dye T-shirts. A few graying heads passed a marijuana joint, looking quaintly anachronistic, but the smell drifting through the room added one more touch of authenticity.

Pilgrim wondered who the soldiers were, faces flashing every four or five seconds, and then gone. None were identified by name. No doubt many of them were survived by wives and children, reflected the reporter, many of the youngsters would probably be his age now. Some might even be part of this crowd. The show would run for a week before moving on to Boston and, in that time, perhaps the thousands who served and died would glow for a moment. We are survived in death only by the individual memory of close friends and family and, if fortunate, by the collective memory of society. But for most of us, sadly, after three generations almost all memory of our existence is wiped from the face of the earth.

"Whatcha thinking of man?" said Bobby.

"Just thinking what a cross section of races these faces represent."

"But not a cross section of American society."

Pilgrim sighed. "You can hardly expect rich folks' sons to be plodding through rice paddies, getting shot at by peasants."

"The day that happens, you know bullets will be sugar-coated and war will be fattening instead of fatal to your health."

Bobby shouldered him as he stared at the wall, faces blinking in the dark like a lonely stoplight in a mid-west town. An anthem by the Byrds played and the voices in the gallery chorused with the musicians.

> Good and bad, I define these terms
> Quite clear, no doubt, somehow.
> Ah, but I was so much older then,
> I'm younger than that now.

Bobby spoke between a sip of wine. "I've been thinking: I'd like to take that whole Zapruder film and enlarge it frame by frame and see if this gallery owner would put it on her walls."

"Must be a lot of individual frames."

Bobby nodded.

"Maybe three or four hundred, maybe more."

"Sounds like you've gotten suddenly inspired."

"Well, someone's got to carry the torch for these fellows who've fallen," Bobby said with a frown; "and it sure-as-hell doesn't look like it's gonna be you."

Pilgrim stared for a moment, saying nothing.

"I saw your man, by the way."

"What man?" Pilgrim said, surprised. "Where?"

"Jeremiah; he's over there, standing in the corner, looking like someone stuck a scorpion in his sock."

The reporter stared into the darkness but found it impossible to see anything. Maybe Smith was mistaken. South Florida was awash with retirees, thousands who probably looked just like Jimmy.

"I saw him talking to the woman at the desk," added Bobby.

"That woman is the owner, Joyce Virden," Pilgrim replied. "I spoke to her earlier, right after we came in."

"You gonna write a review in the Satellite for her show?'

"Maybe."

A brief lull in the music caught the attention of the growing crowd. If the number of people got any larger, Pilgrim thought, the local fire marshal would probably shut the place down. He stared at the walls and the celluloid faces that appeared there became distorted, older, hardened—crueler. A videotape featuring Lyndon Johnson addressing the nation, lips moving but wordless, stained the wall. Nixon and McNamara appeared like a pair of demonic mimes, and then Kissinger too. A familiar guitar riff rose on the speakers, rising as the faces of the powerful men from the Vietnam era appeared. A number of catcalls and boos echoed for the architects of the war but they were replaced by the power and immediacy of the song, replaced by applause, whistles and cheers. "All Along The Watchtower," Hendrix's anthem, seemed to crush the powerful political players and their lackeys simply by the strength of his vocals and guitar chords alone.

> There must be some kind of way out of here,
>   Said the joker to the thief,
> There's too much confusion,
>   I can't get no relief.

Pilgrim's jaw dropped. The videotape spewed forth footage of the war crimes, super-imposed on the heads of the leaders: bombs tumbling from B-52s, spilling across McNamara's head;

napalm roasting the triple canopy of the jungle, Nixon's face emerging from the fiery blob; kids scurrying from the battle zone with flesh hanging from their limbs, rushing from the rotund face of Kissinger; bloated bodies of peasants, bloodied bodies of American wounded, all super-imposed on the heads of Pentagon leaders, accompanied by Hendrix's crashing guitar.

And then Pilgrim spotted the face, glowering off to the side. Jimmy Jeremiah stood in the shadows, looking at the walls, his expression grim, twisted with a mixture of anger or impatience, lit occasionally by flashes of mortar fire, bombs and navy guns.

Chapter 7

Pilgrim awoke, checked his alarm and rolled out of bed.

Although small, the ocean front apartment contained his entire scattered yet compartmentalized life. A poster of Disney World decorated the bathroom. A framed picture of the space shuttle hung above the sink and he stared at it while brushing his teeth. In the small but sunny bedroom, strewn with his clothes, a cityscape poster of New York City hung. The twin towers of the World Trade Center—gone now these past few years--loomed over the most powerful city in the world, overlooking the Hudson River. Framed color photographs of Yosemite and the Grand Canyon, purchased in New Jersey, vied for attention in the living room. Pilgrim rarely ventured out into nature; the vagaries of mankind were wilderness enough for him; he preferred nature at a distance, panoramic and suitably framed.

Taken together, the posters and photographs decorating his apartment, while chosen randomly and without any decorative sense, spoke of Pilgrim's optimism and almost childlike faith in the institutions of America. The Disney castle, the space shuttle Columbia, the twin towers of the World Trade Center epitomized the greatness, zest and creative imagination of the nation. Yet an uneasy feeling--repellent and undeniable--that he was consorting with someone evil and yet somehow more representative of the real America, clung to Pilgrim that morning like the cigarette smoke clinging to the clothes he wore yesterday evening.

Within minutes of leaving his apartment, he padded across the sand, passing sunbathers, until he came to a shady fringe of palms where Jeremiah sat alone on a weathered bench,

"About time."

"Saturday I usually sleep in."

Jimmy grunted, "I don't have too many more Saturdays left. The luxury of 'sleeping in' becomes the final sleep all too soon. You bring your tape recorder or maybe a notebook?"

Pilgrim nodded and produced a small tape recorder. He placed it on the bench between them and they watched the waves while the questions began to flow from the newsman.

"If Kennedy hadn't been killed in Dallas that day, would the Vietnam war have occurred?"

Jimmy shrugged. "I'm gonna give you a list of names and I want you to look them up individually on the Internet or a good search engine and type in JFK with each one."

"Are these names you're giving me more mysterious deaths connected to Kennedy?"

The old man sighed. "If you want to check out mysterious deaths of prominent people who knew too much, whose existence may have troubled those in power, check out the untimely deaths of James Forrestal, Paul Wellstone or Hale Boggs."

"Okay, go ahead," said Pilgrim, "The tape is rolling."

"Edward Lansdale, Eladio de Valle, Bernardo de Torres, Edwin Walker, David Atlee Phillips, Joseph Milteer, H.L. Hunt—"

"Wasn't Hunt an owner of a Texas football team?"

"Hunt was a wealthy, Dallas oil baron with ties to extremist right-wing groups. He said that the best way to remove Kennedy was to shoot him out of office, which we did. Not surprisingly, Hunt was never called to testify about his remarks, as far as I know."

Pilgrim rechecked his tape recorder to verify it was working.

"What about the rest of the names? What about Milteer?"

"Milteer was a wealthy militant with ties to extremist right-wing groups. Are you beginning to see a pattern here? Anyway, in early November an undercover Miami police informant taped Milteer saying that Kennedy would be shot from a tall building later that month. Because Milteer spilled his guts in Miami, the local police added extra security for Kennedy's visit there and the hit we had planned for Miami got cancelled and moved to Dallas. That's why whenever you read about suspects in the JFK murder case—people like me--they're always coming over from Miami, Florida in the weeks just before the assassination."

"But if Kennedy was so hated by the extreme right--didn't anyone ask why an extreme leftist like Lee Harvey Oswald would want to kill him?"

"One of the features of any successful black operation is to make sure everyone and everything appears exactly the OPPOSITE of what it really was. And we did that successfully in Dallas. Ed Lansdale, who had resigned from the CIA on Halloween of 1963, probably planned the entire Dealey Plaza operation—no one knows for sure--with precision so that everything would look the exact opposite of what really occurred."

Pilgrim shook his head. "This is amazing—absolutely amazing."

"Only the tip of the iceberg."

Pilgrim looked perplexed.

"Listen, people like you and me are like a bunch of stupid penguins standing around on an iceberg. We can barely see the top of the iceberg, which is the top part of the goddamn political system, and we certainly can't see down below. But if you dive down you can make out the murky shape in the cold darkness. It's scary and dangerous down there but that's where you and I have to go."

The reporter nodded. He knew that good stories revealed themselves in fragments that seemed to have no coherent shape or form; each person revealing the small part adjacent to them. Jimmy

Jeremiah knew the ominous shape as an iceberg, and perhaps that analogy was apropos: an iceberg could roll over and crush them or drown them at any time without warning.

"Mr. Jeremiah: when did you first hear of the plan to kill Kennedy, and when did you become actively involved?"

"I first heard rumors of an actual plan two months before the assassination, in September of '63." Jimmy watched a pair of policemen in a pick up truck cruise slowly down the beach. "But like I said there had been whispers long, long before. People—powerful people---wanted Jack killed. You see, JFK was a very good man, and yet a very wicked man too. Camelot was a whole lot of camouflage for the media and the average, uninformed man in the street. Perhaps Jack Kennedy epitomized America, he represented a cross-section of our national character--lust, charm, cussedness, generosity, cruelty and a kind of hardheaded idealism. And so he had to be killed."

"Tell me, were many people involved?"

"Oh yeah. You've heard the saying, 'Two can keep a secret, if one of them is dead'?"

"Yeah, I thought some news reporter invented it."

Jimmy laughed. "Well, in a conspiracy like this one, you can have lots of people in on it. Maybe hundreds."

"How can a conspiracy to kill the president have hundreds of people involved in it and not get revealed?"

"Fear."

The reporter looked incredulous. "Fear? Is that all?"

"It's more than enough. Think about it: a hundred people know about a plot to kill a president, even a thousand. Fear of retribution will keep the one person from ratting on the 999. And all the other folks involved will deny the statements of that one whistle blower, ridicule him, deny him. He's dead physically, socially or psychically if he talks."

"So why are you talking?"

"ɔcause I'm not afraid anymore," Jimmy said with a faint "I'm already dead."

"We keep coming back to the question of what proof can you offer of your involvement?"

Jimmy nodded. "Good question, and I've already thought of that. Remember when I said everyone else involved was dead? Well, two other gunners are still alive."

"How many were there altogether?"

"There were four teams of two each. Eight altogether. Four guns and four spotters."

Pilgrim stared in amazement. Eight men in Dealey Plaza that day? Hundreds of others, perhaps, with foreknowledge of the assassination? He hurriedly reached for a pen and pad and scribbled notes while he shook his head in disbelief.

"Tell me more; keep talking."

"We were called FTAP, the eight of us. FTAP was an acronym for our covert operation--which some of us thought meant 'fuck the American president'. Anyway, FTAP was planned for much longer than two months, maybe as far back as a year, maybe even two."

"Who planned it? How high up did it go?"

Jimmy looked puzzled. He stared at a man wielding a metal detector at the edge of the shore. To uncover treasure was a long and laborious process, the sifting of sand a scoop at a time.

"Maybe as high as Helms. He was in charge of clandestine operations. Maybe higher, maybe Dulles. I'm also sure Hoover knew and so did LBJ. Also remember, LBJ and Hoover were friends and neighbors; they lived on the same street. Did you know that LBJ and Hoover were BOTH going to be forced out by Kennedy in 1964? Hoover was going to be forced into retirement and LBJ dropped from the ticket. That was no rumor; that was fact. Also, Hoover exerted tremendous power and had over 2,000 people bugged with listening devices. Without power, J. Edgar Hoover was nothing more than an ugly old man who liked to dress in woman's clothes. Also, Vice President Johnson was politically ambitious and was rumored to have had people down in Texas killed already. Then too, Dulles had the motive for revenge and the connections, but then so did Cabell. The more I think about it the more I believe they ALL were involved and those who weren't directly involved were silent accomplices. Accessories before and after the fact."

"Who was Cabell?"

"Four star Air Force general, born in Dallas. Former deputy director, CIA. He was sent packing along with Dulles and Bissell after the disastrous Bay of Pigs fiasco."

"They got blamed for the defeat at the Bay of Pigs?"

"Blamed and shamed."

Pilgrim thought for a moment. "If they all got fired, then one or all of them had a motive for the murder of JFK. They certainly had the means and opportunity to carry this thing out, at Dealey Plaza."

"That's what Garrison thought too. That was the only time I got nervous we might get found out, when Jim Garrison started snooping around. But all of Garrison's subpoenas to get powerful people to testify were denied by the government. The cabal stuck together for the Cabell". The old man laughed at his pun.

Pilgrim smiled and checked his tape.

"He's never at a loss for words, that's for sure."

Bobby's eyes glistened in the reflected footlights and neon of the strip club. Teresa danced before him on the stage, a brief iridescent thong her only garment. She caught Bobby's eye and he winked.

"I'm beginning to think he might be telling the truth." Pilgrim shouted above the music. "I've tried to check the facts with what he's said and most of it checks out."

The photographer nodded. "Yeah, the more I read about what happened that day in Dallas the more the official government version begins to look too perfect. There were too damn many coincidences. Another thing, a whole lot of eye witnesses in

Dealey Plaza had their camera film confiscated that day, by people claiming to be Secret Service—but there wasn't any Secret Service guys in Dealey Plaza that day."

"The old guy, Jeremiah, said they had quite a few of their CIA people on the ground, playing different roles. I wouldn't doubt if the FBI was there too. Nothing was left to chance. They had to get this guy Kennedy out of office."

"So what now?"

"I'm gonna meet Jimmy tomorrow, on his boat. He's got a friend he wants me to talk to."

"Yeah? Who is he?" Bobby feigned interest but his attention wandered elsewhere.

"His name is Manuel Flores, a Cuban guy. He was one of the other shooters that day."

Chapter 8

"Karma comes around and kicks us all in the ass," said the man in the wheelchair. The last thing the reporter expected to see was a genial old gent with no feet shifting uncomfortably in a stainless steel wheelchair, greeting him from the shelter deck of Jimmy Jeremiah's 40- foot boat. Pilgrim nodded hello and sprung aboard.

"You must be Mr. Flores. I'm Daniel Pilgrim."

"Manny. Don't need to call me mister."

"Call him Many Flowers, or well-the-hell-is many-flowers, like we used to do back in the service." Jimmy emerged from the main cabin carrying drinks.

"Won't be too many flowers left soon," replied the Latin; "And I sure won't get none on my grave."

"Hey!" Jimmy barked, "Shitcan that self-pity."

The two old men laughed. Jeremiah handed Flores a drink and ducked back into the cabin to prepare one for Pilgrim.

"I appreciate meeting and talking with you," the reporter said awkwardly. A gentle breeze drifted over the water and the plume of the canvas awning bulged and swayed.

"What you want to know exactly, Dan?" Manny emptied his glass just as Jimmy emerged from the cabin with two more glasses and a pair of bottles. Jimmy slid into a seat, cocked his head in Pilgrim's direction, and pulled a hinged formica tabletop down and began mixing drinks. The reporter joined him.

"He wants to know everything," Jimmy said. "Whatever you can recall and nothing you can invent."

"Well," Manny began, "Memory and invention kinda get married after forty years, don't you think? Or maybe they live together and, like a couple who argue all the time and don't get along so well, the facts get all mixed up."

"Just get to the facts you do know, Manny; the reporter here don't have all day."

Pilgrim smiled and grasped a pair of fresh limes. He nodded at the rubicund face of the man in the wheelchair, hardly the image of an assassin. Bald, rotund and baby faced, cocoa brown and glistening—Flores appeared almost as the reporter imagined Buddha--seated now cross-legged in the padded chair.

"I couldn't help notice the name of your boat. The Big Lie. Is that a reference to fishing or is it a reference to that day in Dallas?"

Jimmy grinned at his Cuban friend. "Bright boy, didn't I tell you? That's why we want Dan telling our story."

"The legacy of Dallas is built on a foundation of lies; is that true?"

"Not all of it, " mumbled Manny. "But most of the important parts."

Pilgrim nodded. "And you want to set the record straight while there's still time?"

The Latin man spoke. "We were young—I was only 22-- but when we drove over to Dallas from Florida, I don't think anyone said much about the right or wrong of what we were sent to do. When you get older you have the time to ask the questions you didn't ask back then."

"So everyone came from Florida?" Pilgrim pressed his tape recorder. Then he sipped his Vodka Collins.

"At least four of us did," Manny replied, searching the bottom of his glass. "I think those two European fellows were already in Dallas and so were some of the others."

"So how many were there all together in the assassin team?"

"Eight: four groups of two."

Pilgrim nodded, inwardly pleased to see the two had at least gotten their story—if fabricated—straight.

"Who were the Europeans? Why were they there."

"French OAS assassins on loan. You remember their names, Jimmy?"

"One guy who was in Dallas was named Jean Soutre. Also a guy named Michel Mertz was there on the 22nd but later I heard he was the same guy. Now I'm not even sure about either of them."

Manny nodded. "All of us were working under different names. I heard later a rumor that Frank Sturgis and Howard Hunt were picked up in Dallas pretending to be vagrants but by then me and Jimmy had gotten out of there."

The reporter nodded. "But I thought Hunt and Sturgis had alibis?"

The two old fellows exploded with laughter. Manny dropped his glass but it didn't shatter.

"What's so funny?" asked Pilgrim.

"What makes an alibi so damn sacred?"

"Yeah, anybody can get one anytime. A guy gets another guy to alibi for him when he wants to play cards or get a little pussy on the side," Manny confided. "We had airtight alibis that we were both here in South Florida on that Friday, so who-the-hell knows where Hunt was exactly."

Jimmy nodded. "We both knew Hunt through the CIA. Hunt was a political officer and propaganda expert—and what better guy to have in Dallas than a propaganda expert? Do you know, Dan, during Watergate, Mrs. Howard Hunt and some other conspirators tried to blackmail President Nixon, and threatened to reveal to the public what Dick Nixon might have known about Dallas that day in 1963? The blackmailers got away with two million but the plane they were on was sabotaged and crashed and nobody escaped alive and, of course, the media didn't report the story. Anyway, Hunt helped organize the Cuban Revolutionary Council, which was CIA controlled, and which Manny belonged too."

"So was Hunt in Dallas?"

Jimmy looked confused. "I can't remember if I saw him in Dallas. Hunt may have been in disguise. But Marita Lorenz, former mistress of Castro, who escaped through some arrangement of Sturgis, testified under oath she saw Hunt pay off some of the FTAP shooters in Dallas the day before we shot Jack. Now why would Marita, who was later a paid informer for the DEA and the FBI, betray fellow agents Sturgis and Hunt, when we know she was recruited by Sturgis in Havana to be a helluva useful CIA agent?"

"Maybe she wanted to clear her conscience, maybe Sturgis pissed her off, made her jealous, maybe she was just making up a story," Pilgrim offered.

"Maybe. But then maybe Marita was telling the truth. I think she was. But nobody connected with the Company, with the CIA, is to be trusted completely, including me or Manny, certainly not Hunt or Sturgis."

Pilgrim scribbled the name, Marita Lorenz. "I'll check her out."

Jimmy nodded and retrieved the highball glass. "Remember also, the foxes will alibi the wolves, especially if the wolves agree to alibi the foxes, while they all take turns sneaking into the hen house."

The two old men laughed uproariously again. Jimmy splashed some more lime juice into his old friend's glass and jiggered a couple ounces of vodka on top and then swirled the mixture around.

"You got sugar?" Manny said, extending his glass.

"I got Sweet n' Low," Jimmy replied; "I ain't allowed sugar."

"Doctor told me to avoid sugar and alcohol, so I just combine them and hope they cancel each other out."

Jimmy chuckled.

Manny continued. "Sugar rotted my legs; diabetes ate up my feet. Karma comes around and kicks us all in the ass."

"What do you mean by that, Manny?" Pilgrim asked.

"I shot Jack Kennedy in the back and helped put him headfirst into a grave. Now God is dragging me feet first into my own grave. Slow and painful, bit by bit. Karma comes around and kicks us all in the ass."

"We're racing each other to the finish line of death." Jimmy said. "You ready for another?"

Pilgrim nodded. What were the questions that most needed asking?

He unfolded his notebook and watched Jeremiah prepare the drink.

"Where was everybody that day? Where were the European shooters?"

"The company didn't coordinate the teams, so nobody knew where everybody else was," Manny said.

"That's not exactly true, Manny—"

"They didn't want the left hand to know what the right hand was doing," Manny said," In a manner of speaking."

Jimmy nodded. "For security purposes that was true. But I knew where the other teams were that day. We had radios."

Manny looked pensive, his memory under strain. "I think the shooters on the second floor of the Dal-Tex building—or were they on the third floor?--they had silencers on their rifles but I wasn't allowed a silencer on mine. That was also part of the plan."

Pilgrim scribbled the name. "I never heard of the Dal-Tex building."

"On Saturday November 23, one day after the JFK assassination, somebody, whether the FBI or the Dallas police, set up a tripod on the fire escape of the Dal-Tex building, sixty feet across Houston from the book depository, with a rifle or a scope mounted on it. Now why would the Feds do that unless they knew some shots came from there? I think the FBI found some shell cases there, from some of our shooters in that exact same place. I do know that the Dallas cops questioned a couple of guys they caught coming out of Dal-Tex building moments after the assassination. I think they were on the FTAP team."

Pilgrim scribbled furiously. "What happened to them?"

Manny scratched his crotch. "They were let go. Bradley, or Braden, was the name of one of them, I think. That's the thing; nobody knew exactly where anybody else was except Jimmy here."

"That was the beauty of the whole plan."

Pilgrim stared at Manny. "Where were you both at that time? Were you on the grassy knoll?"

"No, that was Tony Lester and someone else." Manny turned to his friend and nodded in the direction of the reporter. "He talk to Tony yet?"

"What are you crazy?"

"I'd like to talk to Tony Lester," said the reporter. "Is he willing?"

The two old men exchanged a serious look that surprised the reporter. Pilgrim had seen that look before. A look of fear.

"Let me rephrase it this way," Pilgrim said: "I'd like to talk to him, even if it's off the record."

"Off the record or not, he wouldn't allow it."

"Over his dead body," smirked Manny.

"Maybe if I wore a wire."

"He'd kill you if you got found out."

The reporter swallowed his drink.

"Okay, tell me, how did you two get away?"

"Manny and I rolled out of the book depository in thirty seconds flat. Oswald had arranged for us to use Ruth Paine's car—Rambler station wagon with roof racks—and Manny had parked it behind the book depository like we were making a pick up or delivery."

Manny nodded. "I drove away, got turned around on Houston Street and when I got back to get Oswald he musta thought I'd left him, abandoned him."

"So Lee panicked," Jimmy continued, "and took a bus. Then he saw the car, got off the bus and caught us in the front of the depository. That's where deputy sheriff Roger Craig spotted the car with Manny driving."

Pilgrim looked up. "He reported you?"

"Sure, but no one seemed concerned. Funny, but according to the Warren Commission Report, the Dallas police were sending out APBs at 12:45, and again at 12:48 and 12:55, to be on the lookout for a white male, approximately 30, slender build, height 5 foot 10 inches, and weight 165 pounds. Now if Kennedy was popped at 12:30—fifteen minutes earlier—and no one knew for sure who did it, how did the police suddenly have a description of a suspect that exactly fit Lee Harvey Oswald when they didn't even know Oswald left work?"

"Maybe the book depository boss fingered Oswald?"

"Nope. Roy Truly was on the roof of the building with officer Baker, who had confronted Oswald earlier and Truly had cleared him. Not until well after 1 PM did truly do a roll call, and not until 1:20 did he notify Chief Curry that Oswald was missing from the premises. Curry was on the sixth floor and I don't think they had even found the alleged murder weapon yet. So how did the Dallas cops know what the suspect looked like—a suspect that fit the description of Oswald almost exactly?"

Manny spoke. "We were supposed to do Oswald later that day."

The reporter perked up his ears. "You mean shoot him?"

Jimmy nodded. "We were instructed to find him at home, get his pistol, and shoot him and make it look like he had remorse. Nice and neat. We even had a suicide note."

"A suicide note? For Oswald?" Again the reporter wrote furiously in his notebook. "Do you know who may have written it?"

"I think I got it from Lester. He passed it on to me earlier that day, but I don't know who wrote it exactly."

"Now I remember" Manny brightened; "his landlady was home that day. We couldn't shoot him."

"That's right, not unless we killed the woman too."

Manny added, "I didn't want to shoot Oswald anyway."

Jimmy shook his head. "Bad enough what happened to him later."

Pilgrim interrupted. "Did Oswald shoot that cop?"

"I don't know who shot Tippit, I really don't."

"Lots happened that day we hardly know about."

"What about this Tony Lester fellow?" Pilgrim clicked his pen impatiently.

"He got away after that woman Jean Hill spotted him behind the fence above the grassy knoll—that's what he told us later. Lester had a spotter who was hanging around at the edge of the trees and that's why some people thought they saw two or three men behind the fence."

"Yeah, he rolled out of there and got away in that black car of his, I guess."

"Was Lester with the CIA; was he part of Operation Mongoose?"

"Yes and no. He was a sub-contractor. I met him either at Camp Peary or Langley, or maybe in Florida. That's where Manny and I met, down here in Florida at Richmond Naval Air Station. It was over forty years ago, remember."

"When you say Langley, you mean CIA headquarters, right?"

Jimmy Jeremiah nodded. "Yeah--Langley, the original Death Star."

The reporter made a notation to research Richmond air station.

The old assassin continued to speak, his gaze distant, fixed on the past, focusing on a single aspect that twisted his features into a grimace.

"One thing I always found upsetting about CIA headquarters was a quotation by Jesus Christ they have there. The inscription is carved in the marble, way up where everyone can see it and says: 'You shall know the truth and the truth shall set you free.' I must have looked at that inscription a half dozen times and always found the words ironic, almost like they were put there purposely to mock me--especially knowing how we secretly lied, tortured and murdered in the name of national security."

Manny nodded. "And don't forget assassinations made to order. I can't remember all of the ones I did. Except late at night, that is. "

Bless me Father for I have sinned, thought Jimmy.

Chapter 9

Bobby Smith slipped the rifle from the zippered leather case and set it on the counter. Joyce Virden stepped closer and admired the weapon, listening to the description while fascinated by the proposal from the two men standing before her.

"Mannlicher-Carcano, 6.5 millimeter, Italian made, bolt action carbine. Model 1938 with attached four power scope. This is the same make and model weapon that killed Kennedy in 1963."

Bobby hesitated for dramatic purposes and then continued.

"Or WAS it really the weapon that killed Kennedy?" Bobby said, before looking at Daniel Pilgrim.

"Forty years ago they killed JFK," the reporter began. "The weapon you see was implicated in the plot. We have reason to believe sinister forces, never questioned in the crime--"

"Due to being in positions of power at the time--"

"—had motives and sufficient means to carry out the assassination far better than Oswald with this ancient, war surplus weapon."

Bobby continued, "What we propose to do is reproduce 300 of the frames from the Zapruder film and blow them up. Every five or ten frames we'll have a white string leading from a photo of Kennedy to a likely suspect in the killing. Dozens and dozens of strings. Guys like Mafia henchman Sam Giancana or CIA boss Allen Dulles; guys like CIA operative and Oswald's best friend in

Dallas, George De Mohrenschildt, or shadowy fellows like LBJ or J. Edgar Hoover."

Joyce arched an eyebrow.

"We'll have strings tying all those guys indirectly to the crime and let people judge them in the court of public opinion."

"And you're a photographer for the Sun Satellite?"

Bobby removed his wallet and handed his card to the curator.

"Do you know there were 75 photographers in Dealey Plaza the day Kennedy was shot. Half of them were professionals. They took at least 500 photographs in the six seconds of shooting but the Warren Commission was permitted to see only about 25 pictures and they only heard testimony from three or four photographers. Why was that? On top of that the FBI only examined about 50 photos. A Navy Commander named Thomas Adkins, an official White House photographer, was filming from six cars to the rear of the motorcade, yet neither the Warren Commission nor the FBI was interested in his film or testimony, and neither was the House Select Committee on Assassinations in 1979. The reason? Maybe because Adkins was convinced the shots came from ground level and to the front of the motorcade. Dozens of witnesses with cameras came forward, offering their precious film, but the Warren Commission and their paid whitewashers wouldn't touch it with a ten foot pole. To make matters worse, amateur photographers like Jean Hill, Norman Similas and Gordon Arnold, along with professionals like WFAA-TV news cameraman Thomas Alyea and NBC photographer David Weigman had there film confiscated and never returned. If that don't indicate a massive government conspiracy, I don't know what does."

Joyce Virden listened with concealed yet growing interest. Passion, idealistic passion full of fury or righteous indignation, amused or appealed to her, depending on the conditions of an individual's combustion. Most artists burned with an intense yet fleetingly illogical passion, fewer still burned with anything approaching commitment. She seldom showed an interest in a project by her expression, weighing instead the merits by a show of objective disdain.

"Where'd you get the rifle?"

"Purchased legally on the internet."

"Each suspect will have a brief bio, including possible motives and past criminal activities," said Pilgrim, with considerable calmness. He stared at the ice blue eyes of Virden and wondered whether he had ever seen her before this weekend at her gallery. As he grew older, Pilgrim became increasingly aware of the cultural shallowness of his life. Wouldn't this woman, with her gallery and her connections to powerful, creative people, be someone to know, someone to add some depth to his life? Pilgrim suppressed a smile. "Additionally we'll have a pair of mug shots of the usual suspects—Nixon, Dulles, Oswald even--to emphasis our point of view."

"Sort of like what detective Columbo would do to get to the truth."

"There were dozens of suspects in the Kennedy murder who had more of a motive than Oswald," added Bobby. "Nixon was in Dallas from November 20th to the 22nd; most people don't even know that. Why was he there?"

Joyce ignored the rhetorical question. "Legally you can't reproduce the Zapruder film."

Bobby shrugged. "The gray area of legality provides we don't try to sell prints. The Zapruder family already made more than ten million dollars on this 18 seconds of film but we don't intend to make a dime."

The reporter nodded. "We're doing most of the work after hours, at our own expense."

Joyce considered the proposal.

"I can probably squeeze you in three months from now for a week or two. I could possibly get some of my Palm Beach patrons to sponsor your show simply on shock value alone. The Kennedys are from Palm Beach, as you know and maybe they'll attend. Then we donate the prints to various collectors and museums."

"You won't be disappointed," Bobby said.

"What are you going to do with the rifle?" Joyce admired the antique weapon as one admires the patterns of a sleeping snake.

Pilgrim spoke: "Get a glass case made for it and display it in the middle of the gallery. You know any cabinetmakers?"

Joyce nodded. "My father can make a display case."

Bobby thanked her and sheathed the ancient rifle. Hardly the centerpiece of the show, the rifle was nothing more than a historical curiosity. But the photographer knew that the rifle—and the predictable media fanfare—would bring in droves of people who otherwise never went to art exhibits simply to stare at the weapon. The real centerpiece in the exhibition would be the photographs with a spider web of string connecting the culprits but people would come to see the rifle. Bobby intended to call the exhibit, "Tied To A Crime".

Jimmy Jeremiah existed for the moment. And those moments were becoming all too few and fleeting.

He lived in a second story shoebox of an apartment along the depressed miracle mile of Lake Worth, Florida. The more the area decayed the better he liked it. A sagging stairway clung to a stucco wall; an attached rail kept the whole thing from collapsing. Jimmy intended to outlive the stairway if not the rail. He had an air conditioner that worked well enough in the winter. He owned the few pieces of furniture, purchased used years ago, attaching that affection elderly humans have for utilitarian objects that have served their owners well for so long. Woodworking, an avocation that became a late-life love, relieved stress like sandpaper softens woodgrain. The wall cabinets, neither ornate nor crude, were polished veneer plywood that contrasted well with the bone white walls. Jimmy made them in the months after he moved in. A few pictures he rarely looked at anymore warmed the room, relieving the starkness.

Jimmy unscrewed a vitamin container, shook a half dozen pills into his palm and swallowed them with a glass of water. Then he stepped to a pair of saw horses in a glassed patio verdant with potted plants. An oblong cabinet lay like a fallen soldier across the saw horses and Jimmy reached inside and removed bronze hardware sealed in cellophane.

A knock at the door startled him. No one ever visited.

"Jimmy?" Pilgrim looked surprised, reflecting the surprise in the eyes of the older man.

"How did you ever find?—I guess you're a better investigative reporter than I gave you credit for."

"I was given this address by your daughter. Without a phone— Joyce said you refused to own one—she said the only way I could reach you was to ring your doorbell."

Jimmy stood aside. "I don't have one of those either. Guess it broke two or three tenants back."

"You daughter said you were a woodworker and you might help a friend of mine with a project."

"I don't do commissions."

Pilgrim glanced around the quadrant of the apartment. Somehow he had expected something different.

"C'mon in. I ain't much of a host."

The reporter stared at the photographs nearest the door.

"What? You expected maybe to see a picture of Dealey Plaza or the book depository? Maybe JFK in his limo?"

Pilgrim shrugged. He didn't know what he expected to find on the walls of a confessed assassin's home. Yet you could tell a lot about a person by the furnishings of his home. Over-furnished: a person who measured himself by the material possessions he accumulated. Over-decorated: a person striving to be fashionable. Cluttered: a person unable to focus in one direction. Jimmy Jeremiah fit none of these categories. There was an austerity that reminded Pilgrim of certain monks; he had once done a story on the monastic life and almost envied the freedom he found in the cloisters. The old man's room seemed to possess that same ascetic sense. Aside from a comfortable couch and an armchair, arranged around a circular rug, there didn't seem much in the way of furnishings. A floor-to-ceiling bookshelf, along an entire wall, caught the reporter's eye. There must have been 500 titles crammed into the shelves.

"I made that," said Jimmy with more than a little pride.

"Looks like you have quite a library."

Jimmy nodded. "And I read most of them too. Well, maybe half."

With an envious eye, the reporter studied the titles. Most of the books were weighty tomes devoted to historical subjects. Pilgrim noticed a copy of the Warren Commission Report. To one side was a thick copy of book called Crossfire and to the other stood a copy of Rush To Judgment. He hefted the book by the Warren Commission.

"A dry read," uttered Jimmy. "The other books are closer to the truth. Lucky for me, people in power swear by the one you have in your hand."

"So why do you want to suddenly upset the people in power?"

The old man heaved a deep sigh and stared at the books lining his shelves for many seconds before speaking. He wore khaki trousers and a faded blue denim shirt and seemed like the curator of a dusty museum, forgotten but not without inestimable value.

"I guess, after all these years, I want to be on the right side of history."

Pilgrim considered the words, not certain he had heard them correctly. "You mean to say, the book I'm holding, the Warren Report, is on the wrong side of history?"

Jimmy nodded.

"How much of it?"

"All of it--it's a crock--I should know. I was there."

"A crock? You mean none of it's true?"

"No, I didn't say that. But the basic premise of the report-- that the commission was conducting an objective investigation--is a complete crock. If the whole purpose of the inquiry was to establish justice and truth, and all of the facts of the case, than it failed. The Warren Report ain't the truth and it doesn't set you free. And what is the truth anyway? Remember what we talked about earlier with Custer and Crazy Horse? The way I see it, the truth can be shaded, facts omitted, testimony ignored, and conclusions drawn until you have a result that supports your position."

"So being on the right side of history might vary from century to century? The official history might be right today and wrong fifty years or a hundred years in the future."

"I think in this case, yeah. Most people accepted the Warren report when it came out in 1964 but now over 80% of Americans believe other shooters were involved. And of course, they're right." Jimmy choked back a laugh before continuing. "There are hundreds of books about what happened that day in Dallas that have more bits and pieces of the truth than all those pages of the Warren Report. And remember, all those other private researchers, working part time out of their own pockets, uncovered important evidence that was ignored or suppressed by the government."

The reporter slid the heavy volume back into the slot. Obviously, never had so many words served so long to fool so many people.

The reporter looked at his subject. "You want to be on the right side of history, but what if history doesn't want you?"

"I guess I got that coming to me then," said the old man. "I had a hand in history; I influenced history for better or worse, and it's funny to think, I'm not in any book."

Pilgrim nodded. More than anything he wanted to write a book. He wanted to place his book alongside these on bookshelves everywhere and have people read what he had to say, his thoughts, impressions and insights. He wanted intelligent people to admire what he wrote, flatter him even, and certainly, if possible, he wanted to earn a small measure of fame and fortune. But what if he succeeded in writing a book that caused such a controversy that people hated him for it—even if he was, as Jimmy Jeremiah said, "On the right side of history?"

"Can I get you something to drink, Dan?"

"No thanks, Jimmy." He turned away from the bookshelf with a tinge of sadness. King Solomon was right. Vanity of vanity, he repeated softly to himself, all is vanity. What did it really matter if he never wrote a bestseller; most of them weren't very good anyway and the histories that might shed light on matters of importance were mostly ignored.

With the practiced eye of the journalist—part voyeur, part busybody—Pilgrim noticed the patio.

"So that's your woodworking shop?"

"Yup, that's it."

He wandered in amid the wood shavings and hanging plants. For a moment Pilgrim stared at the oblong cabinet on the pair of sawhorses, admiring the clean lines and grain patterns of the wood.

"Building another bookshelf, Mr. Jeremiah?"

Jimmy shook his head. Then he spoke, with evident pride in his workmanship. "Nope—this here is my casket."

Chapter 10

He found his office, his cubicle at the Sun Satellite, oddly comforting. Pilgrim adjusted his chair before the computer monitor and inserted a disc. A stack of books rose to the left of his mouse and for a moment the many titles along the spine of each book became one long ominous sentence: 'They've Killed The President Six Second in Dallas Crossfire Accessories After The Fact The Secret Team Rush To Judgment On the Trail of The Assassins High Treason Conspiracy.'

Yet Pilgrim realized, that for all the thousands and thousands of hours of research done, the hundreds of dissenting witnesses interviewed and leads investigated and government files inspected, the official government opinion--and that of the US media--continued to be: Lone gunman, case closed.

How could he, Daniel Pilgrim, a reporter for a small market newspaper in South Florida, overcome forty years of inertia? Wouldn't it be wiser for him, with his modest credentials and a recent Pulitzer nomination, to attempt a more mainstream book? Wouldn't it be more profitable for his career to write an entertaining bestseller? Nothing controversial, adversarial or anything even remotely anti-government. Wouldn't it then be wiser, and in his own best self interest, to write what the public wanted to read, perhaps a colorful history of popular music or maybe an amusing trilogy about a boy sorcerer? What would Mark Twain do, he wondered, if presented with a man like Jimmy Jeremiah and the story he had to tell?

Pilgrim's fingers hovered over the keyboard. The easy way would be to write what others wanted him to write. The efficient way would be write what the public expected, literary diversion with predictable characters and a suspenseful yet romantic plot, while inserting an unexpected twist, and hope the critics called it new or novel. Actually, the easiest way would be to write the official version of the event--as that Wall Street Lawyer had done-- and let the media laud it like another discovery of the Dead Sea Scrolls.

Damn! Why did a man have to possess a conscience that could lead him astray, ethics that induced him down some proverbial "true path" full of briars and overhanging vines, when it would be far easier to take the wider and smoother downhill turnpike to material success? Pilgrim heaved a weary sigh, wishing he knew what to do, regretful that no other literary project--a project luring him with an elusive promise of commercial success--beckoned him at the moment. Thus he began to write, composing rough sentences while the convictions of his heart struggled with the hesitancy of his mind.

> "The amazing story you are about to read will shock, sadden or anger you. Certainly this book--"A Killer Confesses: The True Story Of One Assassin and The Secret Conspiracy That Killed John F. Kennedy"--will stun the world and shake the very foundation of our government. Many will doubt the words of Jimmy Jeremiah, an assassin, conspirator and dying man, and seek to disprove the veracity of this account of his misdeeds. Many in high positions of power and influence, including some with far greater culpability in the murder of John F. Kennedy and the continuing government cover up of the last forty years, will attempt undoubtedly to use their considerable power to silence him. We expect this abuse of power, indeed we

foresee this predictable reaction by those who have been hiding in plainsight for so many years with blood on their hands. We neither fear them nor shrink from their outraged response. Indeed we expect and welcome it, for they are the sinister foes of truth that will cringe from the facts of this crime now that it has been revealed."

Pilgrim shook his head after reading what he wrote. Where, he wondered, did he acquire this capacity for lofty-sounding yet pugnacious prose?

His phone rang, and Pilgrim plucked it before the second ring, inwardly proud of himself for finally making a start. The line went dead while he said hello and Pilgrim returned the phone without a second thought.

Before he could continue, his editor wandered in and gazed at the large laminated map of the Keys.

"I'm pondering if we need another column on the mysterious flotilla of marijuana bricks that continue to appear from Key Largo to Long Key," he said.

Felipe "Phil" Gonzales had lately worked at the Miami Herald, as an associate editor of the Opinion page, before assuming control over the content of the Sun Satellite.

"I thought you assigned the additional follow up to Everett?"

"Yeah, well, the story was originally yours, Dan."

"Okay Phil, I'll get back out there and see what I can find."

Although nearly sixty years of age, Gonzales appeared ten years younger. Bobby Smith dismissed him as a hard-ass 'Republi-Cuban" but Pilgrim saw a glimmer of the old, Pulitzer prize-winning newsman in Gonzales. Twenty five years ago he wrote amazing columns under a tighter deadline than Pilgrim did these days. An autocrat now, apparently unhappy with a management position but tied to a higher salary, Gonzales commanded a tight ship in a crowded, competitive market for news.

"By the way, what are you working on there, Dan?"

Pilgrim minimized the page and restored another column he had begun earlier that morning, before Gonzales turned his attention from the map.

"That piece about the local Café winning historic status to save the building from the wrecking ball. I thought perhaps people would look at our somewhat limited, Florida architectural history with a new interest, Phil."

"Good.... human interest.... History and human interest help sell newspapers every time."

Pilgrim wondered if he should mention his desire to write a story on the John F. Kennedy killing and decided now was as good a time as ever.

"Speaking of human interest," the reporter began, "Forty years ago next month President Kennedy got killed in Dallas. I was thinking perhaps of writing a retrospective for the weekend edition; it might interest our readers."

Gonzales folded his arms while his gaze grew inward.

"From a purely historical angle?"

Pilgrim nodded. "Sure, and also from the angle perhaps of how we've changed as a nation. Plus all that nostalgiac stuff about 'Camelot', of course."

"Nostalgia would be fine but go easy on the politics. Those were some pretty volatile days, especially here in South Florida. Maybe mention how small Miami was at the time; get some interviews with retirees; 'Where were you when you first heard the news about JFK's death and how did you feel,' that sort of thing."

Pilgrim tried not to sound too enthusiastic. "Maybe four or five thousand words with a half dozen photos?"

His editor looked surprised.

"I was thinking more like a thousand words max."

Pilgrim said nothing but perhaps his disappointment showed.

Gonzales noticed. "Okay, maybe a half page in Metro with a couple of photos from the archives. Why the sudden interest in Kennedy?"

The Guns of Dallas

"As you can see I've just been reading a lot of history of that era."

"Looks to me like all of your history books come with a built in conspiracy point of view."

"No—" Pilgrim shifted uneasily and adjusted his keyboard. "These books are just a few of the fringe accounts of that day. I've already read the Warren Report and wanted a dissenting perspective for the sake of balance."

Gonzales nodded but looked unconvinced.

"For those of my generation," Pilgrim explained, "Kennedy epitomized the 'Sixties. The short time he spent in office—during the early 'Sixties—will always be a mystery to those of us born later in the century. The Beatles, birth control, Baby Boomers, the beginning of Rock n' Roll—all of it seemed to have begun simultaneously with Kennedy. So John F. Kennedy--with his easy manner and tousled hair and photogenic family--seemed to fit right in with the particular era. Just like Eisenhower fit the 'Fifties and Nixon epitomized the tumultuous early 'Seventies."

"Kennedy was an anomaly," Gonzales said. "He wasn't presidential material and shouldn't have happened. My parents said he was the cause of Castro achieving absolute power in Cuba. I blame Kennedy more than I blame Castro actually. Not that JFK deserved to die in Dallas."

"I can see your parent's point of view."

"Can you?"

"Well, no, I guess I can't. I'm sorry. I admit that only someone who is of Cuban culture can fully understand."

Pilgrim wondered where the conversation was heading. His journalistic experience cautioned him now to use diplomacy instead of confrontation, especially with his superior, and so he chose his words with delicacy without trying to sound condescending.

"Felipe, do you think a full scale invasion of Cuba in 1961--had Kennedy given the go ahead--would have worked?"

"Of course it would have worked!"

"Okay. Suppose Castro is toppled and his army routed. Castro is now killed or in jail. Mobsters come back and re-open the casinos, the CIA returns and Batista wants to return too. With a power vacuum, the US military would have had to stick around like a referee, like we've stuck around in Iraq, because that's what we always do, Then what?"

"We would have had free democratic elections," replied Gonzales.

"I'm certain of it, even if it took several years."

"Which candidate do you suppose would win: The one who backed the US—as Batista did—or perhaps a Cuban nationalist? I mean wouldn't the CIA select the suitable candidate as it normally does in Latin America?"

"A Cuban candidate with democratic credentials would have arisen from within the ranks of the professional class that existed before Castro wrecked it."

"Okay—but wouldn't this fictitious candidate either have to court the pro-Batista crowd or represent the disenfranchised Castroites in some way to win—or better yet, suck up to the Americans?"

"You're so naïve when it comes to politics, Dan, especially Cuban politics." Gonzales narrowed his eyes. "Castro was the flip side of Batista, cut from the same ruthless cloth. But because Kennedy failed at the Bay of Pigs—he had no balls except when balling actresses like Marilyn Monroe--Cuba has suffered unnecessarily for over forty years."

"Ike had his mistress too and no one faults his leadership."

"But Kennedy got elected by campaigning on the issue of Cuba."

Pilgrim nodded. "I agree, Phil. Cuba has suffered unnecessarily. But weren't the Cuban revolution and Castro simply bound to happen sooner or later and, if not Castro, then someone else? Thus the blame lies not with Kennedy but with the Eisenhower administration, and the CIA, especially the CIA. They propped up dictators like 'Papa Doc' Duvalier in Haiti and that dictator Somoza in Nicaragua and Batista—"

"Bullshit! Early in the game, Castro got support from the CIA. The US supported both sides for awhile, trying to sort out a winner. Castro had the opportunity, after he achieved power, to ask for US aid and UN recognition and announce free elections, but Castro became as bad—No, worse!—than Batista."

"History has two sides," Pilgrim replied. "I'm not an apologist for Fidel Castro but I think Kennedy tried to use military force as the Pentagon hawks wanted him to, and then he tried diplomacy."

"What military force? Only Cubans got captured!"

Unable to focus beyond his sincere passion, beyond the adopted beliefs of his parents and their personal experiences, Gonzales no longer argued with objectivity, but as one who defends a precious territory. Yet he composed himself enough to speak clearly to the reporter.

"You're a fine reporter, Dan; not everyone is nominated for the Pulitzer Prize. But Kennedy was no hero."

"Maybe to some people he was—"

Gonzales shook his head. "As you may know from reading your Kennedy books—have you read 'The Dark Side of Camelot' Dan?—JFK was a compulsive womanizer, a weak man, worse than Clinton. I cannot permit Kennedy to be portrayed in this newspaper in an overly flattering or positive light. You can certainly write a retrospective of his life, and his minor accomplishments—although I'm not sure what those were—but I would like to read your final copy before it goes to print."

Stunned by the prospect of censorship, shocked at his failure of journalistic diplomacy, Pilgrim could only mumble, "Thanks, Phil, I'll get a copy to you."

Pilgrim found the Virden Gallery empty and quiet when he entered later that afternoon. The contrast from the opening night, with a capacity crowd singing to the music and light and imagery reflecting from the walls, impressed the reporter. Amazing how the power of imagery in culture can effect so-called civilized people as well as primitive races, he considered. Stone-age men worshipped fire while we space-age men--flitting about in jet airplanes and automobiles propelled by fiery explosions--worshipped firepower and the bendable, cinematic effects of light. Was there really a difference?

"Daniel!" Joyce swung around a partition. "What brings you here?"

The walls were empty of artwork and the space echoed.

"I'm not sure. Maybe the need to see a friendly face."

Joyce smiled. "You won't find many here, I'm afraid."

She noticed the confused expression on the face of the reporter and Joyce laughed playfully.

"Come look at the portraits that arrived for the next show."

They walked around the partition and entered a smaller room. Racks rose to the ceiling and paintings from past exhibitions were stored for easy access. A young man crouched before an enormous portrait, installing hooks and hanging wire to the frame.

"Let me introduce the artist, Ellis Overman," Joyce said. "Ellis, this is Daniel Pilgrim, the man I mentioned who is doing Kennedy research."

"Lyndon Johnson and I both say hello," said the lanky artist, rising to his feet. He stepped around several packing crates and kicked a swath of bubble wrap into a pile.

"Ellis will be having a show called, 'American Caesar: Fifty Years of the Imperial Presidency' starting next week," said Joyce. "I'm really learning a lot about American history from these last few exhibits and the one you and your photographer friend, Bobby have planned."

Pilgrim stared at the portrait of LBJ, half-listening to Joyce. The painting bore an uncanny likeness to the former president but the dramatic yet unflattering source of light in the painting suggested a powerful man, both the recipient and source of immense evil.

"Joyce tells me you're also a conspiracy buff, Dan," Ellis said lightly. "I'm convinced the American republic got hijacked long before Jack got popped in Dallas."

Joyce laughed, a little uncomfortably. "You'll have to excuse Ellis. His persona as an artist is intended to shock people."

The reporter smiled and Ellis grinned at the curator.

"Dan's not easily shocked, Joyce, after all he's a reporter. The only shock was when Dan got his first job at a newspaper. The shock came when he discovered how easily the so-called free and independent press has become a lackey to powerful special interests over the years."

Pilgrim smiled. Joyce shrugged her shoulders.

"Ellis is a grad student at Yale. His father is CEO of a major electronics firm," explained Joyce. "Understandably Ellis suffers from 'wealth-guilt syndrome' and uses art as therapy."

Ellis laughed. "I use art as a weapon and a mirror, as all great artists have, from Goya to Van Gogh. The rest of the populace is too easily beguiled by the manipulators of levers who continuously intone: 'Pay no attention to that man behind the curtain'."

Joyce shook her head. "Spoken like a man in need of a soap box."

Pilgrim wandered around inspecting the presidential portraits, many still enveloped by packing crates. Nixon looked like a sinister gnome; Ford a calculating bullfrog; Reagan a slick huckster, yet each president looked strikingly lifelike. The elder Bush appeared cast in titanium, hollow and impervious to emotion, the eyes dead pools of toxic, heavy metal. While staring at the portraits, Pilgrim thought of the poem, Ozymandias, recalling the lines from a college assignment, and began to recite them aloud from memory:

"I met a traveler from an antique land
Who said: 'Two vast and trunkless legs of stone
Stand in the desert...Near them, on the sand,
Half sunk, a shattered visage lies, whose frown,
And wrinkled lip, and sneer of cold command,
Tell that its sculptor well those passions read

> Which yet survive, stamped on these lifeless things,
> The hand that mocked them, and the heart that fed:
> And on the pedestal these words appear:
> 'My name is Ozymandias, king of kings:
> Look upon my work, ye Mighty and despair!'
> Nothing besides remain. Round the decay
> Of that colossal wreck, boundless and bare
> The lone and level sands stretch far away."

"Bravo!" Ellis declared. "How apropos. The 'lone and level sands';

I like that. Isn't that a metaphor for our entrapment in the Middle East by our imperial presidents? But we've got to get that oil, never mind the moral cost. I wonder, just because we're Americans, why do we think we're exempt from the lessons of history?"

"I don't think history will treat the Bush Dynasty any too kindly," Pilgrim said.

Ellis spoke, "Has anyone besides me noticed how the head of the CIA and the head of the KGB both rose to power in America and Russia? I mean, isn't that scary and ironic and humorous all at the same time?"

"Maybe it was only inevitable," replied Pilgrim.

"Predictable, you mean. George Orwell might have predicted the inevitability: how the heads of both spy agencies became the heads of their governments. By popular vote, no less! Orwell lives! By the way, do you like my dead presidents?—Even the living dead ones?"

"I'm impressed, but will they sell?"

Ellis appeared stung and affected a tone of wounded yet theatric sensitivity.

"How shallow to measure the value of art by its salability, or lack there of. How very, very American."

"I'm sorry,"

Joyce looked uncomfortable and Pilgrim reddened.

"I'm sure what he really meant to say--," she began.

"Dan said what he meant to say," replied the artist, "and what he meant was valid, for isn't that how we choose our presidents—whether they will sell? Or should I say, whether they will sell out?"

Pilgrim smiled. "Thanks for clarifying my thoughts."

"Ellis is least serious when he pretends to be most serious," explained Joyce. "Maybe Yale tweaked his brain with all that Ivy-league, upper crust education. I'm almost convinced Ellis is a genius but unfortunately so does he."

For once the artist smiled, an awkward smile, finally caught and exposed for being either a gifted imposter or an immature prodigy.

"I apologize for being young but not for being wise. Yale was where I learned how the world really works."

"Oh you poor little boy," said Joyce. "Most of us just work."

"No, listen: my father was a member of 'Skull and Bones'. Ever hear of that? An ultra secret society at Yale, open only to the elite offspring of powerful people. The most amazing thing was, even though my father changed his name to 'Overman' thirty years ago, my grandfather, Augustus Obermann, was a former high level Nazi Party intelligence agent. They must have known that!"

"Fascinating," said Joyce, well aware of Ellis' penchant for hyperbole and exaggeration.

Ellis laughed. "The most fascinating part was that the Bush family also had ties to the Nazi Third Reich, through Prescott Bush—a member of Skull and Bones—and his international banking connections."

Pilgrim's eyes bulged. How much of this was true, he wondered?

"Another snippet of Yale info: the CIA effectively grew to power there and all three of our past presidents were Yale men. Surprised? I now believe that all of our future presidents will have to come through either Yale or the CIA."

Ellis grew silent briefly while he wrenched the lid from a packing crate. President Jimmy Carter emerged, looking harmless and provincial.

"So, Dan, tell me what do you think of LBJ? I mean, what do you think of the man, not the painting?"

"I don't know much about Johnson. Just today I was told I don't know much about politics period."

Joyce came and stood besides the reporter and slipped one arm over his shoulder. Pilgrim liked that and put his arm around her waist.

"Just because I'm gay," Ellis trilled, "you don't have to show off your heterosexuality."

"Just because you're gay, you don't have to announce it to the world," replied Joyce.

"The most powerful man in the world—J. Edgar Hoover—was gay but afraid to out himself. Mostly because Hoover knew that America would boot him out."

The mention of Hoover sparked a thought in Pilgrim's memory.

"Hoover and Johnson were both going to get booted out," he said.

The artist sobered and Joyce looked interested.

"Really? Where did you hear that?" Ellis asked.

"An old history buff told me," Pilgrim explained, "He said JFK intended to force Lyndon Johnson off the ticket in 1964 and force Hoover to retire from the FBI when he turned 70 years old—mandatory retirement age for federal employees-- in 1965. Coincidentally, when Johnson became president, Hoover got to remain in power at the FBI until he died."

"Eureka!" Ellis shouted. "Skullduggery revealed. I knew there was something more sinister in Lyndon's past than just the illegal and immoral war in Vietnam."

"The removal of JFK from office seems like an American version of a Shakespeare play," Joyce remarked. "Like Hamlet."

Pilgrim grew pensive. "I wonder if Johnson was a perpetrator, an accomplice or simply a victim of the conspiracy to remove JFK?"

"A victim?" snorted Ellis. "Give me a fucking break! Where would you get an idea like that?"

"Sounds plausible," said Joyce.

"How convenient for those old conspirators. Johnson arranges to kill Kennedy and suddenly he gets to be president, while Hoover gets to remain in power for life. Excuse me if I don't squeeze out any crocodile tears for the two old tyrants. Victims indeed!"

Ellis removed the other presidential portraits with renewed energy, focusing his vexation on the packing crates. Joyce arched her eyebrows and Pilgrim shrugged. At least Ellis would have more dirt to shovel onto the graves of those with feet of clay, the reporter thought.

"C'mon, Joyce," Pilgrim said, "I'll buy you a late lunch or an early dinner and we can talk about something artistically uplifting."

"A deal," she replied. "Anything but politics."

Chapter 11

He wasn't sure how it happened but Joyce awoke beside him. Rather, he awoke and she remained sleeping peacefully. Wine, fine food, and lovemaking must do that to a woman, reflected Pilgrim. He remembered the previous afternoon ebbed away and the smell of the ocean drifting along Las Olas Boulevard compelled them to walk the few blocks to the shore. From there they watched the sunset with their backs to the diminishing rays, gazing at the whiteness of sailboats offshore and their own lengthening shadows in the sand. Had they kissed before the final patch of sun disappeared from the sand, he wondered?

Joyce stirred but didn't awaken.

He trotted to the bathroom and studied his face in the mirror. Kennedy was fifteen years older when he got killed. He studied his face for lines and his hair for gray. At thirty he felt the first pangs of mortality and watched for signs with bemusement and resignation.

Pilgrim prepared breakfast and squeezed the last few oranges, adding soda and zinfandel to give it some zing. He rattled dishes and dropped silverware in an effort to be silent and the commotion awakened Joyce entirely, for she entered wearing only a thin, sleeveless T-shirt shirt, which he recognized as his. She ambled into the kitchen just as he placed both dishes onto a tray and he tried not to stare at her breasts, their fullness pressed against the fabric. The hem of the shirt covered her hips but just barely. She embraced him from behind and Pilgrim lay the tray down.

"Sleep well?" he asked.

"Perfectly. Aren't you going to be late for work?"

Pilgrim thought of Gonzales. "No, I still have a little flexibility. The prestige of my Pulitzer nod will last another week at least."

"I'm proud of you. I would have given you a bonus."

Pilgrim smiled. "Thanks, I got a small pay raise."

They sipped the orange juice and, between kisses, Joyce picked at her breakfast with her fingers. Pilgrim joined her in an alcove overlooking an alleyway. The ocean was visible as a fragment of blue.

"So what are you writing now?" she asked. "A novel?"

"No. I'm toying with a work of non-fiction. I'm not sure if my heart is in it though."

"Let it go then. Set it aside and let the work ferment."

Pilgrim thought of her advice. Only problem would be whether the idea would ferment before the subject died? On the other hand, Jeremiah might have lied to him about having less than a year to live. Hell, he might be lying about the entire Kennedy assassination and his role in it. The idea made Pilgrim cringe.

"I might just take your advice," he said.

The room was warm, catching the early morning sunlight, three flights up from the street. Pilgrim enjoyed watching Joyce, enjoyed watching her eat, the sensual movement of her mouth as she licked her lips was pleasing to observe. The T-shirt clung to her breasts pleasantly, her nipples plainly visible, and her smooth thighs, now fully exposed, caught the soft light filtering through the curtains. Joyce saw him staring and lay her plate aside. With a deft movement that startled the reporter, she removed the shirt completely and arched her back.

Women fascinated Pilgrim, and alluring women mesmerized him.

Confident women, good-looking women of some complexity, women unafraid or, better yet, fearless, overwhelmed him. And shapely women, suddenly naked, yet with a mischievous grin, devastated him.

"Ready for dessert?" she murmured coyly.

He nodded, and tried not to stare but couldn't take his eyes off her.

They made love all that morning, interrupted only when he made coffee. Pilgrim carried the cups to her and found Joyce reading some of his early work from a file folder. He wondered if Joyce knew the complete history of her father. Perhaps her version would give a completely different picture of the man he would see later that day.

"Did you have a happy childhood?" he asked.

"Much happier evidently than these strippers you interviewed."

"Were you an only child—I imagine you as an only child—or did you have siblings to rival?"

"I have a half sister who I almost never see. She lives in Hialeah."

"Did you take vacations together; did you grow up believing your parents were the best people in the world?"

Joyce put down the sheaf of papers.

"My parents loved each other and we were moderately prosperous. This was during the 'Eighties remember, when the economy was booming and South Florida was leading the charge."

The reporter nodded.

"What did your father do for work: do you remember?"

Joyce got a faraway look in her eye and sipped her coffee.

"He seemed to have been some kind of building inspector or sub-contractor. His friend Manny—have you met Mr. Flores?—worked as a builder. They worked together building sub-divisions and remodeling homes. I don't know what James Virden did before I was born but my father was in the Navy when he met mom. He met my mother in Havana of all places but I'm not Cuban. Then, he worked for the government but I'm not sure how long that lasted. Before that he was in the Navy during the Cuban missile crises. But later I think he was a carpenter and became a contractor. He did build the addition on our house when we were growing up, I know that."

Pilgrim pictured the two feeble old men as younger versions. Perhaps they left the CIA together or—more likely—they never were in 'The Company' at all!

"Your father is an interesting old fellow. I like him. A good builder from what I could see of his work."

"Oh, so he is going to build that gun cabinet for you?"

"Your father, Mr. Virden said, and I quote, 'I don't do custom work', but I convinced him to make an exception."

Joyce smiled, picturing her father's reaction to seeing this stranger at his door.

"Dad's a recluse," she said, stretching and folding herself against the reporter, "but I'll bet he warmed up to you, Mr. Pilgrim."

"We seemed to have a rapport. In fact I'm going fishing on his boat tomorrow afternoon with that guy you mentioned, Manny Flores."

"I'm glad you're going along. I worry about those two old geezers when they're way off shore, although I don't think they do that much fishing anymore. They like to sit on the boat and swap lies now, mix drinks and mix up the facts as they talk about the distant past. By the way, catch me a fish and I'll cook it for you, okay?"

"Sure," said Pilgrim. Then he folded himself into the form of the assassin's daughter and wondered what truths he would discover on a boat named 'The Big Lie'

Chapter 12

"A wheelchair access strip club?"

"That's what he asked for." Jimmy shifted uncomfortably in the leather chair of Pilgrim's office. "Might be his last birthday. I mentioned to Manny a while ago you wrote an expose' on strip clubs and he said that you probably knew of one with wheel chair access."

Pilgrim suppressed a grin. "I know several. When's his birthday?"

"Next Tuesday but its gonna be a surprise. Don't say a word tomorrow when we're out on the water."

"Think we'll catch any fish?"

"Depends on where we go."

Bobby Smith hurried past the alcove, glanced inside and then returned.

"Mr. Jeremiah: How's it going down? Haven't seen you around lately."

Jimmy struggled to rise but Bobby motioned him to remain seated.

The old man shifted, visibly uncomfortable. His hands swept the few folds from the knees of his trousers and continued, restless, to search for hidden wrinkles to smooth.

"I guess I heard Dan say you're working on some photos?"

Bobby nodded. "Blow ups of the Zapruder film."

The old man swallowed, nervous. "I guess you've seen some pretty, uh, gruesome details."

Bobby pretended not to notice. "Someday in the distant future we'll have the technology to dissect each frame of the film enough to not only show the paths of the bullets as they move through the air but to determine the exact caliber of the weapons that fired them, the trajectory and the muzzle velocity."

"Really, is that so?"

"I don't doubt it for a minute. The only problem would be getting the goddamn government and the media of the future to acknowledge—even with scientific proof—that maybe Oswald didn't really pop the prez all by himself."

Pilgrim reclined in his chair and propped his feet on the edge of his desk.

"Hey Smith: what do you know about guns?"

"A helluva lot more than you do," Bobby replied. "What do you want to know?"

"He wants to pose as a badass undercover man so he can tape one of the other mechanics in the Kennedy hit," said Jimmy.

"What's a mechanic?" the reporter asked.

"Shooter. Hitman. Hired gun," Jimmy responded.

"You've interviewed all sorts of shady characters," Bobby began; "Just compile the worst traits and lingo of them all into one person and pretend to be him."

"I used to be an actor in college," Pilgrim said.

Bobby snorted, "Sure, I believe that. You been acting as a reporter ever since you've been here and fooling everyone around. Even Felipe—isn't that right, Phil?"

"I guess so—" Felipe Gonzales wandered past Pilgrim's cubicle before returning. "--whatever you say, Smith."

"I got to go," Bobby chortled. "Greatness awaits."

"See you, Bobby," Pilgrim called; "let's get together later and talk."

Gonzales spoke to the seated retiree. "I'm Felipe Gonzales. I've seen you around before; you a friend of Dan's?"

"We're doing research together," said Jimmy.

"The Kennedy thing?" the editor asked.

Pilgrim shifted uneasily. "That's right. Mr. Jeremiah retired to Florida and lives in Lake Worth, but before that he served in the Navy. I wanted to get a Navy man's perspective on the death of former Navy Commander Kennedy."

"Excellent," said Gonzales. Turning to Jimmy he said, "Where were when Kennedy died and how did you feel?"

"Well, I was shocked to tell you the truth. And I was on a business trip for the company. I worked for a company that sent emissaries all over the world."

"You mean like religious missionaries?" said Gonzales.

"Exactly. But eventually that religion became a cult I no longer believed in or trusted. I regret to say I disagreed with some of their core values and so I left. Now I believe in God the almighty and a fully loaded .44."

Gonzales laughed uncomfortably, unsure whether to take the old gent serious or not. Pilgrim held his breath, hoping the conversation satisfied his editor without provoking unnecessary suspicion. Jimmy smiled genially at the editor before he spoke again.

"Dan tells me you gave him the go-ahead on a story idea about JFK and the anniversary of his unfortunate death in Dallas?"

"Yes, we'll use your quotes if you don't mind, Mr. Jeremiah?"

Jimmy nodded. "What's your own opinion, Felipe? Where were you and how did you feel when Kennedy got shot?

"I was stunned," said Gonzales. He sat down for a moment on the edge of Pilgrim's desk. The reporter kept as silent and watchful as a cat, mindful of every word Gonzales said and the movement his editor made.

"I was in a freshman class at the University of Miami when they came in and made the announcement," added Gonzales. "I was only eighteen at the time."

"Do you think Oswald acted alone?"

"I think he may have had an accomplice but it's never been proven."

"How would someone prove that?" Jimmy offered. "I mean didn't the Warren Commission investigate that conspiracy theory completely to the satisfaction of everybody?"

Gonzales shook his head. "No, many people think there may have been others. Dan and I were just talking about that."

Jimmy smiled. "I've heard those rumors. I don't know if they're true or not. Some people have said—and I don't know if I believe them or not—that anti-Castro Cubans may have been involved. Some of my oldest and dearest friends are Cubans but if there was a conspiracy I don't think they were involved. What do you think?"

Gonzales looked thoughtful, almost conspiratorial. "Listen, this is confidential. Do you both swear you won't say a word?"

Surprised, Pilgrim mumbled assent. The old man nodded.

"When I was still in high school in Miami, many of the fathers of my friends were members or supporters of Brigade 2506. Do you know what that was?"

"Didn't it have to do with the Bay of Pigs somehow?" Jimmy offered.

"Precisely," explained the editor. "Both of my uncles were involved with the brigade and one of them even invaded Cuba in 1961 with the 2506."

"What happened?" asked Pilgrim.

"They failed," replied Gonzales. "They failed because Kennedy called off air support at the last minute. My uncle was captured but over a hundred Cubans were killed in the invasion and over one thousand were imprisoned."

"Damn shame," sighed the old Navy veteran. "No wonder some of them might have had a grudge against Kennedy. I know I would have."

"Yes, that is true." Gonzales turned to Pilgrim. "And that is why I cannot say much that is good about President Kennedy, Mr. Jeremiah. I cannot condone some of the things the brigade has done—support of the dictators Pinochet and Somoza, for example. But there are radicals within any group. Hotheads, as you would call them."

Jimmy nodded. "I know that for a fact."

"The most radical Cubans were members of Alpha 66 and a mysterious group of super commandos called 'S Group' and, while I was a student at Miami—which, believe it or not, was affiliated with the CIA--I heard rumors for many years that some of them might have been involved with the Kennedy assassination in Dallas."

Pilgrim nearly fell out of his seat but Jimmy sighed sympathetically. He had heard it all before. Manny Flores was a member of Alpha 66.

Jimmy walked the reporter to his car but rejected an offer of a ride. The autumn days were too nice and, he realized, he hadn't much more time to enjoy them.

"Information gathering is easy if you proceed in an unorthodox way," Jimmy remarked. "Gonzales was an easy lock to pick; he represents the majority of Americans living in denial but he spilled his guts like a broken gumball machine; I didn't even need a damn key.

"All that stuff about the CIA-Cuba connection I already knew. Hell, three former 2506 brigadistas were involved in the Watergate burglary and were recruited by Howard Hunt, a twenty year veteran of the CIA. Those who were caught got off with light sentences at country club lock ups and sweet book deals or media jobs like Ollie North and Gordon Liddy. The CIA looks after its own, just ask Tony Lester. Certainly the Cubans have many reasons to hate Kennedy but why they ever believed the Republicans cared about their best interests is beyond me. The whole purpose of political parties is to perpetuate their own power and get all of the perks for their followers they can."

Pilgrim remained awestruck by the performance in his office.

"Gonzales never said more than two words to me about the Bay of Pigs before," he said. "How did you do it?"

"Maybe you just never took the time to see his point of view."

The newsman laughed softly. "Yeah, how could I have forgotten: that's one of the cardinal rules of a good journalist?"

"Information gathering is an art. You should know by now, Dan. The way we're gonna entrap Tony Lester is to act like we don't give a goddamn about what he has to say when we finally go meet him."

"You mean it? We might tape Lester?"

Jimmy squinted. "When I'm done with you, you're gonna be one quiet, calculating badass sonavabitch. Tomorrow we're gonna take you down and get you a tattoo. Then over to a gun store for a crash course in firepower. We'll also have to get you a new wardrobe."

"Whoopee! I get to be an asshole!"

Jimmy nodded. "Yup, you can finally live out one of your secret fantasies. Listen, can you borrow a redneck pick up truck on the spur of the moment?"

The newsman looked confused before brightening, "Sure; I know a stripper that owns one."

"Okay. We'll invent a cover story and then I'll grill you like a squad room cop with a grudge until even you don't know your former self."

Attired in a sweatsuit and running shoes, Jimmy stretched his arms overhead. God, the day was beautiful. What a wonderful feeling, preparing for the ultimate black operation against a far superior but unsuspecting force. Could be his last.

"Speaking of journalism," he said; "Don't forget fishing tomorrow. And then on Tuesday, Manny wants you and me to celebrate his birthday with him at a gentleman's club."

"What does any of that have to do with journalism?"

"Everything and nothing. Bring a notebook and pen anyway. You never know when an old assassin or a young stripper might be feeling confessional."

Chapter 13

"Let's cut her loose and get some hooks in the water," Jimmy exclaimed. Pilgrim found the two old men surprisingly sober and the boat idling at the dock in the marina. A stack of fishing gear lay neatly in the shelter deck surrounding Manny in his wheelchair.

"Look out fish, here we come," Manny chortled.

"I hope you ate an early lunch, Dan." Jimmy grinned as he said this.

"Actually I skipped lunch, but I did have dessert."

The two old men exchanged a look of puzzlement. The boat moved powerfully, escaping the shore and slicing through two foot waves.

"As long as we stay out of the trough, you'll be okay," Jimmy explained. "Your stomach that is." The geriatric pair chuckled at Pilgrim's expense.

"What do we hope to catch today? The reporter asked.

"Whatever we're lucky enough to catch," Jimmy replied. "Whatever happens to be running past the boat."

"We'll catch something even if only a dogfish or barracuda," Manny observed. "A marlin would be wonderful or a tuna would do—wouldn't a dorado do wonders for you?"

The trio laughed.

"You ever take Joyce out on the boat, Jimmy?"

The old man looked at the reporter with what Pilgrim thought was a little sadness. "Years and years ago, or at least that's what it seems."

"She sure liked to fish as a little girl," the Cuban said. "Once she hooked a fish bigger than herself."

"A wahoo, if I remember correctly," Jimmy said. "I helped her bring it aboard. You know, now that I think about it, that fish weighed exactly as much as she did. About forty pounds."

They passed a sailboat a mile off shore and continued onward. The tint of the water changed color and gradually they swung around and shut off the engine and let the cruiser drift. The swells gently swayed the boat side to side.

After the hooks had hung idle for several minutes, Pilgrim finally asked: "Did Joyce ever know about Dallas? Did you ever mention it to her?"

Jimmy settled into a folding chair and stared shoreward. A baseball cap shaded his eyes and he seemed more relaxed than Pilgrim had ever known. The gentle slap of the water against the hull of the boat was the only sound for several seconds.

"Nope. What happened there happened long before she was born. I wasn't even the same man; I wouldn't even recognize the man I was before."

"I guess there isn't any reason why she should know. You're James Virden, builder, not Jimmy Jeremiah, in her eyes."

Neither man spoke for many minutes. Manny had gone below, where Pilgrim had carried him.

Jimmy spoke. "Most people--if they even think about Dallas these days--don't realize that what happened there is still happening today. All the events that are taking place in Washington DC are now happening because of what we did in Dallas that day. All the takeovers of countries and the huge deficit spending on weapons, and that fringe group of zealots in the Pentagon making policy, all of that is directly related to what happened that day in Dallas. And I'm not proud of it. Nosirree. But if Joyce finds out one day about what I did in Dallas, I still hope she loves me but I'll understand if she doesn't."

Pilgrim absorbed the words, wondering if he should comment, and then the old man spoke again.

"I almost wished some other person had spoken up long ago. If some top official had bravely come forward and testified, I think I might have spilled my guts for immunity or a reduced sentence. A few times I even thought some high government conspirator like Lyndon Johnson was going to confess and tell the whole story. Maybe someone has talked, but their confession probably got hushed up or destroyed. Or maybe just before they were about to talk, they got killed, like Bill Colby, former CIA director. Or George De Mohrenschildt, Oswald's mentor. George supposedly committed suicide with a shotgun blast to the brain, right here in Florida, but four people there at the house never even heard a sound. He was gonna spill his side of the story to a reporter and maybe even a House sub-committee but that shotgun blast cut his confession short. Anyway Dan, promise me that you won't destroy my confession, not even if Joyce eventually reads it, okay?"

"Okay."

Jeremiah pulled his cap lower on his head as Manny rolled out of the cabin. "I made a pitcher of margaritas and I hate to drink alone to celebrate my upcoming birthday but if I have to I will," said the Cuban.

The trio laughed and Pilgrim fetched the glasses while Jimmy raised the hinged table.

"I heard you talking about Dallas," Manny said. "I think you two should go."

"Go?" Jimmy replied. "Go where?"

"Go on over to Dallas and take Dan around and show him where it all happened. I hear they haven't changed a thing. You can still walk around the plaza and even go upstairs in the book depository like we did that week almost forty years ago."

The reporter pricked up his ears. "I think it's a great idea. I could get away around Thanksgiving."

Jimmy rubbed his chin. "I don't know…..maybe."

"You might get rid of some of your demons, Jimmy. And take some of mine and get rid of them too. Shit, you might just run into some of our old compadres up in the book building. You might even find my old rifle."

The trio laughed. Pilgrim refilled the glasses. The boat drifted with the current. Were they in the Gulf Stream, the reporter wondered? Two miles across the water, the skyline of Fort Lauderdale resembled a row of distant headstones glistening in the sun.

"Why did the ambush at Dealey Plaza work so well?" Pilgrim asked.

"Because we were so good," Manny said, before swallowing his drink.

Jimmy shook his head. "Because of all the planning that went down weeks and even months before the event. And because Kennedy had so many enemies who wanted him dead, nobody could be blamed. Imagine a half a dozen very rich and very powerful men sitting around a table after a round of golf, in an exclusive, private membership club outside Houston or Dallas or Washington DC. The sun is going down. An oilman says: 'I hear tell old Lyndon may get the boot and if that happens then that sonofabitch Kennedy will kill our oil depletion allowance'-- which was worth millions by the way. Another fellow, a retired general says: 'And I heard from all my friends at the Pentagon that Kennedy intends to close two dozen bases and move troops out of Southeast Asia. Are we going to let all of goddamn Asia fall to the Communist bastards?' And a third fellow, a Southern banker says: 'If Kennedy had his way, he'd force integration on us all—like he did down in Mississippi--and make interracial marriage a federal law, him and that brother Bobby and that nigger, King.' Finally a fourth fellow says: 'Someone needs to do something now before it's too late. Why I heard old H.L. Hunt say Kennedy should be shot out of office.' And the whole table laughs--and the following day all of those rich and powerful men are on the phone to other

The Guns of Dallas

men like themselves. So then it happened—JFK is shot out of office--but by a lone gunman with a shitty Italian, bolt action rifle with a scope that wasn't even true, from the sixth floor window of a building, at a moving target, in an automobile traveling under a tree. So, surprise, surprise—that's the official version. But before all that could happen the FBI had to do their very best in Dallas to coerce testimony from scores of eyewitnesses in Dealey Plaza who might have disagreed with the lone gunman scenario. And before that could happen, someone had to shoot Oswald, who was too damn trusting to get himself killed in a shootout in that movie theatre. And also, thanks to wholehearted media participation, Oswald got all the blame. So Dan, the beauty of the entire operation--besides the superb planning--was that the assassination could never precisely be blamed on any one group or individual."

"Except Oswald, that is," remarked the Cuban.

Jimmy continued. "But remember, all of those shadowy groups--Big Oil, Pentagon, FBI, CIA, LBJ, Wall street bankers—all of 'em had a hand in the killing, since all of them profited directly and none spoke out later."

The reporter flipped open his notebook. "I still want to talk to this Tony Lester fellow."

Jimmy Jeremiah looked disgusted. "Do you know how dangerous that is?"

"But if I can get Lester's confession on tape--since you said he fired from the Grassy Knoll—his corroborating testimony blows the whole Warren Report and forty years of media suppression right out of the water."

"Are you aware that Tony Lester is still well connected to the CIA?" Jimmy exclaimed. "His son works there! He has mob connections all throughout south Florida!"

"Look, I can pose as a Right wing gun nut. It worked for that informant that got Milteer to talk in Miami."

Jimmy chuckled. "What do you know about guns?"

"I could learn!"

"Sure, you could learn just enough about guns to get yourself killed by one."

Manny spoke. "I still think you should take the boy to Dallas and show him how the whole operation happened."

Jimmy looked thoughtful. "Maybe. Let me think about that idea. We just might do that after all. What better way to show him what went down."

Jimmy pulled his hat further over his eyes, scarcely concealing a wide smile.

"Gun nut: that's a laugh."

Chapter 14

"Get some new old clothes?" An expression more of dismay than disbelief flitted across the reporter's face. "Why should I?"

"You heard me, Pilgrim," affirmed the invigorated old veteran.

"Look at your clothes: what do they say about you?"

"I don't know—I guess they say I'm dressed presentably and professionally yet without undue ostentation."

The collar of his polo shirt brushed against his neck with reassuring softness; the satin lining of his sports jacket lay against his back with a refreshing coolness; the brushed cotton of his trousers and lightness of his socks enveloped his legs with a wonderful feeling of compatibility; his leather shoes bespoke a sense of style and dignified bearing.

Jimmy laughed derisively, shaking his head.

"To me and Tony Lester they say: I'm a geek; I work forty, fifty or even sixty hours a week for The Man; I mouth his opinions because I'm too afraid to express my own; I wear clothes that are a uniform of conformity and so-called good taste, designed not to offend the boss or any of his advertising clients. I know because I wore those clothes too."

The reporter snapped. "What do you want me to wear? Navy togs?"

The comment drew a suppressed smile from the old Navy man. At the traffic light he pointed to a mini-mall.

"Up ahead on the right you'll see a gas station and then a Salvation Army thrift store. Next to the thrift store is an Army surplus store. Everything we'll need is in those two stores."

Pilgrim swung his late model Toyota into the parking lot. He slowed to squeeze the compact car between a two tone, 1969 Oldsmobile station wagon with massive chrome bumpers and an advanced case of leprosy and a sagging 1973 Volkswagen van with bald tires and dusty windows.

"Watch that little old lady; she probably doesn't see you," advised Jeremiah.

"I didn't know you cared."

"Sure I care," said Jimmy. "She's probably a member of AARP like myself."

They entered the surplus store first and the old vet led the reporter immediately to an aisle of camouflage trousers and shirts. Distracted, Pilgrim gazed at the stacks of helmets and mounds of woolen socks and gloves. A row of rain ponchos exuded an odor of mold, while on the floor beneath the uniforms reposed an assortment of metal ammo boxes.

"Get two pair of trousers," Jimmy instructed; "One pair each, desert and jungle camouflage, cotton fatigue pants in your size. Get the used ones, in well worn condition but not torn.'

Pilgrim followed the old fellow to an aisle of boots. Jimmy handed him a pair of Doc Martens.

"Pre-owned. Steel toed. Try them on. Get ones that fit."

Next they wandered down an aisle of used fishing gear. Jimmy selected a serviceable deep sea fishing pole with a reel.

"Do you have any poles that may have been stored for a long time or, better yet, dropped in salt water?" he said to a clerk.

The clerk looked puzzled for a moment before he spoke.

"I have a fine old split bamboo pole with a corroded reel that just came in, probably hasn't been fished in thirty years, but you couldn't fish with it now. The reel is frozen solid."

"I'll take them both, that one and the one my friend has in his hand."

Jimmy waited at the cashier's counter while Pilgrim wrote a check.

A rack of shiny chrome Zippo lighters doubtless appealed to the veterans of the last several wars but another, more practical item, caught the eye of the old serviceman. Jimmy tossed five dollars onto the counter and plopped an olive drab web belt with a brass buckle onto the pile of goods.

"You need something to keep those surplus pants up," he said. "Consider it my treat."

Pilgrim angled the poles into the car and followed Jimmy into the thrift store. What in the world would he be compelled to buy next, he wondered?

The overflowing aisles were blocked by Latin ladies with children, Haitians in bright colors conversing in Creole or solitary old gentlemen searching for bargain slacks or shirts. A heavyset couple occupied parallel rows while passing items of clothing back and forth for inspection and appraisal. Impeded by the obese woman, Pilgrim tried not to crinkle his nose at the smell issuing from a cardboard box on the floor overflowing with athletic shoes, until finally he slipped past, seeking his mentor.

"You come hear often?" Pilgrim asked when he finally found Jeremiah.

"Sure. As a playboy with a limited income I'm always seeking to upgrade my wardrobe to impress the ladies."

"What are we looking for exactly?"

The old fellow arched an eyebrow and Pilgrim followed his fingers as they probed a rack of long sleeved shirts and sweaters. Northern residents migrate to Florida every winter seeking warmth and sunshine while bringing with them boxes of heavy clothes more suitable for Buffalo or Long Island in December. A mixture of thrift, uncertainty and Puritan pragmatism accompanies each migrant as they depart their former winter homes--an inbred caution against complete abandonment of sweaters and stylish yet heavy winter coats. Suppose Florida disappoints them—as often the case--and they return again to the north? So each season more winter clothes migrate south in cardboard boxes and suitcases to Florida, more than can ever be used, given the tropical weather, and eventually the clothes find its way here, to thrift stores from South Beach to West Palm. Pilgrim thought of this amusing yet all too human tendency while he watched the gnarled hands of Jimmy Jeremiah deftly slide the hangers aside, aware that he too arrived from New York with three cardboard boxes of winter clothes.

"Here take this," said the old man. "And this one too."

Pilgrim held up the two garments. Sweatshirts, embellished with imprints, logos and slogans, they appeared unlikely garments--in the reporter's opinion--to compliment camouflage pants. One carried the slogan: "Make My Day" together with the emblem of the National Rifle Association. The other sweatshirt carried a faded silkscreen imprint of a backhoe and the name of the company. On the rear of the sweatshirt a bold slogan announced: "We'll shovel it wherever you say."

"Why these?"

"They tell people that you're a working class hero, unafraid to get your hands dirty yet ready, willing and able to carry a gun," said Jimmy. "Or have you never noticed how people wear their opinions on the backs of their shirts?"

"You mean that big guy over there with the Gold's Gym T-shirt is making some statement?"

"Aside from being a walking, unpaid billboard for that gym, he's probably saying: 'I work out with weights and I'm better and stronger than you.'"

The reporter shook his head. "A journalist wouldn't make that simplified assumption. That muscle guy might actually work there at the gym and the owner gave him the shirt for free. That's like saying that fat Haitian woman over there actually went to the University of Miami just because she's wearing that Hurricanes jersey."

Jimmy smiled indulgently, as a parent would to a child.

"Maybe her son goes to school there. Maybe she wears it proudly because that's his jersey. Or maybe she's the aunt of your friend, Bobby Smith. He played football at Miami, didn't he? Hell, how do you know that woman's not his mom?"

"Yeah, maybe you're right. I never thought of it that way."

"At least when trailer trash like myself, or southern rednecks and immigrants wear a shirt with a slogan, they either work for the company, migrated from that country, or they believe in the product, whether Jamaica, NASCAR, the Steelers or Joe's Diner. As long as I live, I'll never figure out why yuppies like you wear slogans or swooshes from companies that make billions and pay you nothing."

"I guess we all must be brainwashed," chuckled Pilgrim.

"I don't see any other explanation."

"Okay, I see your point—and the point about the reasons some people wear certain clothes."

"Good. Maybe only an old, burned out, intelligence man like me, or maybe a sociologist, would read into the clothes we wear. Clothes make the man, remember? But why we wear the clothes makes other men assume that is what we are. Tony Lester must assume you are the good-looking, redneck asshole with a ten cent brain we want him to believe."

"Okay; I'm convinced," Pilgrim said. "There is a scientific method to your madness."

"I should mention that Tony Lester is a fag but--like J. Edgar Hoover--not overtly so."

"Doesn't bother me unless I have to sleep with him to get information. And the polite terminology is 'gay'."

"You'll need some baseball caps too," said Jeremiah, ignoring him.

Pilgrim almost asked why he needed a hat but thought better of it.

"Okay. Let me try some of these on."

"That one there. The one with the chewing tobacco logo,"

The reporter pushed it onto his head gamely. The cap reeked of sweat and cigarettes. The old man noticed and his face beamed.

"Perfect! Whatever you do, don't wash it."

Crestfallen and disgusted, Pilgrim replied, "What if Lester offers me a chew of tobacco?"

The hefty Haitian women waddled past, staring at the hat with evident distaste affixed to the reporter's head.

"Tell him you had to give it up," said Jimmy. "Tell him you gave it up because of mouth sores and because you're afraid of cancer. Tell him a friend of yours died of testicular cancer, a friend who chewed tobacco since the age of twelve. Tell him you only smoke medicinal marijuana now."

The two exchanged a conspiratorial smile and Pilgrim added the soiled hat to his stack of sweatshirts.

Bobby Smith placed a series of 8x10 color photographs on the reporter's desk and Pilgrim examined them with covetous pleasure. The dark blue Lincoln limousine enshrouded a smiling couple in a single suspended moment of time. Another six seconds and America would be changed forever.

"I'll take this one but I want it autographed," he said.

Bobby smirked. "I'm afraid Jack Kennedy's got writer's cramp and Abe Zapruder's joined him in the big hereafter."

"No, I meant your autograph," Pilgrim insisted. "Artists sign their works and number them. How many photographs did you make?"

"Only about forty so far but I plan on over three hundred, including thirty of the fatal head shot."

"Have you shown these to anyone else?"

"Only Teresa. She's been helping me after hours."

Pilgrim stared at his best friend. He wouldn't let a woman come between their friendship. Not even a woman like Teresa.

"Can you have the rest of the photographs done in time for the show?"

"I probably can but I hope Gonzales doesn't catch me."

"You don't like him much do you, Bobby?"

The walnut shade of the photographer's face darkened.

"The feeling is mutual, I'm sure."

"I may be going to Dallas with Jeremiah in a week or two. Returning to the scene of the crime, so to speak."

"Vacation time or do you think Gonzales will pay you?"

Pilgrim thought a moment. "Definitely the newspaper won't pay me. I don't even think Gonzales will let me write a Kennedy retrospective from a conspiracy viewpoint."

"That's a damn good indicator the cover up continues," Bobby said.

He gathered his assortment of glossy assassination photographs and returned them gently to a protective box, the faces forever frozen in the radiance of blurred fleshtones. Jackie would forever hold her stricken husband with an expression of shock and puzzlement; Jack moments from his death about to be dealt the death blow; Mary Moorman and Jean Hill somewhere in the background, their lives also about to be changed forever, not to mention the several hundred million humans outside the photographs, further in the background, also about to be effected.

"Yeah, I guess the death of one important man in 1963 enriched thousands while endangering or impoverishing millions," Pilgrim remarked. "You know Jimmy Jeremiah was here the other day and he had a very informative conversation with Felipe."

"About what?"

Pilgrim tapped a finger to his forehead. "I was sworn not to tell."

"What! Why?"

"Off the record and very confidential information," replied the reporter. He wasn't sure whether his friend took him serious.

"Was it about Jimmy's role in the assassination?"

"No, just some personal history of Gonzales I never knew about."

Bobby seemed satisfied. "I can live without knowing."

"I thought so. Still-," continued the reporter, swiveling in his chair and hoisting his feet onto his desk, "I wonder what Gonzales would say if I mentioned to him we had an actual eyewitness to history? I wonder what Gonzales would say if I offered him an exclusive interview with the hitman who changed American history?"

"Jimmy Jeremiah? You want to do an exclusive interview for the paper about Jimmy, the man who popped JFK?"

"I know it seems farfetched--"

"Unbelievable is what it seems. Dangerous, maybe not body-wise but certainly career-wise."

"Why? Jimmy's the one with the most to lose."

"Not if you protected your source. Or do you plan to give him up? Would you identify him by name?"

"That decision would be his to make."

Bobby looked unconvinced. "If you do that, I think you need a bigger forum than this here South Florida Sun Satellite newspaper if you intend to do that. I think you need TV."

Chapter 15

The reporter and the former assassin stood in the underground parking garage of Pilgrim's apartment building. Earlier Pilgrim had told his landlord he was rehearsing a part for a play, a very dramatic part, very impassioned, and not to be too surprised if he heard occasional shouting or even an occasional profanity.

"So tell me again why you want a shipment of drugs?"

Pilgrim spoke without the hint of tremor in his voice. For the tenth time this morning he offered the same explanation.

"The people I represent are finding their former supply has dried up. The local prosecutor has been on some kind of crackdown."

"Why didn't you pay him off?" Jeremiah inquired.

"I guess they tried."

"Good, keep your answers short; don't offer more information than needed. Don't try to be evasive and don't try to be helpful."

Pilgrim nodded.

"Jimmy, does this Tony Lester fellow, did he deal drugs while with the CIA? Or did he get involved in the drug trade afterwards?"

"Tony Lester learned how easy it was to run drugs from a position of power. Low risk, huge rewards. Many of those Cubans affiliated with the CIA and 2506 also learned how easy and profitable drug smuggling was and began operating out of a seafood import business in Miami. Local law enforcement have known for a long time that some Bay of Pigs veterans—like Tony Lester--dealt drugs, and all throughout Reagan's war with Nicaragua, planeloads of illegal payola were filtering back from Central America destined for the streets, nightclubs and penthouses of America in planes piloted by CIA sub-contractors.

"Former Panama strongman and fellow CIA friend of George Bush, Manuel Noriega, was eliminated because of what he knew about the drug trade and the CIA connection but not before channeling huge shipments of cocaine through Panama and laundering millions of US dollars. A graduate at the US Army sponsored, School of the Assassins, in Panama City after Kennedy's assassination, Noriega learned every new method of torture and probably taught a few to our own black operation boys. By 1972, the DEA had a thick dossier on Noriega but the CIA, with Bush as director, chose to look the other way. Some say Tony Lester played a substantial role in drug shipments all through the 'Eighties, still under contract with the CIA. By the early Reagan/Bush years, Noriega had completely seized power in Panama with help from the CIA. He had popular Panama President Omar Torrijos assassinated--a mysterious mid-air explosion of the plane carrying Torrijos--reportedly again with help from the CIA. Sound familiar? However, Noriega was becoming a huge liability. Even after he brazenly stole the 1984 elections in Panama, his days were numbered. Remember, as a major drug kingpin and former CIA operative, Noriega knew too damn much and now, as an unpredictable loose cannon, he was an extremely dangerous embarrassment to new President Bush, his former mentor. So, in 1989, the US invaded and Noriega was toppled and now old "pineapple head" sits quietly in jail. Tony Lester, meanwhile, learned extremely well not to make waves.

Okay, anymore questions?—Good, let's try again--What's your name?"

"Luke Gorman."

"Luke's a funny name, ain't it?"

"I ain't laughin'."

"Gorman? Is that Jewish?"

"Fuck the Jews—they're worse than the Cubans."

"What's that shitty tattoo on your arm say? What's TMVL?"

"Timothy McVeigh Lives."

"What-the-hell does that mean?"

"McVeigh was set up for Waco, to take down the militias."

Jimmy nodded. "Expect the unexpected. If Lester asks you a difficult question, just squint your eyes like Clint Eastwood, maintain a posture of pissed silence, then say: 'What exactly does that mean?'—Even if you heard his question clearly."

"So I shouldn't seem to be too bright?" offered Pilgrim.

"Why should you answer just because some old fart asked you a question? What grade did you finish in school?"

"Uh—I don't know?"

Jimmy exploded. "Don't know! What-the-fuck! Pilgrim, you fucking shithead! Didn't I just say squint and remain silent while you concoct an answer? Now ask me the same question?"

Stunned, Pilgrim asked the same question.

"Why do you wanna know?" Jimmy retorted. "You opening a school or something?—Or you can simply say: 'Tenth grade'. In that outfit you look like a tenth grade dropout."

Pilgrim smiled. For a retiree, Jimmy Jeremiah was still full of fire. The reporter had never seen a man his age so animated or full of intense physical energy. The old man pacing before him wore an outfit of black sweats and canvas sneakers, a style of shoe Pilgrim had never seen before and probably hadn't been made in forty years. Each day Pilgrim felt he was growing irreversibly older; was it possible for a person to grow younger again, inspired by some new goal or sense of direction?

"Now Lester drinks to excess but he can hold his liquor. He does not, I repeat, he does not lose control. However, he likes to brag when he's been drinking, but the quickest way to get a braggart to elaborate is to doubt his story. Details will flow."

"Okay. How do we get on the subject of guns?"

Jimmy explained, "The subject of guns will arise. Quick, what guns do you own?"

"I used to own a Glock automatic but it got stolen by my best friend who denied it."

"What else?"

"Now I own an M4 Stinger. But if I join the Special Forces I'd like to get a Heckler Koch MP5. The M4 cost me $600 used; all I could afford."

"What's a clip hold?"

"I use 30 shot clips. Takes .223 caliber ammo. The MP5 takes 9 millimeter but it ain't as accurate as my M4."

"What are you gonna do in the Special Forces?"

"Go fight in Afghanistan?"

"Where the fuck is that?"

"How the hell should I know?—On the map somewhere!"

Jimmy smiled. "Good response. You need to be a normal guy, not a newsman. You need to represent the great majority of Americans who know nothing and are proud of their knowledge. To the great mass of Americans, ignorance is bliss as long as they have ass, gas, and bass."

"Thanks."

"But I think you're a piece of shit!" Jimmy bellowed, his face inches from the reporter's. "I think you're an undercover cop, a narc! I think I'm gonna waste you right here and now! Give me one good reason why I shouldn't!"

Stunned, Pilgrim grew silent for a second, tightened his jaws and then spat.

"Goddamn, If you think you're man enough, then bring it on! There ain't nothing between us now but air and opportunity!"

Disarmed, the old intelligence agent whooped with delight.

"Where in the world did you ever hear that expression, Dan?"

"I overheard an old redneck say it to some asshole in a bar."

"Damn fine comeback. I'll have to file that away for my own use."

"Remember," Bobby instructed the pair of old men, "Don't spend all your money at once. Let the ladies come to you and certainly you can smile in return but not too wide. A dollar will do as a tip--that's why I gave you that wad of singles—five dollars is too much unless you just cashed your Social Security check. Now fold the dollar lengthwise, like so, and put it in the waistband of her thong when she enters your airspace."

Pilgrim pulled his Toyota into the entrance of Hoodwink n' Hijinks, a Broward county strip club. Pink and baby blue neon dappled the glass of the car and a valet took his keys and the four exited the car and entered the club.

"Ten dollars, please," said a shapely blonde wearing gold hoop earrings and a tight pink spandex dress that fit like a second skin.

"Do you have a senior discount?" Jimmy asked.

"No sir, I'm sorry, we don't."

"I'm paying for the four of us," Bobby said. He removed a pair of twenties and passed them to the woman, ensconced in a booth with protective glass, a security camera mounted above her head, and an intercom at mouth level. An assistant outside the booth, a perky brunette with shapely legs and four inch platform heels, attired in a T-shirt bearing the nightclub's name, stamped their hands and gave them complimentary passes for half price well drinks on the upcoming Thanksgiving holiday.

"Let's sit in the back," suggested Manny. "That way we can see everything for free."

Bobby nodded, adjusting his eyes to the interior of the club. "You sure you haven't been here before, Manny? I could swear you got the system down pat."

Pilgrim ordered a pitcher of beer and four glasses. The two old gents ordered shots of whiskey and the four of them formed a semi-circle of chairs facing the stage.

"How long do you think my twenty dollars will last?" the Cuban asked.

"As long as you keep it in your pocket," Bobby replied.

"Yeah, let the younger guys pay," suggested Jimmy to his friend; "it's your birthday."

A beautiful Latin girl with tresses specially woven by her hairdresser earlier that afternoon brought the beer and a blonde followed in her wake. Tanned and toned with perfect sculpted breasts, costumed in a red, white and blue spangled thong, the blonde approached the table with manufactured joy.

"How are you gentlemen all doing tonight?" she chortled. "Would anyone like a table dance?"

"I would!" replied Manny.

"Would you like a single song for twenty dollars or a three song lap dance for fifty?"

Manny looked perplexed. "I'll have to think about that."

"Well when you decide, honey, please let me know," the blonde said and trotted away.

"Don't act too interested," Jimmy coached. "When I met my wife in Cuba, she was a real blond sweetie, a cigarette girl in the swankest casino, but I acted like she didn't even exist."

"That's not the story Carolina told me," Manny replied, more confused than exasperated.

"Was Carolina a Cuban girl?" Pilgrim asked.

Jimmy leaned in close. "No, she was a European, Norwegian, who happened to be traveling to Cuba just before the Revolution. That's when I met her, at one of the casinos. She was broke before she got the job but after she started making money she shared a little place. And that's when I met her. I was on holiday leave. I guess it must have before '59 or '60. Hey Manny, when did Castro close the casinos? Anyway, Carolina and I were married within two weeks back in Florida."

Manny hadn't heard the casino question, distracted by the flora of scantily clad females in high heels. Bobby began pointing out the various women he knew by name and added brief biographies. The photographer brandished a flash camera and set it on the table before pouring the Cuban a beer.

"We'll get some photographic evidence of your birthday celebration before we leave tonight," Bobby said, "I even ordered us a cake."

"The kind of cake where a girl jumps out of?" Manny asked eagerly.

"Nope, sorry my man. Unless they got a girl whose only ten inches tall."

Bobby waved to Teresa but she didn't see him. She stood next to the bar, engaged in an animated discussion with a pair of heavyset bikers.

A shapely girl with short dark hair and almond eyes, wearing a one piece string maillot that concealed little in the front and even less in the back, winked at Manny and he waved her over.

"Today's my birthday and I'd like to buy you a drink," he said.

She smiled, exposing perfect teeth. "Aren't you the sweetest!"

"Yes, and that's my problem—sugar diabetes," Manny explained.

"But I intend to sign up for the Special Olympics next summer; will you come watch me perform the hundred yard dash?"

She giggled. "Would you like for me to dance for you?"

"You bet," he said, and she flashed those perfect teeth again.

She pressed her supple body against his thigh, holding the chrome rail of his wheelchair steady while she did so, the aqua gleam of a five carat cubic zirconium in her pert navel glistening only inches from the Cuban's face.

"We have a half-price special for birthday boys," she explained. "Two dances for the price of one."

Many nodded vigorously while the trio watched the transaction, appraising the girl and her business acumen.

"Let's wait for this song to finish and I'll begin on the next one," she said.

"What's your name?" Manny inquired; "Where are you from?"

"Carmen," she said; "Originally from Costa Rica."

Bobby raised the flash camera, just as the song begun and snapped a picture as Carmen arched herself backwards over the seated form of the Cuban. Pilgrim smiled, before turning his gaze wistfully to Teresa. A year ago he had met her by chance in a Laundromat and, through her story as a stripper, had begun both his Pulitzer nominated series and a torrid if short-lived love affair. But it all seemed like a century ago instead of only a year. When drunk, depressed or filled with carnal desire, Pilgrim became either philosophical or self-pitying . Now he became both.

"That you girlfriend?" Jimmy uttered.

"Used to be," Pilgrim replied.

"She's very attractive; I think I remember seeing her at my daughter's art show."

"Yes, that was her; Teresa." Pilgrim said. "She was also identified in that story I did, that three part series you said you liked."

Jimmy gazed approvingly. "Why'd you leave?"

"That's something I wonder myself." The reporter paused and then laughed softly. "Maybe I wasn't man enough for her."

"Smile," Pilgrim heard Bobby say. The camera flashed and Carmen began to vamp for the photographer, draping her arms around the Cuban, pressing her now naked breasts into his face, aglow with perspiration. A pair of smiles blossomed, the camera flashed again, and the petite dancer swung her naked thigh across the lap of her admirer and straddled his hips. The trio laughed as the girl rocked on her willing victim, her trim little bottom oscillating in time to the music. The wheelchair rolled back and forth while Bobby shot several more photographs.

The music ended and Carmen became a shy wisp of a girl tugging at the tendrils of her costume before another song began. A cake appeared, a dozen candles lit, and Carmen exuberantly rushed to appropriate the prize and present it to Manny herself.

"Look, only a dozen candles," Jimmy exclaimed. "Hey Flores, they must have got you confused with some twelve-year old kid playing hooky."

Carmen frowned at the remark. "Who wouldn't want to be twelve again?"" she said, sticking out her tongue at the good-natured tormentor.

"I feel like twelve again," Manny admitted. "My heart's beating like I just ran a mile."

Carmen cut the cake, posing nonchalant on her high heels and near nakedness, while Bobby folded a twenty dollar bill under her waistband. Then Carmen excused herself to get forks and napkins, slipped away, and didn't return.

"Feel like a game of eight ball, birthday boy?" Jimmy dropped his full shot of whisky into a glass of beer and swallowed the contents.

The Cuban licked the icing from his fingers and rolled toward an empty table. Pilgrim watched the duo go and wondered if he had the talent to write a story of one segment of their lives. A good story must have a beginning, a middle and an end. The middle offered little indication of the beginning and end. Never having been a military man, Pilgrim didn't know their mindset. Was it enough to point them in the direction of the enemy and order them to kill? Or was it something more basic, some instinct he lacked?

A commotion behind him at the bar, a shout, a shrill response, and Pilgrim turned. Bobby glanced up at the same instant, the smile fading from his face. The animated conversation between Teresa and the bikers escalated into a shouting match and Pilgrim watched the trio like an episode from a seamy, weekday soap opera.

Bobby's jaw dropped as Jeremiah crossed the room with his pool cue in hand, the Cuban twirling along in his wheelchair right behind him. Before either the reporter or photographer could react, Jimmy fronted the first man and Teresa sidled away. A bouncer gazed in their direction but the figure of two geezers confronting a pair of stout bikers must have appeared comical rather than threatening. Bobby began to rise at his chair, but not before a biker swung at—and missed—the face of Jimmy Jeremiah.

The old assassin swung the pool stick with brute force and a series of compact swings. Pilgrim remembered having seen martial artists on television swing a stick as skillfully as Jimmy swung his, but not with such swiftness. Before Bobby dragged him away, the elderly figure of Jimmy Jeremiah tensed for a moment with the pool cue extended towards the fallen bikers, like an ancient samurai. Pilgrim, awestruck by the swiftness of the action, half expected him to bow to the beaten men on the floor.

"They started it," Manny chortled, "But Jimmy and I finished it! We had our cake and ate it too!"

"I hope you got pictures of that," said Jimmy, as they were escorted from the club.

Manny Flores beamed. "Best birthday I had in a long time: A big pitcher of free beer, a sexy floor show, a fine ass lady on my lap serving me cake, all followed by a helluva fight!"

Chapter 16

"One day you may awaken from a dream and know exactly what to do and how to do it," said Bobby Smith, towering over his desk. "And consider yourself lucky for having that knowledge even if it means more hard work to do."

"I envy you, man."

Pilgrim turned his eyes once more to the screen of his computer. The uncensored version of his Kennedy retrospective emerged into a complete working draft.

Bobby slid into the leather chair. "I get into work now at 5:30 AM. Sometimes I'm here almost until midnight. I may be the first and only black 'buff!"

Pilgrim smiled. "I never thought you'd become a JFK conspiracy theorist, Bobby, I really didn't."

"Oh sure; it's in my genes. My uncle believed a conspiracy killed Martin Luther King and now I believe him. They killed Bobby Kennedy too. You know why those three leaders died in five short years?"

Pilgrim shook his head, certain Smith would inform him.

"JFK getting popped at Dealey Plaza was just the beginning. Dallas was the cornerstone in the quest for American empire and signaled a definite shift in US foreign policy. JFK and MLK were too damn progressive for the rich and powerful people behind the scenes and those two leaders wanted peace to be more than an abstract idea. When Jack Kennedy signed that test ban treaty with the Russians in '63 he was signing his life away. When he mentioned a pact with the Russians to explore space, and his intention of closing a few overseas bases, man, the powerful people in this country just went ballistic!"

"Literally," remarked the reporter.

"You know how many military bases we got now, forty years after Kennedy threatened to close down a few? Maybe one thousand military bases all over the world, including those here in America, but the Pentagon doesn't really know. We've got over 700 bases in 130 foreign countries. Now don't tell me they exist to keep America safe."

"Okay, you tell me why they exist, Bobby?"

"Evidently they exist to exert pressure--none too subtle--on any foreign leader that don't toe the party line, the Pentagon party that is."

Pilgrim swung in his chair. "Hate to interrupt but listen to this."

"Okay, read me what you wrote; I got a minute."

"Jack Kennedy died for our sins. One shining moment in the warm sunshine of Dallas became a nightmare on Elm for the nation and, particularly, for the man who uttered these idealistic words at American University just months before his death in 1963: 'What kind of peace do we seek? Not a Pax Americana enforced on the world by American weapons of war. Not the peace of the grave or the security of the slave. I am talking about genuine peace, the kind of peace that makes life on earth worth living, the kind that enables men and nations to grow and to hope and to build a better life for their children—not merely peace for Americans but peace for all men and women—not merely peace in our time but peace for all time.' A few short months later, Jack Kennedy was dead. Forty years later, let us neither forget his words of hope, nor the man who spoke them. Nor should we lose faith in that idealism. For if we fail we sacrifice that secure vision of the future for an insecure form of hysteria, thinly disguised as militarism and an ill-defined war on terror."

Bobby nodded his head appreciatively. "And that, my man, was exactly why they killed him. For making statements like that."

"You think Gonzales will approve?"

The photographer scowled. "Probably not, but fuck him."

Pilgrim stifled a laugh.

"Keep on keeping on, is what my uncle used to say. I never knew what that meant before but now I do. Your readers expect Pulitzer Prize quality work from you now, Dan. Ain't no going back to hack work now."

Bobby rose and, for the first time in Pilgrim's memory, shook his hand. The reporter watched him go and then returned to work. Pilgrim's mind tried to return to the battlefield of ideas, where men were slain for adhering to unsafe opinions, but he couldn't concentrate fully on the essay before him. In an hour he would meet Jimmy Jeremiah for lunch and then drive to the marina where Tony Lester agreed to see them. Kennedy was killed for expressing lofty ideas in public, killed because he was found out, exposed; would the same thing happen to him, the reporter wondered?

Jimmy conducted the ride to the marina like a last minute intelligence cram session before they were dropped into enemy territory. The reporter guided the borrowed truck and tried to focus both on the traffic signals and the clipped inquiries of his mentor.

"So, where'd you grow up, Luke?"

"Outside Moultrie, Georgia."

"What'd your father do there?"

"Grew onions."

"What kind of onions?"

"Sweet Vidalia onions—the best in the whole wide world."

Jimmy chuckled. "Don't overdue the accent too much, Dan. Your pronunciation of 'wad' for the word wide was good but don't come on too strong. You do have a convincing Southern lilt though; you've been studying."

The cherry red Chevy pick up with raised suspension, wide tires and dual exhaust, tattooed with Confederate flag decals on front and rear bumpers, swung into the parking lot and braked to a halt. Pilgrim shoved the truck into reverse and backed to the boat that Jimmy indicated. Emerging from the truck, Pilgrim pulled his cap down firmly on his head and appraised the fiberglass cruiser before him with a four sticks of chewing gum firmly wedged against his unshaven jaw.

"James!" hailed the vigorous older man from the deck of the boat. "Come on aboard and bring your young friend."

Pilgrim fetched the gear from the bed of the truck, including the pair of fishing poles purchased at Jimmy's insistence days earlier. A small tackle box, cooler, and a daypack rounded out their equipment.

"Helluva boat, Mr. Lester; helluva boat," said Pilgrim as he swung aboard the sixty foot fiberglass cruiser. He piled the gear on the teak deck and brushed his hands on his camouflage pants. Tony Lester offered his hand and grasped the sturdy grip of his guest. The vigorous owner grinned approvingly at the logo on the sweatshirt and spoke.

"NRA? I'm a member myself. How long have you been with the organization?"

The reporter looked puzzled for a second and then grasped the breast of his sweatshirt with a smile.

"Oh, you mean this? Naw, I got it at a yard sale. Of course I had to shoot the man wearing it."

The two old fellows laughed and Lester patted him on the arm

"That's a good one," he said. "C'mon, I'll show you both around; stow your gear over there. Jimmy: how long has it been? Two, three years?"

"Not that long," Jimmy protested.

The reporter followed wide-eyed but pretended not to show it.

"So you're a friend of Jimmy's," said Lester, motioning the men to sit. Inside the main cabin, an alcove of leather seats encircled a free form table bolted to the floor. A brass barometer hung on the wall near the reporter's head. Pilgrim slid in and removed his cap, cupping the crusted object like a precious scroll.

"Where exactly did you meet?" Lester asked.

"I'm dating one of his daughter's," Pilgrim blurted.

Tony's eyes widened with interest. "Oh? Which one? I always thought my friend and colleague, James, only had one."

Jimmy Jeremiah squirmed.

"What? Did I let the cat out of the chicken coop?"

Tony chuckled at the colloquialism.

"What Luke means is—I have an adopted daughter aside from my natural daughter."

Tony Lester gleamed. "Why you old pirate! Where had she been hiding all this time?"

"Hialeah," said Jimmy. "She's Cuban. Her father was a friend of Manny's, died a dozen years ago. I'm just sort of godfather."

"Probably one of our old comrades."

A silent Cuban of early middle age, attired in a starched whites and deck shoes, surveyed the table without emotion from an adjacent cubby. Finally he entered and offered a tray of entrees.

"This is Ramon, my steward and right hand man," Tony said. "If you have any request or drink preference, he will try to accommodate you. Shall we adjoin to the flying bridge?"

The trio ascended a teak staircase to the upper wheelhouse of the boat. The view of expensive waterfront property and yachts moored nearby from the windows impressed the reporter. Few of the people he interviewed ever lived so lavishly. The marina was private and the enclosed lagoon retained a feeling of a wealthy nature preserve, a sanctuary for privilege and power. Even the shorebirds seemed of an elite sub-species, groomed for wading in moneyed waters.

From below, Ramon started the engine but the sound seemed distant, almost as the hum of a powerful turbine. The reporter noticed the boat moving slowly past the moorage and assumed Ramon was at the controls.

"Jimmy tells me you're quite a character, Luke."

"When I was growing up in Georgia, a character was always one of those fellows on wanted posters down at the post office."

Lester laughed. "I like this fellow, Jimmy. He reminds me a lot of a southern version of your old friend, Manny. How is Manuel Flores?"

"Manny is still kickin', even though he hasn't any feet."

"That sounds like a Mannyism, itself," said Lester.

Jimmy appraised the passing scenery, the sun warming him while washing the waterfront condos a dazzling shade of white. "He hasn't much longer to live. Have you ever heard that saying: 'Elvis is dead and I ain't feeling too well myself'? That describes him and me both."

Lester looked thoughtful, even pensive, trying not to think of encroaching mortality, before staring at Pilgrim with a critical eye.

"So what do you do for a living, Mr. Gorman?"

The reporter finished a mouthful of food. "I do lots."

"Houses on those lots?"

"Not yet," he said, with a puzzled expression.

"Like what? Could you be a bit more clear?"

Pilgrim shifted uneasily, and caught the encouraging glance of his mentor. Ramon hurried up the stairs with a tray of drinks, placed them on the table and took the mahogany wheel of the cruiser. The boat moved past a channel buoy and out into the ocean and Pilgrim heard the engine accelerate.

"I'm into export import," he said. "But not into the scale we would like."

Lester exchanged a look with his old compatriot.

"We?"

"Well, the people back in the area of Georgia I work for," Pilgrim splashed a soda into a glass filled with ice and took a sip. "We would like to expand, if you know what I mean."

Jimmy explained, "His people are into herbals but would like to expand into other regions." Jimmy pressed a forefinger to his nose. "We deal in ounces now but we'd like to deal in pounds or kilos." "I could put you in touch with someone in your area, but I only do business in sizeable shipments of hundred of pounds." said Lester. "But if you can eventually get your people interested in quantity and Jimmy can vouch for you, I believe there are business possibilities. Ramon?"

Lester tilted his head and Ramon approached and stepped behind the reporter.

"If you wouldn't mind, Luke; please stand."

Jimmy nodded perceptibly and Pilgrim stood and allowed the Cuban to frisk him. The reporter lifted his shirt and then lowered it. The old Company man noticed the taut torso and the tattoo.

"A person in my business can't be too careful, not that I suspected you of wearing a wire, Luke."

"I understand. You can search my boots too if you'd like."

Lester shook his head. "You obviously keep in good shape; I notice you work out. But what do the initials TMVL on your forearm mean?"

"Timothy McVeigh Lives."

The wealthy host smiled. "A man of few words; I like that. We speak the same language. More actions than words, right Luke?"

Pilgrim nodded. "Isn't that how things get done, sir? With a word if necessary but with a gun if need be."

"You are almost a philosopher; isn't he Jimmy?"

"It drives my daughter crazy sometimes, Tony, but once in awhile I see a younger versions of yourself in Luke."

Lester leaned in close. "You like guns?"

"Shot 'em since I was about ten. Got a .22 on my eleventh birthday."

"I sure hope you've moved up in firepower, son."

"I got an M4 Stinger. Paid only $600 for it. Not stolen either."

Lester whistled under his breath. "That some kind of assault rifle?"

"Best one made for the price. SWAT teams use it. M-16 but better muzzle velocity. Mine's been modified to fully auto."

"Sounds like you're the regional salesman."

The two old intel men laughed. Lester swallowed his drink and rose to glance at the course and the compass and then returned with a pair of bottles.

"You don't seem to be drinking, Luke," he said.

"Only on the return home; I'm not sure what my stomach wants to do right now."

"Good man." Lester poured himself another.

"Luke's rarely been on the ocean, and never to fish. My daughter—her name's Marie, by the way—talked me into taking him fishing but my boat's been kind of balky lately. Starter problems I think."

"Well, we'll get you a fish to take home," said Lester, "Even if we have to hook one out of my freezer."

The reporter smiled. He found the continual need to remain under cover and in character, as Luke Gorman, stressful at first and then almost second nature. A man becomes whatever character his mind convinces himself to be, he surmised.

"Of course, Luke's fishing equipment isn't the best—a couple of poles and reels from another era—but he's mechanical. I watched him take apart and put together a rifle once in the dark."

"Shall we retire to the stern and wet a few lines, then?"

Tony Lester rose and his two guests followed, descending from the bridge through the galley. Ramon descended the gangway and, from the main cabin, put the boat on auto pilot in trolling gear. Before the guests appeared Ramon arranged three deck chairs on the spacious rear deck and unfolded a table. The weather remained calm, the winds light. With silent efficiency, the steward arranged three poles with attached lures and placed them into mounts angled over the transom.

Drinks in hand, the trio ambled to the stern of the boat. Pilgrim was surprised to see Ramon again; the man seemed to be everywhere. Instead of a tray of drinks he held a camera in hand. Tony Lester noticed and signaled the steward. With a garrulous embrace, the host herded his guests into a tight group near the rail, the three of them standing stiffly with awkward smiles, while Ramon shot a quick pair of shots. Just as suddenly and efficiently, the steward disappeared.

"What does your boat name mean, Mr. Lester?" Pilgrim broke the silence a moment later. "The Covenant: doesn't that word have to do with witches?"

Lester smiled warmly. "I guess it could. But covenant means a promise or a contract between two or more people, an agreement usually entered into secretly and sealed."

Pilgrim stared dumbfounded, jaw gaping.

"You and I may eventually have a covenant, Luke; Jimmy and I, and many other powerful men, already have had a covenant now for the last forty years."

Pilgrim shook his head.

"I don't know what covenant has to do with fishing," he replied, "but then some boat names are more puzzling than others."

"Does he know about Dallas?"

Jimmy Jeremiah nodded. "He knows bits and pieces. But like most folks his age, Dallas is old news."

"Does he know about your involvement?"

"He knows most of the details."

"Dallas happened last century, just after the Civil War." Pilgrim strolled to the rail and retrieved his fishing pole. Intently he unwound the tangled lines of the bamboo pole with the frozen reel, muttering curses under his breath.

"What's your frank opinion of politics, Luke?"

"Frankly, my dear, I don't give a damn," the reporter drawled.

The pair of old men chuckled. Jimmy poured them both another drink, a single for himself and a double for Lester.

"I have other poles, Luke," Lester said. "If you're really determined to fish."

"No sir. It ain't about the fishing. I'm stubborn and loyal when it comes to an object or a thing, or even a covenant. This here thing belonged to my father and I intend to fix it."

"I don't know where your daughter found this fellow, Jimmy, but he's a keeper."

"Manny and Luke are now like two peas in a pod," Jimmy confided.

"Our friend the Cuban is like a mentor to young Mr. Gorman."

"That true, Luke?"

Pilgrim pretended to concentrate on the fouled fishing pole in his hands, remembering some long-forgotten advice a drama professor once gave him. An actor must occupy his space with such convincing force that all eyes of the audience are upon him even when he performs a mundane task in silence. The reel in his hands and the attached pole were as important now, if he were to succeed, as Don Quixote's sword or Yorick's skull in the hands of Hamlet. Finally, exasperated, Pilgrim slipped the pole into a mount and tightened the clamp.

"Jimmy, could I borrow your Leatherman?"

The leather sheath tumbled through the air and the reporter caught the combination tool, opened it and quickly released the frozen reel from the bamboo pole. Carefully he cradled the large antique in both hands and carried it to the table.

"I learned a lot from ol' Manny." Pilgrim said finally. With an expression of content on his face the reporter sprawled into a folding chair between the two men. Ramon brought him a Mai Tai and he sipped the cool liquid before placing the half-filled glass on the table.

"Damn, that's good," he continued. He placed the frozen reel on the table and began to remove the smaller screws. "Manny and I talked a lot about weapons, a lot about sniper scopes—which ones

The Guns of Dallas

are the best. Myself, I prefer the most expensive scopes—Schmidt & Bender—but my budget says second hand Bausch & Lomb."

The pair of old men listened and observed with fascination. Like theatergoers in a private box, they watched the performance, hung on each word, one unsuspecting yet entertained by the taciturn monologue and the other fearful of possible miscue.

"What's one of those expensive scopes cost? Smith & Wesson, was that it?"

Again Pilgrim acted like he hadn't heard the question. His face contorted by degrees as the seconds passed and he focused on the task before him. His hands steadily examined the reel until he gently set it down in the center of the table like an oversized can of sliced pineapple. Finally he spoke.

"Schmidt & Bender. German made. Ballpark figure? Maybe $1200. Sure, the Norwegian army and the British military sometimes use S&Bs but c'mon, the taxpayers of those countries pay for 'em. Me? I ain't got no taxpayers."

"Suppose someone were to provide one of those scopes, with a rifle attached to it?" Lester drained his drink. "I could always use a good man with weapons, someone loyal and stubborn and good with his hands."

"I'll sure think about that offer. You and Jim, here, and Manny—well, Manny told me he used a Zeiss in Dallas. I believe he said 4X but I could be wrong. If someone were giving it away, even a top of the line Zeiss would be nice."

Jimmy Jeremiah spoke, as if remembering something important.

"That's right, now that I recall, a 4X was what he used," Jimmy said. "Just like the scope on Oswald's rifle."

"Oswald had a piece of shit rifle and a piece of shit scope," Lester declared. "How the Warren Commission ever got people to believe in that fabrication is beyond me."

"I heard the scope wasn't sighted true," Pilgrim observed. "A 4X Ordnance Optics brand. That scope cost all of seven dollars."

"Oswald couldn't have hit shit even with my rifle," Lester declared.

"Especially from the cafeteria of the book depository. Ramon, another drink—make it a double."

"Yeah? What were you using, Mr. Lester? Hunting rifle?

Tony Lester glared at the reporter and Jimmy Jeremiah grew afraid the old fox had spotted the snare. Lester's glare bored into the younger man, idly intent on disassembling a corroded lump of metal. Just before Jimmy broke the silence, Lester laughed aloud.

"Hunting rifle! That's good. I guess you could call it that. I had a custom Remington .270 Magnum with a 3X Schmidt & Bender scope--quality all the way--a rifle that could knock a buck on its ass at 500 yards." Pilgrim chuckled like a backwoods buffoon. "My, Oh my! 500 yards! Is that how far Kennedy was from you?"

"No, he was 25 yards at the most. I propped that rifle on the picket fence and drew a bead. That car of Kennedy's was traveling less than ten miles per hour—and then it rolled to almost a complete stop. Sure, Kennedy had already been struck from behind and when that happened I thought that Secret Service driver, Greer, would put the petal to the metal. But nope; he stopped."

"So that Kennedy shot of yours was like bagging a buck at point blank range," drawled Pilgrim. "Lucky shot is all."

"Luck!" Lester nearly fell off his seat. The color of his face darkened, and Jimmy almost interceded but before he could the younger man retorted.

"Well how much skill did that shot take as a sniper? I don't even think I'd feel right about taking the money, if it had been me."

Jimmy watched the color darken through several shades of crimson while Lester poured off his drink. The sound of the empty glass crashing down on the table startled Ramon and he hurried over with another double.

"Luke, just shut the hell up for a minute and listen," Jimmy calmly ordered. He watched the face of his old friend gradually compose, color draining away. "You weren't there with Tony; it wasn't as easy as you make it seems, was it?"

"No and I'll explain why. There were four or five rifles trained on Kennedy that day and two of them had already missed once and hit once. On the rooftop of the County Records building a guy with a 30.06; Manny and Jim in the Texas Book Depository with a 7.65 Mauser; A mechanic on the third floor of the Dal-Tex building. The two of us behind the fence were the last line. Charlie had already hit Kennedy in the neck. He was using a .223 with a silencer and flash suppressor. I had neither. I was young and dumb like you, Luke. But that last shot, the kill shot, was mine, the shot everyone heard and remembers from watching the Zapruder film."

Pilgrim listened without interrupting while the old assassin recounted the story.

"Charlie had already knocked apart his weapon and handed it to a fellow, a railroad man, who stashed it in a tool box near the railroad tracks. Then Charlie ambled over to some box cars where he was apprehended. Now he's in jail. I tossed my rifle to a fellow dressed as a cop standing at the front of a parked car near the fence."

"What'd he do with it?" Pilgrim asked.

"You know those heavy chrome bumpers of the 'Sixties? Well, we had devised a pair of spring clamps attached under the front bumper. They flipped down when empty and flipped up and out of sight when holding something, like a rifle. Hours later, a guy drove out of that parking lot and corks were popped at private country clubs all over America."

Jimmy interjected. "What sort of ammo were you using that day, Tony?"

"Like everyone else, I used a hollow point round. That's why the head exploded." Tony laughed quietly. "The head exploded when my bullet hit and then Manny and I went to Vietnam. They never looked for us there"

"What was in Vietnam?" Pilgrim asked.

"Only Operation Phoenix. We helped the CIA liquidate 60,000 troublesome Dinks. I was attached to the Special Forces then."

Pilgrim whistled appreciatively. "I'd like to join the Special Forces but I don't think I'd pass the drug testing."

Tony Lester gazed at the coarsely dressed yet good-looking man in his torn sweatshirt and camouflage pants, tinkering with an antique reel, appraising him with more than a little fondness and amusement.

"I could probably find a special place for you, Luke, and I wouldn't even require a urine test."

The reporter smiled awkwardly and Jimmy applauded the final performance with his eyes as the curtain fell.

They drove back from the marina in the borrowed truck, silently, with exhausted smiles of satisfaction flitting across their faces.

"I don't think Tony suspected a thing," Jimmy finally said. "Not for a moment."

"I was pretty good then?"

"You were damn good. Even I was convinced at times."

The reporter basked in the praise.

"Where'd you learn all that stuff about rifle scopes?" The old intelligence man asked.

"Internet and the local gun shop and, of course, Manuel Flores."

Pilgrim pulled into the alley behind the Lake Worth apartment in the last reflected glimmer of sunset. The reporter helped unload the gear and carried the heavier items up the sagging stairs to Jimmy's apartment. Almost forgotten in the cab of the truck, the damaged reel was the last item he retrieved. Pilgrim set the piece gently on the table and folded into a chair, suddenly drained.

"Let's open her up and listen," Jimmy said.

"Maybe we should wait; maybe there's nothing there and all of our efforts were wasted."

Jimmy placed a beer before the younger man. Pilgrim stared at the bottle.

"What we did was a fine work, Dan. A pair of professionals couldn't have done better. I say let's listen and decide what we're going to do with it later."

Pilgrim took a deep pull on the beer and smiled, the glimmering smile of a man having done worthwhile work well, and at last at rest.

"Okay, I'm dying to hear it," he said.

Jimmy drew the fishing reel to him and within seconds broke the seal of epoxy and separated the inner components of the spool. Like a scarab nestled in a ball of dung, a tape recorder lay hidden inside.

Chapter 17

By the time Pilgrim had finished his third beer, they had listened to the thirty-minute tape play from beginning to end twice. At times the conversation sounded clear and nearby—every voice recognizable--but at others the recording became almost inaudible. Several times the reporter rewound the tape briefly, especially during responses by Tony Lester, and the two men listened carefully to the words at full volume.

"Yeah? What were you using, Mr. Lester? Hunting rifle?

"Hunting rifle! That's good. I guess you could call it that.

I had a Remington .270 Magnum with a 3X Schmidt & Bender scope, quality all the way, a rifle that could knock a buck on its ass at 500 yards."

Pilgrim fast forwarded and they listened to the words come tumbling out of the tiny speaker, incriminating words, descriptions and details of events that happened forty years ago, that people in power who knew better had denied ever happening.

"He was using a .223 with a silencer and flash suppressor. I had neither. I was young and dumb like you, Luke. But that last shot, the kill shot, was mine, the shot everyone heard and remembers from watching the Zapruder film."

They played that part twice more, neither man speaking. The reporter listened to his own remarks and the responses of the old assassin. Pilgrim didn't know exactly what he intended to do with the tape, what he could do legally, but the simple fear and excitement of even listening to such a confession—"but that last shot, the kill shot, was mine, the shot everyone heard and remembers"—left him inert, wondering.

"You should have two or three more copies made immediately," Pilgrim heard the old man say. "That's what they did with that Zapruder film that very same evening, made two or three copies."

"Good idea," the reporter mumbled.

"Then they locked up the original for safekeeping."

Pilgrim considered the idea. He could rent a safe deposit box.

He could keep another copy hidden somewhere in his apartment.

A third copy he could give to Bobby for safe-keeping, with a letter stating that if anything happened to him...

"Don't go blabbing to everyone," Jimmy said. "This is one of the most dangerous pieces of information ever to be caught on tape. People have disappeared for having something like this in their possession."

"You will not believe what you're about to hear," Pilgrim said to his friend when he met him in the corridor of the Sun Satellite the next morning. The reporter hustled the photographer back to the limited sanctity and isolation of his office and removed a tape player from a desk drawer. Since Bobby had heard such words before--and since what followed usually was startling and filled with juicy details of scandal and corruption in South Florida--he sat down.

"Listen to this tape, especially listen to this one part."

The photographer tried to picture the setting and kept his questions to himself until the end. Toward the end he heard some words that made him exclaim.

"Turn it back! Rewind that part and turn up the volume."

Pilgrim hit the rewind button for three or four seconds and the fragment of confession issued out in graphic detail.

"Like everyone else, I used a hollow point round. That's why the head exploded....The head exploded when my bullet hit and then Manny and I went to Vietnam. They never looked for us there"

The pair remained silent for several seconds, each man pondering his own thoughts. Then Bobby spoke.

"Do you think, maybe, we could have parts of this audiotape enhanced and then, perhaps I could use the confession along with the exhibition of motorcade photographs? I'd like to have the visual impact of the pictures and then the spoken confession—even if we never identified the name of the shooter. Maybe we could even have a composer set a score to the confession, or use available classical music, and then the voice over that."

The reporter pictured the shock and disbelief. He pictured the scandal and recrimination and outrage. Then he pictured the enormous publicity.

"Not a bad idea, Bobby," he said. "By the way, this is your copy of the tape. I made three altogether. Keep it somewhere safe."

The photographer smiled. Bobby accepted the tape proffered like a rare piece of ancient jewelry. He noticed the blank label and reached for an ink pen.

"What shall I title it?'

Pilgrim thought a moment. "Call it the Luke Gorman interview."

"Was that the name of the fellow speaking?"

"Nope, that was my alias. The other fellow will have to remain anonymous for awhile. I'm not sure what I want to do with the tape, exactly. Jimmy told me not to let anyone know I have it but I think the more people who know, the better."

The pained expression on Bobby's face offered a different opinion.

"You should talk to a lawyer first," he suggested.

"Not a bad idea. What kind of lawyer would I talk to?"

"Maybe a criminal defense lawyer. Start by asking him a theoretical question, Dan. Unless you're a police informer, I don't think you can lawfully tape anyone without their knowledge. Also, they might want you to identify the other voice on the tape—Jimmy Jeremiah. Anyway, doesn't Morgan & Marsh represent the newspaper when we have all sorts of legal problems?"

Pilgrim shook his head slowly. "Bad idea. They might want me to identify the others on the tape or get a signed release form before I could even try to use the tape. They might want me turn over the tape. Or worse still, destroy it."

"Yeah, too close to home for objectivity."

"I like your earlier suggestion, Bobby, to try to get this stuff out to television. Print media failed for the last forty years-"

"And now video and film media can fail for the next forty years. I was joking when I said you needed a bigger podium, like TV. Television today is only a legal narcotic, a government approved, billion dollar, drug-of-choice. No, Dan, instead of one big podium, I think you need lots and lots of little ones."

Pilgrim smiled. "Houses on those lots?"

"What? What houses?" Bobby said.

"Nothing. Just a lame joke."

"Maybe you should have a complete transcript of the audio tape made—like those PBS programs always offer—and then have it signed by Jimmy Jeremiah and notarized. Start a paper record. Make as many copies as you can. Get all the documents you can; find out if there's any record of this fellow you interviewed in the Florida newspapers; call up people, people like the district attorney. In other words, cover your ass."

Pilgrim smiled uncomfortably. Knowledge is power. But with great knowledge comes great responsibility. Especially secret knowledge, dangerous knowledge, then the human inclination is to suppress the knowledge or use it for sinister or personal ends. The reporter suddenly pictured the Warren Commission, each commissioner gradually realizing the depth and breadth of the conspiracy and how they must have each agreed—arguably for the good of the nation—to suppress this shocking, secret knowledge, agreed to cover it up and keep it secret forever from American citizens. Heroically—at least in their own minds—they kept the truth from leaking out. But the truth had seeped out anyway, or bits and pieces over the last forty years and what they intended to do, reaffirm trust in American institutions, had the opposite effect. Few Americans now trusted anyone in power, and the lasting reputation of the commissioners as a whole was tarnished, while the once-lauded Warren Commission had become synonymous with the word whitewash.

"What did Mencken say?" Pilgrim asked rhetorically. "I believe that no discovery of fact, however trivial, can be wholly useless to the race, and that no trumpeting of falsehood, however virtuous in intent, can be anything but vicious. I believe that all government is evil, in that all government must make war upon liberty."

"Well, I don't know nothing about virtue, but you uncovered some facts that could get you killed, so all I'm saying is you best cover your ass."

"Yeah, maybe you're right, Bobby."

"I know I'm right. And if I was you I'd make out a will too."

Chapter 18

"Dan?"
"Yes?"
"Sorry to wake you."
"Who is this?"
"Jimmy."
"Jimmy? Where are you calling from? What time is it?"
"Late. I'm calling from my daughter's."
"Is she okay? You don't sound too good. Is anything wrong?"
"Joyce is fine. But Manny's dead."

Early the next day Pilgrim told Gonzales he had an appointment and drove to the Lake Worth apartment of his friend. He took the stairs three at a time, unsure and a little afraid of what he might find, knocked, and pushed the door open without waiting. The figure on the couch looked shrunken, collapsed, as if an atmosphere of incredible gravitational weight exerted an unearthly pressure on him alone. A single line of cardboard boxes along the wall, like debris from a shipwreck swept there by a high tide, held the last worldly effects of a tragic soul.

"I knew he didn't have much time left," Jimmy gasped, "but I never expected it to be so sudden."

"Death has its own timetable, I guess." the reporter sighed.

Pilgrim regretted the bluntness of his words but the old man seemed not to have heard them. Death is sudden and blunt, reflected the reporter, even when the destruction appears imperceptible and catches up to us, frightened and cornered finally, in our old age.

"He died of a heart attack, I guess," said the stricken old man. "Inside I think he died long ago."

"I liked him," Pilgrim remarked, immediately aware of the callowness of his words. What condolences can anyone offer, what honest heartfelt words can anyone utter, who remains outside the pain? "I sorry; he didn't seem like the man who did all those things in Dallas when you got to know him."

"Oh, he had remorse but he didn't show it. Unlike Tony Lester, Manny knew he'd lost his moral compass long ago and couldn't figure out how to get it back."

"He didn't have any relatives did he?"

"None that I know of; none that he ever mentioned. Maybe he had them and kept that part of himself hidden. You see, I knew the bloody side of him but maybe somewhere Manny had a clean side, decent and good. At least I like to think so."

Pilgrim stood in the middle of the spare apartment, in the center of a building constructed seventy-five years ago, wondering how many other tragedies the room had witnessed in that time. When Jeremiah was dead—this year or next or five years down the road—the room would clasp others to itself, others destined for tragedy of some sort. The earth was a world filled with millions and millions of rooms, and each room was haunted by a small measure of joy and a large measure of sorrow.

"He left you something personal though," said Jimmy. "There on the table; something important he said."

"What is it?"

"Something you can use. Something you always wanted. Something you once demanded of me. Proof."

Pilgrim opened the thin billfold, not sure what he expected to find. Inside he found only two items, an identification card with an image of a younger, intense Manuel Flores and the bold, double white bars on a red background insignia of the Secret Service.

Chapter 19

They headed south on I-95 from Lake Worth with the windows down in Pilgrim's Toyota, and the radio playing tunes from another ear. Sinatra sang of a very good year, the song melodic yet sadly moody and somehow apropos. Jimmy stared out the window at the passing urban sprawl and the miles slipped past into a second and third song. Then he finally spoke.

"Manny and I were given identification badges, exact copies of those issued to the Secret Service men on the Dallas/Fort worth swing."

"How many other men had them?"

Jeremiah turned his gaze directly to the freeway in front of the car. He stared at a bumper sticker on the rear of a large black SUV, staring in silence at the vinyl American flag and the slogan, These Colors Don't Run. Then he replied.

"We had a signal, those of us with fake badges. We would raise our hand with a forefinger extended, like so"—Jimmy raised his hand as if holding an imaginary pistol—"almost like a friendly wave, and if a guy raised his hand and shot back, like so, with his forefinger, then we knew he was one of us."

The scale and complexity of the operation amazed the reporter. He had read reports of fake Secret Service agents on the grounds around Dealey Plaza that day in Dallas but he had always thought the reports were simply rumors. How many other fake credentials, he wondered, were stuffed away in shoeboxes all over the country?

"The beauty of the plan was that it was well thought out—like all of us having authentic, forged Secret Service identification—and except for a few fuck ups, which are to be expected, it worked to perfection."

Pilgrim lowered the radio.

"Was the real Secret Service involved?" he said.

"I've wondered that myself for forty years. For example, why did the Secret Service allow the motorcade to make a series of slow turns on Houston and Elm? Why did the driver, Greer, slow down after the first shot instead of speed up? Remember, that first shot wasn't fatal. All the driver had to do was accelerate downhill under the bridge on a straight road; why didn't he do that? Why weren't there any real Secret Service men in place--or deputy sheriffs or US Army troops from Fort Sam Houston—in Dealey Plaza that day? Why were the office windows in tall buildings along the parade route allowed to be wide open? Why was the bubble top removed? Who authorized it? Why was the motorcycle escort ordered to the rear of the limousine? Why didn't the agents in the following car—code named 'Halfback'—dismount, spread out, and assault the area of the Grassy Knoll with guns drawn after Kennedy was killed and arrest all the men--Tony Lester included—skulking around back there? Why wasn't the book depository, at least, surrounded in the first minute after the assassination? All of those precautions—why were they ignored?"

"Who authorized all those changes?"

The old man shook his head. "I don't know."

"Didn't the Warren Commission demand to know?"

"They only wanted to know about the evidence that would neatly fit into the scenario of a lone gunman. The threat of an assassination in Dallas was well known to the Secret Service. Hell, half the Dallas cops hated Kennedy, including sheriff Decker; retired General Edwin Walker hated his guts; Mayor Cabell resented the fact Kennedy canned his brother; Lyndon Johnson raged after learning he was getting the boot; Nixon was in a snit—and conveniently already in Dallas, as was J. Edgar Hoover, the night before the assassination. Hell, you have a handful of likely suspects right there and every one of them with more than enough motive, means and opportunity for a murder."

Pilgrim drove in silence for awhile. The singer on the radio crooned the song Route 66 and the reporter remembered what he wanted to ask.

"But if that driver--Greer was his name?--had been secretly involved in a conspiracy, wouldn't he have put himself in mortal danger of being hit in the crossfire as the driver of the limousine?"

"He'd have been in far less danger if he slowed down almost to a stop like he did. Listen, if I was one of those Warren commissioners I would have been grilling guys like Greer and Kellerman and offered them complete immunity from prosecution for testimony leading to the conviction of us conspirators, otherwise one or both of them would have been sent to prison for a very long time."

"On what grounds?"

"Negligent homicide. Suppose you leave the gate around your swimming pool open and the neighbor's toddler falls in and drowns? You can be convicted and sentenced to prison for negligent homicide. Abraham Bolden, the only Negro Secret Service agent in 1963, offered to testify to the Warren Commission about some of the negligence—drinking on duty, etc-- but the commission refused to hear him and later he was fired."

"Harass the whistle blower?"

"Damn straight! Harass his ass for trying to tell the truth."

"But some of the Secret Service agents on duty in Dallas must have wondered about a plot."

"Of course they did; they talked about a plot later that evening. They talked about the number of shots and the direction they thought they came from. Remember, most of the agents were idealistic, underpaid young men. In their reports to Secret Service Chief James Rowley later that night they mentioned their belief that three or four professional shooters may have been involved. And they were right."

Pilgrim nodded sadly. "FTAP: four teams of two men each."

"Five according to Tony Lester."

The reporter wondered if he shouldn't be taping these remarks.

"I brought my sleeping bag like you asked," Jimmy said, completely off the subject.

The reporter sighed. There would be plenty of time later that evening, he realized, to question the old man at length around a campfire; no need to dampen his excitement now by dredging up the past.

"I'm looking forward to seeing all those old historical spots I never knew existed," Pilgrim replied.

"Some of them might be swallowed up in concrete but I'm sure we can find a few reminders."

"I can't believe I actually got my editor to agree to that story you recommended: The Forgotten, Historic Navy Bases of South Florida."

"Well, Dan, there are a lot of retirees down here in Florida and you know how some of us folks love to read about history in newspapers."

Pilgrim nodded. "The good old days, a time when history takes on a rosy tint, when even disasters take on a golden, nostalgic glow. Everyone loves a good story of yesteryear."

"As long as you stick to the accepted version," said Jimmy with a sly gleam in his eye.

They took the exit for the Miami zoo and parked near a towering obelisk of concrete bristling with antennas. Instead of following the others to the zoo, the two men wandered toward the assortment of concrete structures, stepping carefully over the uneven concrete.

"This was once the largest blimp base in America," said Jimmy.

"Part of Richmond Naval Air Station. Built in 1942, the base covered 2,000 acres but what was really amazing about the place were the structures on it."

"Like that giant, fifteen story gun platform over there?"

The old veteran chuckled. "Wasn't anything like that. Like I said, even more fantastic were the buildings on this base. The Navy built three huge wooden hangars right here out of Douglas fir, with rounded roofs, each of them 160 feet tall. They were at that time some of the largest structures in the world, enclosing seven acres of space."

"So where are they now?" the reporter noticed a gradual animation overcome the older man. Pilgrim began to take notes for his newspaper while he listened with growing interest.

"There were 3,000 men stationed here, along with twenty five blimps. The helium-filled blimps—none of that dangerous hydrogen gas for our American boys--were flown over the Florida coast looking for Nazi submarines but remember, this was before my time. Anyway, in 1945, exactly three years to the day after the base was officially opened, a powerful hurricane headed for the area. All over Florida and out to sea, airplanes were flown here for safety, to seek shelter inside the three giant cocoons. Over 350 airplanes—Grumman Hellcats, P-51 Mustangs, F4U Corsairs, PBY and PBM flying boats--plus one hundred cars were crowded under the roof, along with those twenty five balloons."

"And then what happened?"

"The hurricane winds blew, 150 to 200 miles per hour, and the structures withstood the weather but an electrical short started a fire. The flames whipped over the buildings in horizontal sheets until by the following day only smoldering ruins and smoking ashes and the skeletons of the former structures stood. That and six massive concrete door pillars like that one over there."

"Nature's fury," remarked the reporter, busy scribbling.

"They cleared the rubble and dynamited all the pillars but this one refused to fall. Just as well. Today it's one of the tallest structures in Dade County and a convenient antenna platform, as you can see."

Pilgrim listened as the old man continued.

"Richmond never sheltered any more blimps—how could it—but the war with Germany was over anyway. When I got here, over forty years ago, it was a sleepy little outpost and now it's almost overgrown."

They wandered around the remnants of the former base, Pilgrim trying to picture the exciting launch and recovery of airships from the middle of a sawgrass and palmetto wilderness, the torpid clouds sharing the sky with the porcine shapes of observation balloons.

"Then one day in early 1961, a whole lot of activity sprang up, all over the Gulf Coast but mostly here in Florida. Remember when your editor, Gonzales, said the University of Miami may have been affiliated with the CIA? He was right. This is part of the UM campus. The CIA took over some of the buildings—that building over there was one-- and under the name of Zenith Technological Services operated a command post with hundreds of agents. Imagine the excitement."

"I notice they still have a chain link fence around some of the abandoned structures."

"Maybe to keep the spooks in," Jimmy said with a sly grin.

"When the Bay of Pigs invasion failed," he continued, "the former mood of--what was the exact word, exhilaration?—changed to gloom. Worse than gloom; outright grumbling, dissension. Then those eleven hundred Cubans we lost had to be bartered, if I remember correctly, for one thousand tractors and medical supplies. Castro wanted a tractor for each man in captivity."

"But what about the base? Any more historical significance?"

"Sure. In 1962 another invasion plan was underway, plus covert plans like ZR-rifle, to eliminate Castro by assassination or whatever means possible, even trying to use Mafia connections and former Batista henchmen. Crazy schemes, really, absurd plans devised by extremely ambitious men, each with his own agenda. Imagine Cuba today if we had succeeded, a crazy quilt of corruption? Anyway, most of it was planned right here, right where we stand, on forgotten Richmond Naval Air Station. But damn, Kennedy foiled us again there. He cancelled another invasion attempt."

Pilgrim's cell phone rang. He picked it up but got a garbled response. The reporter listened for a moment and then closed the connection. He watched in silence as the elderly veteran ambled over the former launch site, scraping his shoes on the worn pavement, trying to determine the exact boundaries to a place that no longer existed except in his mind. Pilgrim suddenly saw the diminished shape of his father in the form of Jimmy Jeremiah, the inward existence more real than the outward, day-to-day life. He looked like a little boy, lost in his own imaginary world, perfectly content to wander for an hour among the weeds and remnants of a ruined military base, more real a place to him, in his childlike state, than the modern yet artificial zoo that existed nearby now.

"I wonder what happened to most of the other buildings Jimmy?"

Jeremiah had sauntered back after wandering the perimeter, making mental calculations, and the reporter noticed an expression of freshness or a fullness of composure about the old man. Pilgrim had posed the question with his pen and pad in hand, ready for one last quote or crumb of colorful information.

"Got blown down by hurricane Andrew in 1992, I guess. Or carried away piece by piece. Isn't that how our whole life goes, Danny boy?"

Pilgrim nodded twice, staring at the wistful yet contented face before him. A smile began to form there, reminding the reporter again of his father on one of his last few days, when death and the man had negotiated a truce. Jeremiah looked around one last time before he spoke again.

"Carried away piece by piece or blown away all at once; what-the-hell difference does it matter? That's the story of life, isn't it? C'mon; let's get out of here."

Chapter 20

Pilgrim was aware of what was happening, uncertain of when the change had begun. They drove south on the Turnpike after leaving the site of former Richmond Naval Air Station and passed the sprawl of Miami, heading toward the Keys. The lively fellow beside him no longer seemed like the odious assassin he had met several weeks before but, to the reporter, a genial old gentleman, almost a beloved uncle now. What had occurred, Pilgrim realized, was something he referred to as the "Patty Hearst Syndrome."

In 1974 the heiress of the Hearst newspaper empire, Patricia "Patty" Hearst, had been kidnapped in Berkeley by a group of militants known as the SLA: The Symbionese Liberation Army. Held for several weeks in a closet by her captors, she gradually became persuaded to adopt their lifestyle and—to the shock of most normal Americans—appeared to embrace the revolutionary viewpoint of her coed kidnappers, even so far as changing her name to Tania and participating in a bank holdup armed with an assault rifle. Brainwashed according to the mainstream media (but wiser heads knew otherwise), Patty Hearst had begun to identify and bond with the armed militants of the SLA. When finally caught more than a year later, long after most members of the SLA were killed in a fiery shootout in Los Angeles, Patty Hearst appeared unrepentant and told the police her occupation was "urban guerilla".

Pilgrim concentrated on the road ahead. When exactly had he begun to view Jimmy Jeremiah more as a flawed but distinctly sympathetic individual and less as a cold-blooded assassin? And could he, as a reporter, still maintain an objective distance now that his emotions became involved? Eighteen months ago, when he was halfway through the series of interviews with strippers, bouncers, nightclub managers and proprietors that eventually became his Pulitzer-nominated series, he felt his emotions shift perceptively, sort of a sympathetic bias, to some of the women, dancers like Teresa who worked nights and attended community college by day, and also to a few—very few—of the men, mostly an occasional bartender or cook. The emotional and physical involvement with Teresa either made his writing better—or worse, he still wasn't sure.

"I haven't camped outside in, well, it must have been forty odd years," Jimmy said with noticeable excitement in his voice. "But if you camp inside a tent, ain't that still sleeping under the stars, at least technically?"

Pilgrim shifted a map on his lap, passing Homestead and heading south for Key Largo.

"Seeing the stars is okay but sleeping out means peeing outside in the bushes as soon as you wake up, in my opinion."

"Thought so."

"Doesn't matter whether you sleep on the ground," added Pilgrim. "Having a tent is okay because the Indians had tents and they were the first American campers."

"You ever notice, Dan, how most white folks brag about having a little Indian blood in them but you never hear too many Indians brag about having a little white man's blood in them?"

The reporter laughed. "Everybody respects the freedom of the wolf but prefers the domesticated dog."

"But who would we rather follow—the guy who says, 'I'm part wolf', or the guy who admitted, 'I'm just a dog'?"

"As a reporter, I'm just a seeing eye dog for the status quo."

The Guns of Dallas

"Society counts on you, Dan, being a dog—I was a dog, most of us are dogs--easily threatened or beaten, caged up if we don't comply, thrown a few treats for obedience. 'Promoted', we call it."

Pilgrim shifted uneasily. "Just as long as I don't become a lap dog."

"That's the name Manny and I gave all the top magazine and newspaper people after the assassination: lap dogs. They lapped up the official version—lapping up whatever Shank and Rank fed 'em."

"Shank and Rank?"

"Gordon Shanklin and Lee Rankin. We even began to use the term 'shank and rank' as a slang phrase, meaning to switch or deceive."

"Who were they?"

The old man's eyes brightened. "J.Gordon Shanklin was head of Dallas FBI in 1963 and J. Lee Rankin was high counsel of the Warren Commission in 1964. Maybe it had something to do with that J-hook initial in their first names, but one way or another, very little dissenting evidence ever got past those two guys. Manny and me came to realize that as long as Shank and Rank were covering our tracks we had nothing to fear."

"Give me an example?"

"Okay. About a week or two before the assassination, Oswald passed a note to a Fibbee named James Hosty at Dallas headquarters. Two hours after the assassination, Hosty destroys the note on orders from Gordon Shanklin. Now if that note was truly incriminating to Oswald—like the FBI claimed it was--they would have preserved it in their files like the Gettysburg Address, and ballyhooed to the press with a lot of fanfare, to prove what a nutball Oswald was, right?"

"Okay, I follow you."

"But what if that note was really a warning about the upcoming threat to President Kennedy's life? How embarrassing would that be?"

"Major embarrassment."

"Kind of like another recent FBI embarrassment, you'll recall, when one of their own agents in Minnesota reported in August of 2001 that maybe Saudi students were learning to fly for terrorist reasons—and FBI headquarters ignored that warning too. And we all know what happened on September 11, 2001, don't we? Ironically, just this year the brand new FBI headquarters in Dallas, Texas was dedicated. The name of the building? J. Gordon Shanklin."

Pilgrim could hardly conceal his shock. "You mean Oswald might have been a paid informant for the FBI?"

"Might have been? When Oswald was arrested he had a scrap of paper with Hosty's phone number on it! How many assassins carry the names of FBI agents and are denied lawyers for almost 48 hours? The CIA and FBI were trying to disavow any knowledge of Oswald, don't you get it? He was way in over his head; they were expecting him to shoot it out with the Dallas cops at the Texas Theatre."

"No wonder Shank and Rank couldn't allow the truth to get out."

"Shanklin had orders from headquarters to contain the damage, especially after Texas Attorney General, Waggoner Carr dropped a bombshell on the media that Lee Harvey Oswald was a paid FBI informant. Now if a guy is paid to inform, what is he expected to do? Didn't I say, when we first met, that this story had more twists and turns than a South Florida canal?"

"Speaking of canals, where will I be turning up ahead?"

The quizzical expression on the face of his passenger hardly reassured Pilgrim. He slowed the car and kept to the right while faster traffic sped past on the way to Key West.

"I believe it was called Lost Key forty years ago—or was it Alligator Ridge?--but maybe those were just local names. Now that I think of it, the place I remember was neither a key nor a ridge but more like a nameless peninsula. Maybe none of those names are on the map at all."

Pilgrim passed the map to Jeremiah and the old man stared at the colorful page for more than a minute before flipping it over and gazing at the reverse with rapt attention. In between memorizing the map, the old man stared out the window, trying to get a sense of place in a landscape as devoid of permanent features as the middle of the ocean.

Jimmy brightened. "I'm sure we have to turn right and head west before we get to the bridge for Key Largo." He watched the passing canals and occasional lagoon for a road he might recognize.

"Up ahead," he said, a tone of hope rather than certainty in his voice. "No, keep going; my mistake."

"How did Jack Ruby fit into all of this?"

"Jack was a mobster from Chicago who ventured south sometime in the 'Forties, I believe. Dallas was wide open and the local cops were very accessible. One hand washes the other, you understand? Anyway, Jack owned a couple of burlesque clubs in Dallas, one named the Carousel, and since he was gregarious guy he became very chummy with all the Dallas lawmen. They packed his nightclub, met the girls, drank free liquor, and rubbed shoulders with out-of-town mobsters. Reports are that Jack funneled mob money to the police in exchange for protection against harassment or prosecution for his mob bosses."

"But I don't see how that ties him to Oswald?"

"Okay, when you play chess, what do you call those little fellows up front that can only move forward?"

Pilgrim thought for a second. "Pawns."

"Yeah, that's it. Both Ruby and Oswald were pawns. They were told when to move forward, and where, but they couldn't move backwards. Jack was told by the mob, and Oswald probably by his CIA mentor, George De Mohrenschildt, a wealthy, well connected Dallasite who mingled with other powerful Texans like Clint Murchison, Lyndon Johnson and George Bush. Now why would George De Mohrenschildt waste his time with a bit player like Oswald if he wasn't grooming him? As I said before,

De Mohrenschildt allegedly committed suicide right here in Palm Beach, Florida and if he did bite the bullet I believe it was because of remorse for setting up Oswald."

"But how did Jack Ruby fit in?" Pilgrim remarked, growing exasperated.

"Many folks believe the mob had a hand in the Kennedy hit. Remember, the CIA and the mob worked together against Castro; each had a vested interest in getting Cuba back and getting rid of the Kennedys. Hell, George Bush had the troop transports all ready for the invasion, even had one of them renamed after his wife, Barbara, and his oil company, Zapata, but Kennedy cancelled the second invasion. Ruby himself may have been CIA connected. The mob and the CIA are joined at the hip; they are both business organizations, like the Elks or the Masons but with less morals and a helluva lot more guns. Now if the mob leaned on Ruby, and if Jack used his influence to get access to the Dallas police lock up—which he did--and if certain influential people told Ruby how he would be a hero for plugging Oswald, then he had to do it. He was a pawn. Anyway, the old mobster died in a Dallas jail cell and Earl Warren, who coulda busted open the case but was afraid to, declined to transfer Jack back to Washington to testify about what he knew, which was considerable."

"Do you really believe Jack Ruby died from an injection of cancer causing substance?"

"Shit yes! You give me a needle and I could inject you with a few ounces of radioactive water from the Three Mile Island nuclear power plant and you'd be dead in a month. I could add a few drops of beryllium and you might keel over that same day. David Ferrie, another co-conspirator who turned up dead before he could testify in New Orleans for Jim Garrison, was working on just such a cancer project for the CIA under Project Mongoose."

The reporter shook his head. "C'mon, we're the good guys. Maybe the mob might arrange a killing but does the CIA really resort to dirty tricks like that?"

"All the time if they could get away with it," declared Jeremiah.

"Inside The Company we called it Terminate with extreme prejudice. We perfected ways to make a death look just like natural causes, so that bodies could either be so mangled that no autopsy could be preformed, or bodies were made to look like accidental deaths or drug overdoses or we could simulate a heart attack or a massive coronary. We have the technology. Jack Ruby knew what was happening to him. After all, we did the same thing to many, many others before him."

"Poor Jack," the reporter sighed, "Dying like that in jail must have been pure agony."

Jimmy concurred, clicking his tongue. "For a Jew, Jack Rubinstein was alright, but he knew he really didn't fit in with most of the rednecks in Texas. He always wanted to fit in and maybe he thought--by killing Oswald--he would fit in finally. I liked Jack but he got what he deserved, just like I will. Karma comes around and kicks us all in the ass."

The reporter gasped in amazement, listening to the cold objectivity of the sensational account. Maybe this was as close to being a war correspondent as he would ever become, glimpsing the liner notes of history while seeking a forgotten battlefield of the Cold War, with an old soldier afflicted with just a hint of remorse, an absence of self-pity and an uncanny power of recall.

"That's it!" Jimmy screamed. The reporter slammed his brakes, thankful that no other vehicles followed directly behind him and guided the car over to the shoulder. "That road back there looks familiar."

What were the odds, Pilgrim wondered, that the rutted trail disappearing into a thicket of pine and tamarisk, could lead to a site existing vividly in the memory of a man who hadn't seen it in forty years? He reversed along the shoulder for fifty yards and then turned his car onto the track. Immediately he checked his gas gauge and the odometer. At least if they became lost, he could calculate roughly how many miles he had driven from the highway.

Thankful for the dryness of the season, Pilgrim rolled over the ruts in first gear before shifting into second. Beside him, Jimmy became as attentive as a deer in a meadow, all eyes and ears and nostrils. The soft branches of the trees swished against the car and sunlight dappled the single lane with a picturesque quality. The mesmerizing effect of nature--the sense of serenity coupled with the thrill of wildness and a slight feeling of danger—appealed to Pilgrim. He realized, as a city dweller entering nature, how excited yet out of place he felt.

They passed bogs and isolated islands--or hammocks--of vegetation, mostly palmetto or prickly ash, strangler fig or wild lime with an occasional, spindly bald cypress. Few trees of any size grew but groves of slash pine and the bright berried Brazilian pepper flourished. He knew his South Florida trees from a distance, learned from a book and, like most Americans, admired them from the highway inside a speeding car. Now they swished and scraped a greeting as he guided the car down the narrow lane.

They passed a moldering pile of trash at the edge of the road: a broken chair, smashed toilet, rotting mattress and mildewed clothing left there by some slob. Several bald tires lay scattered about and the sight of trash strewn along the road distressed the reporter but clearly enlivened his passenger for a moment.

"That shit doesn't look recent but I don't think it's forty years old either," he remarked. The car slowed for a deep rut and bounced over. Pilgrim noticed the road angling southwest; a parallel trickle of ditches carried little water while a hedge of trees bowered the road on both sides. Occasionally a path, hardly more than a pair of wheel tracks, led into the thickets on one side of the road or the other. Jimmy stared straight ahead. Soon a brackish pond appeared on the left and the sight seemed to indicate to the reporter perhaps they were near the coast. Another stretch of swamp appeared on the right and then the roadway seemed to become a dirt causeway coursing through marshland before entering a dry patch of scrub forest, the land becoming slightly elevated—rising as most South Florida terrain varies--by a matter of inches rather than feet.

"Find a turnout or somewhere to pull into the forest," Jimmy commanded. "There, on your left, looks like what used to be a road."

Pilgrim peered at the undergrowth, even for the narrowest of slots. Finally he spotted a faint track and eased the car deep into a forest that seemed to open up, expand, once he left the road. Completely shaded now, the car rolled along the faintest memory of a road, a shadow of some long ago byway that once lead men to a destination, since abandoned, perhaps decades in the past.

"Park anywhere," Jimmy suggested. "I have a feeling I've been here before."

Pilgrim switched off the ignition and the pair exited the car. They stood beside the silent car without moving, breathing in hushed breaths, beneath the eaves and buttresses of wetland trees. An occasional birdsong broke the cathedral of silence, an occasional angel wisp of wind rustled the autumn leaves overhead, but no earthly choir of urban traffic or din of industrial pipe organs intruded within the sanctuary where they now stood.

For almost a minute they stood still, neither speaking. Then, while the reporter unloaded the trunk, Jimmy Jeremiah shuffled away from the car, hesitant at first but striding more purposeful after several steps. The sound of leaf litter underfoot pleased Pilgrim and he listened as the sounds diminished, the searcher, like an archeologist seeking evidence of past life, moving farther away. Suppose the old man became lost, Pilgrim wondered? Likely he knew the area far better than himself; likely the old man became part wolf again after forty years and communed now with the ghosts of fellow comrades.

He raised the tent, feeling akin to Crusoe and Boone, Lewis and Clark. Jimmy returned with a piece of lumber in one hand, his eyes gleaming like an adventurous boy having uncovered a clue to a lost treasure.

"I'm almost certain this is the place."

"Where are all the alligators?" Pilgrim asked.

"Never was any gators, that I recall. This slab of chestnut board might have been part of a target and surely means men were hereabouts."

"It looks old."

"Suns going down soon," observed Jimmy. "I'll build us a fire."

Pilgrim pulled the sleeping bags from the car and unrolled them on the soft forest floor. He propped his pillow over a five gallon jug of water and leaned back, watching the most basic of human labors.

The old man scraped the leaf litter aside with the chunk of lumber, exposing limestone sand. "Scaffold," he said aloud. Slowly a pyramid of twigs and sticks rose and then larger limbs. A dancing ghost of smoke arose, drifting parallel to the ground before rising.

"I brought hot dogs, Polish sausage, steaks and potatoes, plus a cast iron skillet," said Pilgrim. "In that cooler beside the car is cold beer, wine and cream and for our coffee. Plus an aluminum lawn chair for armchair admirals and toilet paper when our bullshit gets too deep. I think I'll have a beer."

"My contribution is a pint of whiskey, a bottle of brandy, coffee and two cups and two spoons."

"Camping: primitive man's gift to modern civilization."

The sun dropped lower until skewered by the bare branches of the trees. A squadron of mosquitoes on their first foray of the evening circled at the edge of the fire, and the temperature dropped several degrees when the sun disappeared at last. Pilgrim claimed the first sighting of a star but Jeremiah informed him it was the planet Venus. The old man mixed a couple of cups of Irish coffee and passed one to the reporter.

"Here's to Manny, wherever he may be."

"And to all of his victims," added Jimmy.

"Jimmy, you think there's a God up there in the great big sky?"

"God, I hope not."

Pilgrim awoke from a sound sleep in the morning and realized Jimmy was gone. He slipped out of his sleeping bag and pulled on a pair of sweat pants. The forest in the morning is a more welcoming place than at night, he realized, and forest birds were more active, more vocal, than the night before. He walked several yards from the campsite to pee, wondering how long Jimmy had been gone, debating whether or not to holler and then decided not to.

He looked at his watch and noted the exact time: 7:35. The campfire was cold so the old man couldn't have cooked breakfast, nor even made coffee. Surrounded by trees, without a single urban sound, Pilgrim became nervous. If Jimmy didn't return by 8AM he would sound the horn. He fingered the keys in his pocket and accidentally set the car alarm, the single, electronic chirp startling him.

"You don't really expect carjackers way out here in the forest, do you Dan?"

Pilgrim jumped again.

"Look at these. I found them in a clearing not far from here."

Tarnished green and brown, the brass shell cases rolled in Jimmy's palm, and Pilgrim didn't see the significance.

"Hunters?"

The wrinkled old face broke into a wry grin. "Hunters of men! Do you know what these are? These are brass cartridges from the rifles we used to practice with out here. This is where we practiced for the invasion but there weren't any trees then. This is where we practiced with our sniper rifles on stationary and moving targets."

Pilgrim plucked a shell case from the pile.

"What caliber is this one?"

Jimmy squinted and then removed a pair of reading glasses from a breast pocket. "Give me a moment while I open my knife," he said.

The reporter observed as the old man carefully scraped the base of the shell with a couple of swipes.

"30.06."

"And that smaller one there?"

Jimmy scraped away the dirt with the point of the blade, the brass still gleaming in places.

"6.5 millimeter."

"Wasn't that the caliber of Oswald's rifle?"

"Millions of bullets were made, but so what?" said Jimmy. "C'mon, I want to show you something even more amazing. Bring your camera."

Pilgrim returned to the car and retrieved his camera and then hurried after the spry older man. What if they both became lost and never found the car again. He fingered the keys and wondered if he could trigger the alarm through the forest.

"C'mon, Dan. Look at this!"

"Frameworks?"

"Nope, scaffolding."

Jimmy Jeremiah danced around the rusting piles of scaffolding as if he had discovered Captain Kidd's treasure.

"I can't believe it's still here after all these years. We used construction scaffolding to build towers twenty or thirty feet off the ground in three or four places. Then a target, I believe it was a wooden buoy, was pulled along a wire at a constant speed and I remember several Cuban shooters practiced everyday to hit the damn thing, 'La Cabeza de Castro', we called it. Castro's head. Manny had the best score."

"Where did Lester fit into the picture?"

"Then one day, after the second invasion of Cuba was cancelled, a handful of Special Forces from Fort Bragg toured our makeshift base. Tony Lester among them. They all took turns with their custom rifles from both the scaffolds and ground level. Only Lester beat Manny's score. Tony couldn't speak Spanish then, so the name Cabeza had to be translated, but he fully understood the word Castro. Then during one pass, he shouted 'Cabeza de

Kennedy' and from then on everyone referred to the moving target as Kennedy's head."

"Did they know how prophetic that would be?"

"Not really. The handwriting was on the wall. All over US military bases in 1962 and 1963, Kennedy was being raked over the coals, from boot privates to three star generals."

Pilgrim stared at the stack of scaffolding.

"I still don't see how this stack of rusty pile of metal has any significance," he said.

"Don't you see, Dan? Everything was in place for a hit on a moving target—Castro—and our group was going to do the honor, maybe from tall buildings in downtown Havana. This was an Executive Action training base, a covert sniper school for the CIA and our secret team, ZR-Rifle. When the Castro plan was abruptly cancelled along with the second invasion, most of us found another target, a scapegoat for our resentment and wounded nationalism."

"Kennedy?"

Jimmy Jeremiah didn't answer, his gaze encompassing the pile of rusting metal and the scrubland but surveying the last forty years of his personal history and the effect he had on the nation.

"We were dogs who went to Dallas, attack dogs, highly trained and programmed but dogs just the same. Perhaps I'll find some answers in Dealey Plaza before I die."

Chapter 21

Gonzales greeted him warmly at the newspaper upon his return from the overnight trip. Pilgrim decided not to tell his editor everything he had learned about the history of Richmond Naval Air Station. Instead he mentioned the blimps and the fire and the wonderful wooden buildings in glowing terms but not a single word about the CIA. Gonzales suggested he write the story using ample quotes from the veterans once stationed there, especially Jimmy Jeremiah. The reporter assured him he would also locate a few living Navy men from the World War II era still living in the South Florida area.

"Whatcha find out, man?" Bobby sidled up just as Pilgrim entered his cubicle.

The reporter trashed the junk mail on his desk and stashed the rest in his drawer, except an invitation from the Virden Gallery. He tore open the envelope with scarcely concealed excitement. Disappointed the contents were not more personal, Pilgrim glanced at the invitation to Ellis Overman's art exhibition and then tossed it on his desk.

"I got one of those too."

"Looks like I'll be out of town on that date," said Pilgrim.

"How long you intend on being in Dallas?"

"Three days max."

"Returning to the scene of the crime with the mastermind himself."

"He was just one of many."

"I wonder if anyone will ever really know for sure who did it?"

Pilgrim shook his head. "Even Jimmy Jeremiah doesn't know who instigated the plan in the first place."

"But I'll bet he knows more than he's telling."

"Maybe I'll get a deathbed confession out of him."

"I wish I was going with you guys; I'm convinced LBJ and Hoover planned the whole thing along with Nixon. Now that's an axis of evil."

"Yeah, I think it was entirely political and the Mafia is a convenient smokescreen. Like Jimmy said, as long as everyone is a suspect, no one and everyone is a suspect, but nobody will ever get convicted."

"How convenient for the conspiracy."

"I'm beginning to believe they planned it that way from the start."

Pilgrim turned the key in his apartment and walked in wearily. For some reason he thought perhaps he had left the light on in the bathroom before leaving yesterday morning. Scratching his head, he walked in, deposited the mail on the kitchen counter and then checked his few messages. There were none. He rinsed his hands at the sink and then opened the refrigerator. An obsessive arranger, he had positioned the beer with the newest ones in back, exactly as grocery stores arrange items in their coolers, and now had the distinct feeling the bottles had been shifted. He stifled a laugh before he removed a bottle, opened it and began to look for a lime.

The phone rang and he forgot his search.

"Welcome home; how was your trip?" she asked.

"A lot of fun; your dad is good company."

"When do you plan to leave again for Dallas?"

"Our plane leaves day after tomorrow."

"Wish I was going too."

"I got your invitation today," he said. "Guess I'll miss the opening night and all that champagne and lively art banter."

"I'm sure Ellis will be disappointed."

Pilgrim imagined she had more on her mind. "Want to come over?"

"Sure, what time?" she said.

"I already had something to eat but I could chill a bottle of wine."

Joyce purred, "Tell you what: let me pick up something and I'll be over in an hour."

"I'll be looking forward to seeing you," he said.

The reporter pushed his camping gear into a closet and stripped off his clothes and tossed them atop his other gear. After he showered, Pilgrim shaved in the steamy bathroom. He could scarcely see himself in the mirror, standing with his face pressed nearly to the glass. He opened the cabinet and replaced his razor and shaving foam. Closing the cabinet, he remembered the need for deodorant and toothpaste. He shifted a bottle of aspirin and there, between the deodorant and the aspirin, stood a shiny brass rifle shell. Perplexed, Pilgrim picked it up and examined the base as he had seen Jimmy Jeremiah do in the forest.

Stamped into the brass cartridge he saw the caliber .223 and wondered if Jimmy might have put the bullet inside as a joke. The reporter smiled, realizing it hadn't been the work of the old spy after all. No, only one man could have pulled that prank, a man with a macabre sense of humor and an eye for the dramatic. Bobby Smith.

He replaced the bullet just as the telephone rang. Before he could answer, the phone stopped. He dressed and switched on some music, soft jazz playing just above the level of the outside, city noise.

The sound at the door excited him, the possibility of sex and distraction from the world of journalism; to leave the world of writing for the world of art, even for an evening, was very enjoyable.

"Look at you," he said when he opened the door, unable to take his eyes off Joyce. "No, look at you, " she said, playfully, holding a bottle of champagne in one hand. Instead he held the door and watched while she undulated into the room. Her hair buoyant, her face glowing, radiant as the highlights in her hair, her full lips glossy, animated, even without words being spoken; he appraised her with fresh awareness. She had chosen a casual yet provocative look: high heels with just the hint of a strap, shoes that elevated her to match his height; thin white blouse over a lacy, half bra, the blouse tied rather than buttoned; tight hip hugger trousers of some thin stretchy material, which accentuated her ample curves and exposed her navel, bejeweled with a faux gemstone. From the look of desire in his eyes, she had evidently chosen well.

"What are we celebrating?" he asked.

"Your overnight expedition, I guess. Your homecoming. The missed art opening." She gave him a look of affection that conveyed any reason was valid. "Well, homecoming and departure, if you want to be precise."

He opened the champagne and the foam dribbled over her hands as he poured into a glass. She giggled and slurped at the tide of champagne overtopping her glass. Then they toasted and Joyce wandered into the living room, aware of the effect she was having on him. A woman knows instinctively when and to what degree a man is attracted to her by her presence. Joyce felt his eyes all over herself. She began to study—or pretended to study—the artwork on the reporter's walls, posing before each framed print or poster before moving to the next. Her subtle movements, a slight twist of her torso or arch of her legs, mesmerized the reporter. He approached her with the champagne bottle and glass in his hands, alternately pouring and drinking.

"Would you like to see my etchings?"

She saw through his seductive mirth. "Do you keep them in a safe?"

"Yes, safely in my bedroom."

They kissed, champagne glasses curling around the other,

offering little sips, teasing each other with desire. He emptied the bottle, filling each glass to the top, and then set it on a table. They embraced and danced to a slow sensuous tune, alternately kissing and sipping, the taste of champagne on their lips. He slipped one hand to the small of her back and gently caressed. She pressed one hand to the small of his back and then rubbed his hip. Pilgrim could feel her body meld to his, the awakening of desire like a flower opens in the morning. He untied the loose knot of her blouse in front and she slipped it off and she deftly removed her bra. In the warm light of the room she looked like a bronze statue come to life.

They undressed each other in the bedroom, almost in slow motion, prolonging the sexual tension purposely. New lovers explore, advance, indulge, retreat and eventually conquer each other, every small physical act heightening the pleasure of the others.

After they made love twice, she asked him—almost as a humorous aside--what do you two men do together? Without spoiling the mood, what romantic women call the afterglow of sex, he replied leisurely: We bond. And he meant it, whether she took it seriously or not.

"What about Dallas?" she continued.

How much could he tell her, he wondered; how much of the truth was too much for her to bear?

"Dallas was part of history, the forty year anniversary of the assassination, and your dad remembers the details. I wasn't born then, and since we both like history-"

"What's to like about history? It was my worst subject in high school."

"The past is prologue," he replied.

She giggled. "I've never understood that; please explain what it means."

"What happened in the past lays the groundwork for the present," he began bravely. "What happens in the present effects the future."

She smiled, still playful. "Then why not simply say, 'the past is prologue to the present and the future'? What does prologue mean anyway? Sounds like a football term for one of their playbooks."

"Prologue is like foreplay; no one can define it but everyone thinks they know what it is."

They wrestled playfully, a residual energy left over from lovemaking; neither wanted to fall off to sleep immediately.

"My father is looking forward to this," she said and he knew she meant the Dallas trip.

"I was scheduled to take him to the VA hospital for more treatment, she continued, still upbeat, "but the old coot refused to go until he got back from Texas."

"We had a lot of laughs together out in the woods."

"I guess he wanted all of his energy; chemo would have left him too tired to enjoy all the historical sights there."

One day, he promised himself, he would tell her everything.

"If I was my father, and I didn't have long to live, I'd probably be the same way: stubborn until death." She laughed. "That should be our family motto."

Chapter 22

They boarded the plane for Dallas and took seats in first class. Neither had traveled first class before but, weeks earlier, Pilgrim found discount fares on the Internet and decided to splurge. Immediately Jimmy Jeremiah retrieved an enormous hardbound book from his carry on bag, slipped into his seat and opened the book. A printed page slipped out and Jeremiah grabbed it before it fell to the floor. The reporter dug a book from his own bag, adjusted his seat and table before glancing aside.
"What are you reading?" he asked.
"An Internet page I printed. I wasn't aware that Kennedy intended to begin withdrawing troops from Vietnam until I found this but it says here in The Stars and Stripes--which is a US military newspaper—that in October of 1963 President Kennedy wrote National Security Action Memorandum #263 calling for the first thousand troops to come home by 1964. Now wouldn't you think most military men would applaud any leadership that kept them from the line of fire in a potentially disastrous war? Instead JFK's memo had the opposite effect with the top brass. Years later a retired Colonel named Fletcher Prouty, who also worked for the CIA, posed the question: Who benefited most by Kennedy's removal from office and who continues to benefit? Well, the answer to that question is military contractors, many of them who also employ former Pentagon bigwigs as consultants. The removal of John Kennedy was not a question of a few millions of dollars

in profits, but hundreds of billions, whether we won the damn war or not."

A pair of young men glared at Jeremiah from across the aisle but he hardly noticed. Businessmen, they arranged their laptops and cell phones on the tray before them.

Jimmy continued, "Corporate ambitions disguised as patriotism probably killed more people in history than Hitler and Stalin combined."

"I think you're exaggerating slightly," Pilgrim replied. "What book are you reading there, by the way?"

"A fascinating account of what really happened in Dealey Plaza that day. Called 'Case Closed', the book uses selective evidence very ingeniously and has almost convinced me that Oswald acted alone."

"Oswald did act alone," said one of the businessmen. "I'm from Houston and I ought to know."

An older fellow in the seat in front of the Jeremiah's turned and spoke. "I was in Dallas that weekend—I'm originally from Austin—and as a hunter, no way in holy hell could Oswald have gotten off those shots like he did, with two hits out of three. The FBI tried to reenact that feat and failed. They couldn't do it then and they couldn't do it now--and neither could Oswald."

Jimmy grinned with delight. A round table discussion of the event was totally unexpected. He folded the page into a bookmark, then lay the book aside and listened.

"If Oswald didn't do it, then who did?" said the other businessman.

Pilgrim spoke. "Why not a conspiracy involving the Secret Service? They had people in the plaza that day with badges, confiscating film from bystanders--and then they denied ever being there."

"Why not just blame the Dallas Police while you're at it?" The laptop screen folded down.

"People see conspiracies where there are none," added the other man. Neither of the two appeared older than thirty. The

Wall Street Journal lay open near a laptop. "They see government plots behind every act of terrorism."

"What if the evidence of a conspiracy is so obvious that—"

"Most people want to tear America down with their negativity," said his partner.

"Skepticism is hardly negativity--not until it's met with hostility."

"Exactly!" said an elderly woman, agreeing with the reporter. "Whenever you question authority now, most people think you're being unpatriotic, but that was exactly how out country was founded in 1775."

"Really? And were you there? I didn't think so. Now we hear conspiracy talk about how some Pentagon insiders planned the whole 9-11 attack on the WTC and how a secret group used that as a pretext for what they call a phony war with Iraq."

"Makes sense to me. There weren't even any Arab hijackers on those planes, according to the passenger lists provided by the airlines."

"The hijackers were very real, just as terrorism is very real," said the other colleague with a determined shake of his paper. "Just as Oswald was very real—and very guilty."

"Bullshit," said the hunter. "Oswald had to have had accomplices. Besides, the government lies all the damn time—like the lies they told us for going to war in Iraq—So why should we believe them when their evidence looks shaky? Just because they say so?"

"Because!" shouted an exasperated business suit. Almost at once, the pair flushed deeply, whether out of anger or embarrassment. They exchanged a look of disdain for the fools around them, donned earphones, and ended the discussion before it began.

A stewardess offered drinks after all the economy passengers passed their seats and Pilgrim ordered a whiskey and offered one to Pilgrim but the reporter declined.

"Miss," the old man said: "May I smoke?"

"No!" The reporter heard the stewardess' abrupt reply and Pilgrim turned to Jimmy and said, "I though you didn't smoke; I thought you had to give it up?"

"I only feel like smoking in places where it's not allowed."

The fellow in front chuckled. "I'm Sanders." He turned and offered his hand. "I remember clearly when we could smoke in airplanes and restaurants. Those were the good old days."

"I'm dying of cancer but I'd still like a cig."

"You said you were a hunter, Mr. Sanders?" Pilgrim asked.

"Used to hunt. Bad hip now; I'm sixty and beginning to feel it."

"Why couldn't Oswald have made those shots?"

Sanders looked thoughtful. "He might have made two hits on Kennedy coming toward him on Houston Street, if he really had a mind to, before the car sped up and kept going. Those were comparatively easy shots and the target would have drawn closer to him not away."

Pilgrim noticed the old man beside him listening intently.

"But when that Lincoln turned onto Elm the degree of difficulty was multiplied greatly. Now why would Oswald want to do that, make things more difficult for himself?"

"Maybe he wanted to give Kennedy a sporting chance?" said an overweight man in the seat behind them. "Maybe Oswald still hadn't decided to actually shoot him?"

Sanders ignored the suggestion. "So now you have the car going downhill and away from the shooter and under a tree. You couldn't have planned for a worse combination."

"Why didn't most Americans question those circumstances?" Pilgrim asked.

"Because most Americans never shot a gun of any kind, and certainly not a rifle with a scope. Also, in 1963 most Americans trusted the government. If the government said Oswald shot the president, we believed them. I know I did and so did everyone else I knew."

"When did you stop believing them?"

Sanders laughed. "When I went to Vietnam. Maybe after the first week over there."

Jimmy Jeremiah nodded and Sanders turned around. Then the old assassin returned to his weighty book. He opened 'Case Closed' and began to read avidly, chuckling under his breath from time to time all the way to Dallas.

They rented a car and headed for the first stop. Pilgrim drove.

Jeremiah held a street map in his lap and the reporter followed his directions.

"Turn here," he said and Pilgrim turned down West Neeley in the Oak Cliff area and drove two blocks until he reached a dead end. He drove with one hand on the wheel while reaching into a valise and removing his tape recorder. Pilgrim turned the recorder on and set it carefully on the padded dash where he could watch the reel unwind.

"Now where?"

"214 Neeley must have been right there." The old man squinted into the sun. The lot was vacant, a grassy slope with a fringe of trees. "I guess they tore the place down, but this was the address where Oswald 'supposedly' posed for those pictures of him holding a rifle with a pistol on his hip. Only problem was, Marina told the Secret Service in December 1963 her husband didn't own a pistol, but there it was, on his hip in the famous photographs she 'supposedly' took eight months earlier."

Pilgrim backed the car around. The neighborhood appeared as a forgotten backwater, the cul-de-sac street with the empty lot, where an infamous figure in American history once lived. Jimmy directed him next to Tenth and Patton and he navigated the streets until he reached the intersection. He stopped and got out of the car. Another mystery, another series of empty lots in a quiet, tree-shaded, residential neighborhood, offered him little to see.

"This was where Oswald 'supposedly' shot Dallas policeman, JD Tippit," Jimmy noted.

"I notice you're using the word 'supposedly' more often, Jimmy."

"Well, most of the witnesses here failed to identify Oswald as the shooter. One fellow, a car salesman, who actually chased him for a block, said the murderer didn't resemble Oswald. Two days after he testified to the Warren Commission, that car salesman, Warren Reynolds, was shot in the head with a rifle from a distance but luckily he recovered. They caught the man who admitted shooting Reynolds. Almost immediately a stripper from Jack Ruby's nightclub came forward and offered an alibi that the fellow had 'supposedly' spent the night with her and that shooter got off. A week later that same stripper was arrested on a minor charge and while in Dallas jail she 'supposedly' hung herself with her pants, committing suicide. Warren Reynolds wisely changed his testimony and declared that, yes, Oswald was the man he 'supposedly' chased that day and yes, he admitted changing his testimony out of fear and yes, I have been using the word 'supposedly' more often."

Pilgrim stared at the intersection but realized there wasn't much to see. Not a single house remained on any corner. Even if he wanted to ring a few doorbells, there weren't any doors in sight.

They drove a few blocks to the Texas Theater, the building forlorn, empty and surrounded by chain link fence at 231 West Jefferson. They parked, fed quarters into the parking meter and walked to the theater. A sign near the locked door said a restoration of the building was planned. Pilgrim took a few pictures while pedestrians passed him on the busy street without giving him any notice.

"Oswald holed up here, probably thinking he was safe," observed the reporter.

"Oh no, he knew he was in danger," Jeremiah said. "His cover was blown; he was like a spy hoping for rescue but no rescue would come."

"Why didn't Oswald give himself up peacefully?"

"They were hoping the opposite would happen, hoping he would come out shooting."

"He killed Tippit, right?"

"Probably not but who knows? We were instructed—me and Manny--to find Oswald at his place and kill him ourselves and make it look like a suicide but his landlady was home."

"What do you think Oswald said, down at police headquarters?"

"Probably nothing much for awhile. Then, after they beat him up pretty badly, Oswald might have told them he was an undercover FBI man. Notice how convenient it was not to have any tape recordings or have a stenographer write down what Lee Harvey Oswald actually had to say for almost 48 hours? Notice how he never got that lawyer he requested? He was dead meat and the Dallas cops were just waiting to hear how the higher powers wanted to dispose of him."

Pilgrim looked at the façade of the movie theater, remembering the oddity of the titles. At the exact time Oswald was arrested, a double feature was playing. "War Is Hell" and "Cry Of Battle." Ironically, a year after Kennedy and Oswald were murdered, both terms would apply to American soldiers destined for Vietnam. The reporter scrawled a few lines in his notebook and listened to Jeremiah's observations.

"Most assassins are proud of their attempt to kill a powerful leader. Oswald always claimed he was innocent. Hell, John Wilkes Booth jumped to the stage of Ford's Theater and broke his leg after shooting Lincoln and shouted to the crowd, 'Sic semper tyrannis', which means 'Thus always to tyrants'. All Oswald said was, 'I'm just a patsy,' which he was."

Pilgrim snapped a picture of the movie house with Jimmy Jeremiah glowering at the camera in the foreground.

"What do you think, Jimmy: If Oswald had lived to stand trial, would a good lawyer have won the case and gotten Oswald off?"

"There is no doubt in my mind, no doubt at all."

They parked near a sports bar, three blocks from Dealey Plaza and walked through the warm sunshine angling down Elm. The old man withdrew with each step, Pilgrim noticed, growing silent but acutely observant.

The first thing Pilgrim noticed about Dealey Plaza was how small everything looked. The second thing he noticed was how exactly like all the photographs everything looked. The third, and most lasting impression, struck Pilgrim powerfully. Here an epic, history shaping assassination had occurred, transpiring in this bucolic park, with fountains and rolling green lawns and shade trees, before crowds of welcoming people on a warm sunny day exactly like this one. If Shakespeare had written an English tragedy about a king--betrayed and then brutally slain--he could not have picked a more picturesque setting for the slaying.

The reporter held the tape recorder in one hand, hoping his witness would utter even a few choice lines. Would he brood, silent as a ghost?

They crossed Houston at an angle and wandered past the fountain. Here Jimmy turned and Pilgrim followed his eyes. The sunlit, seven story brick building might not be the most famous structure in America but it certainly was one of the most mysterious.

"Somehow it all seems smaller," Jimmy uttered at last. "You expect historical places and people to be larger than life but you find out different."

"Does it seem very long ago?" the reporter heard himself ask, in a voice that wasn't his.

Jeremiah gave him a strange look. "What sort of question is that? Sure, it seems like forty years ago! It seems like forty centuries and seems like forty minutes ago, both!" The old man shook his head and began to walk.

Pilgrim followed, embarrassed and ashamed he had fallen into the role of a newsman. He felt almost as if he were a television reporter interviewing fire victims or earthquake survivors on camera in Los Angeles. He switched off his tape recorder and put it in his pocket.

"Damn, nothing has changed, and everything," he heard Jimmy say, as they crossed Elm. "Almost like time has stopped and I'm back and Kennedy is due here any minute."

"Looks just the photographs," Pilgrim mumbled.

"No, they took down the giant Hertz clock from the top of the book depository. They removed the fire escape from the Dal-Tex building. And there used to be a locked barricade stopping traffic going into that parking lot."

The reporter looked puzzled. "You mean cars couldn't just drive in or out?"

"No, you had to have your own key."

The reporter hurried along, amazed and indignant at the apparent slipshod detective work. "Lee Bowers, on duty in that train tower, saw three cars with out of state license plates circle the parking lot ten or twenty minutes before Kennedy was killed. Who gave them all keys?"

Jeremiah laughed. "Shank and Rank didn't think that question was important, I guess."

Jeremiah strode into the parking area, threading his way around cars, striding purposely to the fourteen foot tower and Pilgrim followed. At the wall they turned and counted off the yards to the picket fence.

"Ninety yards!" Jeremiah exclaimed. "Bowers could see both of our shooters clear as day. I'll bet not one commissioner came down here and walked off the distances after the assassination. Lester told me once that ten minutes before the assassination they pretended to have car trouble and even opened the hood. That's when he removed the rifle."

Pilgrim pressed the tape recorder; the old man was on a roll.

"Look over the fence," he said. "We're hidden pretty well in the trees. Remember, all eyes will soon be on Kennedy and the approaching motorcade. People can hear it coming, they're excited, the roar of the motorcycles, the distant cheers. You raise your rifle carefully, between your torso and the fence. You see the big blue Lincoln turn slowly onto Houston. Then you hear that first pop while the car is still out of your sight. Then another shot, from the direction of the book depository and the car appears. Now every eye is absolutely glued to Kennedy, in pain and agony in that car—and it's slowing down! The car is slowing down! Bang! You fire and so does the fellow next to you. Bang! Kennedy's brain spews all over the trunk of the car, blood and brain matter all over the motorcycle escort; people are aghast and falling, and your heart leaps and in a split second the rifle muzzle swings away from the fence, swings up under the front of the car and the spring clamps under the bumper secure it. And you take a deep breath and light a cigarette and the first motorcycle policeman roars up and people are shocked and puzzled and pouring over and around that fence because of course that shot that killed Kennedy sounded like it came from the Grassy Knoll and the picket fence but of course there's only a trim fellow in a nice shirt and raincoat smoking a cigarette and the cop notices he has greasy hands but he produces Secret Service ID to calm the cop and says, No, no one came back here."

Pilgrim took a deep breath and gazed at the tower ninety yards away and then over the picket fence to the street where Kennedy was struck finally.

Jimmy continued. "That's pretty much how it all happened, according to Tony Lester's account that same evening."

Now Pilgrim grew silent, forgetting every question he intended to ask. They walked around the picket fence, graffiti carved and scratched into the wooden slats, and entered the peristyle overlooking the Grassy Knoll. Jimmy stood next to a man smoking a cigarette and the smoke drifted past him, triggering a memory.

"Everyone said they smelled gunsmoke drifting from the trees above the Grassy Knoll. And of course they did. They saw the flash, they smelled the smoke, they heard the shot—remember Lester wasn't using a silencer like he was supposed to—and some of them even felt the blast. Think of all the witnesses ignored, all the testimony discarded."

Pilgrim watched a man with a movie camera attempt to film a passing automobile from atop the same pedestal Zapruder had used forty years ago. He stepped off and Pilgrim took his place. For a moment the reporter wondered how steady his hand would have been at that moment. He was certain he would have lowered the camera at the sound of the shots. How did Abraham Zapruder ever resist the urge to verify the assassination with his own eyes? The old man seemed to read his mind.

"Curiously, Zapruder belonged to a couple of CIA fronts and his former business partner, Jeanne, married Oswald's CIA mentor, George DeMohrenschildt. Small world, huh? Anyway, Abe Zapruder may have been instructed to go film the whole damn thing right here, that's what I think. How else do you explain his ability to film right through the entire assassination?"

Pilgrim turned and saw Jimmy frowning from the peristyle, cigarette in hand. The old man seemed to shrink with each successive puff, people wandering past him unaware how close to history they stood.

Without saying a word, they walked to the entrance of the book depository and entered the building, taking the elevator to the sixth floor. Several dozen other people lingered at displays; the entire sixth floor now a museum. Like entering a tomb or a shrine or a sanctuary, Pilgrim thought, or a combination of all three. Jeremiah ignored the displays and looked at the floors and the ceilings. Then he looked at the support pillars and finally wandered to the windows where the reporter followed, tape recorder ready.

"What were you looking at, Jimmy?"

"Trying to visualize how it was. Back then the entire floor was dark, pretty claustrophobic, boxes stacked floor to ceiling, only a couple of weak light bulbs. Tremendous hiding place for Manny and me. You could hide a half dozen people in among the boxes. They were putting down new flooring so they had pushed boxes around to the east wall. Manny and I got here early, before the place opened. We had keys. We had our Secret Service ID, just in case we were stopped, badges like that one Manny left you."

Pilgrim raised his camera but Jeremiah pointed to a sign, forbidding photographs or filming. They wandered to a glassed area, containing stacks of books. The sign informed them they were looking at the corner window known as the sniper's lair.

"Supposedly, that's where Oswald popped the president," Jimmy continued. "But Oswald was downstairs. We told him to keep a sharp lookout and act normal but we were setting him up. Lee Harvey had been set up precisely for months if not years."

"And what did Oswald think you two were going to do?"

"We told him we intended to shoot at JFK and Castro would be blamed and then another, full scale invasion would topple Castro. Not kill Kennedy, just maybe wound him. Oswald was as shocked as everyone else in Dealey that day when our guys behind the picket fence blew Kennedy's brains out and Lee found out later at the police station. You could tell he was genuinely shocked, just by looking at him in the TV camera—that deer-in-the-headlights expression he had. I felt pretty bad about that, amused but a little ashamed. Still do."

Jeremiah sidled to the windows and Pilgrim followed. He stared at the skyline before Jimmy continued.

"Manny had smuggled his 7.65 Mauser up here—a tremendous weapon--and together we tried to figure out where exactly we wanted to position ourselves. At first we considered the southeast corner, the so-called sniper's lair, but that damn tree down there got in our way. We had been instructed--all the teams of FTAP--not to fire until Kennedy's car turned the corner onto Elm completely and the following car in the motorcade blocked his way behind."

Pilgrim peered out the window at the overspreading leaves of the Texas live oak. When he turned to look at Jeremiah again, he was surprised to see the old man holding a rifle scope to his eye, staring outside at the traffic coming toward them on Houston Street.

"The best shots are the approaching ones, like that hunter fellow, Sanders, said on the plane." Jimmy handed him the scope. "But when Kennedy turns on Elm the shooter must swivel the gun, lead the target and then—just as you've got him in the crosshairs—the target disappears into the trees! Quickly you get off a round, as Manny did, that first round everyone heard, but you've missed! Then you pan through the tree, trying to follow the shape of the car through the branches, but as the car enters you've lost your target! Quickly now, you swing the rifle and wait a second but as the car reappears you haven't locked onto the target in your crosshairs. You shoot and score a lucky hit but if you're the lone gunman the target is now almost one hundred yards away, moving downhill. You chamber another shell, which throws your aim off also."

"Sounds difficult to do."

The old man nodded. "Manny always thought he had killed the president but I knew otherwise. The first shots that wounded JFK could have come from Manny or from the third floor of the Dal-Tex building, a perfect place of ambush with a direct line of sight. The throat shot to Kennedy was frontal, from the picket fence. The wounds to Connelly were probably done by Flores or the guy atop the County Records building with the 30.06, or the guy in the Dal-Tex. Every shooter used hollow points or frangible rounds for maximum effect, that's why they only found fragments in the car. One report said 46 grams of fragments, which is a lot of lead fragments if true, but the Lincoln was immediately cleaned on orders from LBJ himself so we'll never know for sure."

"And then what happened up here in the book depository?"

"I yelled for Manny to move even before that last shot was fired and we got the hell out and left the rifle. All those first reports by the police said they found a 7.65 German Mauser here in the book depository but then they discovered that the weapon of Oswald's--the one that's now in the display case--was an Italian Carcano so they quickly changed their story. Like I said, there were a few untidy loose ends."

Pilgrim turned back towards the exhibit. The drone of narrators describing the events of that day echoed throughout the museum. Videotape played, flickering against screens for viewers mingling in silent clumps, but the footage held little interest for the old assassin. Window dressing for a historical event that had been as well planned and executed as any political murder in history.

Pilgrim noticed Jeremiah remain standing by the window, not the least bit interested in the displays, while the reporter wandered away and looked closely at every exhibit. What measure of remorse or contrition, if any, coursed through the mind of the man instrumental in killing Kennedy, he wondered? A month ago the pair of old assassins had confided to the reporter how much they had been paid. Ten thousand dollars for each of them on successful completion of the FTAP operation, and twice that amount in ten years time to each of them if the covenant had not been broken by any of those involved. That ten thousand went quickly, they admitted: new cars and clothes and a spree in Vegas and soon it was all gone. Manuel Flores added ruefully that the shadowy group who had hired them for the hit used the Watergate investigation as an excuse to cancel the second payment in 1973. Howard Hunt's wife had tried to blackmail more money out of the shadows that same year. She managed to get two million, and even had the money in her possession on the seat beside her, but the shadows sabotaged her plane and killed most of those on board. The very real threat of death--if the FTAP team ever talked-- served as an additional incentive to the men, to guarantee forty years of silence.

For whatever reason—remorse, bitterness or his fatal disease--Jimmy Jeremiah now looked exactly as Pilgrim imagined Judas Iscariot to have looked, as that Biblical conspirator contemplated suicide by hanging or death from a great fall.

Pilgrim wandered away and tried to convince himself, one last time, that maybe the old man was mistaken, and worse, maybe he was mistaken for believing him. Maybe what occurred here on the sixth floor was exactly what the authorities had concluded: Oswald

The Guns of Dallas

acted alone; motives unclear; case closed. And all that background noise of dissenting voices claiming second and third gunman was simply idle conspiracy theories.

But the more he looked at the exhibits the more doubts he had. There lay the Mannlicher-Carcano rifle with the misaligned 4X scope, supposedly sent to a mail order box with a fictitious name used by Oswald, but no cleaning kit or extra rounds of rifle ammunition were ever found among any of Oswald's possession. There lay Oswald's pistol, the one he supposedly used to kill patrolman Tippit, but the shell cases at the scene didn't match and eyewitnesses couldn't identify Oswald conclusively. There were the famous photos of Oswald posing with two weapons, taken at the house on Neeley Street that didn't exist anymore, supposedly by a woman who claimed her husband didn't own a pistol, and who wasn't aware that scopes could be mounted on rifles. There were the cameras that recorded the famous footage that day, footage that seemed to indicate a headshot of JFK from the front; there was the sixth floor window Oswald supposedly aimed through with a large tree blocking the shooter; there was the pageantry for the slain president, the swearing in of Johnson, the poignant salute by John Kennedy Jr., the flag-draped caisson, the widow in black, the bereaved nation. Where in all of this, Pilgrim wondered, was the truth?

Chapter 23

For a couple of days Pilgrim didn't see or hear from Jimmy Jeremiah when they returned to Florida. Joyce called in that time and said she had taken her father to the VA hospital in Miami and he would remain there over the weekend. Her voice had sounded subdued and Pilgrim surmised the prognosis wasn't good for the old man. Karma comes around and kicks us all in the ass eventually. Manuel Flores was right. There are various levels of justice and karmic justice may be somewhere near the top, just below that of divine justice. The sentences may seem harsh or lenient but certainly less skewed by favoritism than human judgment here on earth.

For an entire day Pilgrim wrote about Richmond Naval Air Station, dancing around the truth, thoughts of Jimmy Jeremiah and Joyce never far from his mind. Gonzales assigned him another story with a historical angle--aging motorcycle gangs and the colorful assortment of people who belonged to them. His editor commended the story he finished the previous week, about a local café winning designation for National Historic status and saving itself from the wrecking ball.

As long as he avoided controversy he flourished, the reporter realized. Readers loved the picturesque and nostalgic. Perhaps for the next thirty years of his life as a journalist, until he retired, he could write according to the dictate: To get along, go along; don't rock the boat. Another few weeks or months and Jimmy

Jeremiah would probably be dead. Better that Joyce never knew about that chapter of her father's life. Better still if he never wrote a single word about FTAP. Let the Bobby Smith's of the world tilt at windmills like Don Quixote, with the same frustrating results. Maybe he was destined to write a wonderful children's book.

But in the back of his mind something wouldn't let go.

The phone rang and he picked it up with a brisk, "Sun Satellite."

"Luke Gorman, please."

He nearly dropped the phone in shock but regained composure three seconds later and said, "I'm sorry you must have the wrong number."

He hung up quickly and stared at the phone, fearful of another ring. When the phone remained silent for many minutes, and his breathing returned to normal, Pilgrim suddenly realized that perhaps Jimmy Jeremiah had been trying to call him, or that prankster, Bobby Smith. One had probably disguised his voice to fool him, or the other's voice had become unnaturally harsh due to medication. He laughed weakly at his own fear.

But what if neither had called? That meant only one thing.

He bolted from his chair and hurried across to the photographer's space and found him gone. The darkroom, someone suggested and he hastened there. A brisk knock at the door produced the face of his friend.

"Just the man I wanted to see," Bobby said, "C'mon in here and close the door. Thought you were Gonzales they way you were knocking."

"Did you call me a moment ago?"

"And how and why would I do that, Dan, with everything but my toes immersed in chemicals?"

"I thought you had just called. Someone called me and asked for Luke Gorman."

"Uh oh. That don't sound too good."

Pilgrim shook his head. "How many people on the staff have you told about my little sting operation, Bobby?"

"That's a question you should be asking yourself?"

The reporter did a mental calculation and lost count after half a dozen, including the lawyers, but not including Bobby.

"That's what I thought," Smith said. "You couldn't abide by your friend Jimmy's advice and now that other guy, Lester, knows."

"No, he doesn't know!"

Bobby hung an 8x10 color photograph of Kennedy clutching his throat, seconds before his death, on the line to dry. The reporter caught his breath, overwhelmed by a feeling of claustrophobia yet sensing some security in the darkness and concealment of the closed room.

"You wanna borrow my Beretta? Beautiful little weapon, 9mm automatic, purchased legally."

"I really don't think that's wise."

"Okay. Suit yourself. It's a mighty brave man who carries no weapons in America. Mighty brave or mighty foolish."

Was he being facetious, the reporter wondered? Pilgrim spoke, "This is serious, man."

"I'm as serious as a tax audit and as sober as a ghost. Listen, a gun in your hand gives another man something to reconsider. Next time he calls asking for Gorman you tell him you'd like to meet, man to man."

The reporter shook his head.

"I'm not saying you need to do anything with the gun once I give it to you. Once you start waving a gun around, then you might have to use it, and since it's registered to me, I could get in trouble. You dig, man?"

Pilgrim considered the offer. Wondering what Jimmy would do.

"Yeah," he said. "Okay. I'll keep it at home or in my car—but you'll have to show me how to load it."

Pilgrim drove home early, checking his mirrors to see if he was being followed, and locked his door once inside the apartment. The

Beretta sagged in the pocket of his sport jacket like a cannonball. A loaded clip in the other pocket hardly compensated for balance. Bobby instructed him how to slide the clip in and out; how to snap the safety on and off; how to chamber the first round: and how to instinctively aim and shoot.

Inside the door he snapped the clip into the butt of the pistol grip as Bobby has shown him and, with the weapon ready, he crept through the apartment checking closets for intruders.

The phone rang and he nearly shot it.

He recognized the number and snatched the phone from the cradle.

"Just wondering if you would like some company later?" Joyce said. "Because I know I would."

He stammered out a reply. "I could go for some company; sure. Come over whenever you like."

"Good. I'll make us some dinner and we could watch a movie or whatever. I'm picking up my father tomorrow and I'm stressed."

"I thought he was spending the entire weekend?"

"He called and pleaded for me to get him out of there."

The thought of company soothed him for a moment. Safety in numbers, he thought. But Kennedy had been killed surrounded by thousands and numbers were an illusion. He wished he could talk to Jimmy.

"Okay," he replied. "Knock twice hard, pause three seconds and then knock once—only one time—more. Got that?"

Joyce giggled. "Sure. I can remember that, agent 007."

An hour later when Joyce arrived, he pulled her inside on the second knock, peering down the alleyway as she stepped across the threshold.

"My, aren't we a little jumpy," she said. "You forget to pay your rent or something?"

He smiled weakly. "No; nothing like that. I'm just more safety conscious is all." He closed and locked the door and helped her with the bags of groceries. She had come directly from work and looked very composed, very businesslike. He wanted to ask her about her father but embraced her instead. She felt the metallic bulge at his waistband and inquired instantly.

"I'm doing a story on motorcycle gangs and Bobby gave it to me for security."

Joyce clicked her tongue. "You should get in my father's line of work. It's safer."

"And what is that?"

"Remodeling houses," she chided him with a crooked smile. "I'm sure I told you all about that. He was a building contractor, remember?"

Pilgrim shrugged. "Sorry, I'd forgotten."

"My father wanted to send his thanks again. He's not well, but he has a stubborn strength."

"I envy him for that quality."

Joyce sorted the groceries, laying out the vegetables. "You two are an odd pair," she said with good-natured puzzlement. "Tell me again how you met?"

"He came into my office one day and we started talking about history, politics, things like that. My editor loves him."

Joyce washed the mushrooms and spread them on a napkin and began to slice the vegetables.

"Has he ever talked about a time in the past when he may have done something—uh—I don't know?"

Pilgrim looked at her, a smile concealing his uneasiness. "What man doesn't have something in his past to hide?"

"I sometimes get the feeling he wants to tell me something."

"All fathers want to tell their children something more but don't know how. My father was exactly that way. Maybe fathers can only tell complete strangers, I mean people they're not related to."

"My mother said he once worked for Navy Intelligence but I don't think that has anything to do with it."

"Listen, would it make a difference how you felt about him?"

"Probably not. I don't know."

"Maybe he prefers that you don't know, because he wouldn't want you to love him for whatever he might have done. Or feel like you had to love him. Or maybe he's afraid that you wouldn't. Bad enough that we ourselves know what we've done. Only the very young are without some crime or cruelty to be ashamed of."

He opened the bottle of wine she brought and poured two glasses.

"So much about his past I don't know; what's one more chapter, more or less, I guess?" The look on her face said Joyce hadn't given up the effort.

Pilgrim laughed, trying to lighten the mood. "I wish people had lights, like gas gauges, on their foreheads, that let us know when they were completely empty or morally bankrupt, and when they were full of decency. Then we wouldn't waste our time on assholes, whether we were related to them or not. Diogenes was looking for an honest man but we can't tell the difference between a good and decent person and an extremely evil one if we passed them in the street."

"You sound like a philosophy professor. The problem is, most of us alternate between honesty and deceit in our day to day lives." And then Joyce laughed too. "Besides, the real criminal masterminds would find a way to give a false reading to any measuring device soon enough."

"And make a few dollars by marketing them besides."

Joyce tossed the vegetables and mushrooms she had cut, scattering them into sizzling olive oil. Pilgrim liked the sharp, crackling sound.

"I don't think my father is any kind of saint," Joyce continued.

"Sainthood's overrated," Pilgrim said. "Just being a decent human is hard enough."

Chapter 24

The presidential portraits resembled a rogues gallery of sinister, modern day Machiavellis. The exhibition at the Virden Gallery drew only a smattering of viewers on Saturday afternoon, Daniel Pilgrim among them. Yet the quiet power of the assembled works—"American Caesar: Fifty Years of Imperial Presidents"--in the near empty room overwhelmed the viewer. The eyes of each president followed the viewer, like wolves in the wild surrounding weakened prey, muzzles red and eyes glistening, some predators more voracious than others. Pilgrim wondered how history would view each man, not histories written by the present generation but generations far in the future. Even then an honest overview would be impossible since, as Jimmy Jeremiah inferred, so much intelligence information was hidden or intentionally destroyed.

"Looking to buy or just browsing?" Joyce sidled up to the reporter and touched his arm. "We've already sold the Jimmy Carter and, of course, the Kennedy to some people in Palm Beach but the others might be harder to move."

"Not too many people would want Nixon or LBJ staring at them from their living room wall, I guess."

"I don't think Ellis Overman thought of that."

"Did your dad get back okay?"

Joyce sighed. "This morning; I picked him up before I opened."

"How's he feeling?"

"I don't think he allows the doctors there to do everything for him. For some reason, I think he actually feels guilty for being at the VA hospital, taking up 'valuable bed space', as he calls it. I'm noticing a lot more younger veterans walking around the halls, guys younger than me or you. He was angry about that too for some reason."

"Still full of piss and vinegar. Glad to hear he hasn't changed in that respect."

"You should go see him at home; I know he'd like that."

Pilgrim shifted uneasily. "I might just do that later today."

"He's probably resting now but I know he love to see you."

The phone rang and Pilgrim excused himself while Joyce answered it, hurrying away, inwardly thankful for the opportunity. Troubled by his involvement with Jeremiah, unsure how to extricate himself, he swept out the door. Once outside he looked carefully in all directions for anyone suspicious.

Pilgrim spoke into his cell phone. "You didn't leave an M-16 shell in my medicine chest, did you Bobby?"

"Now why the hell would I want to do that?" The voice crackled.

The reporter checked in his rearview mirror twice since turning off Las Olas Boulevard in Fort Lauderdale, heading for the freeway.

"I thought you were playing a prank. You have a set of keys and I assumed you let yourself in the night Jimmy and I went camping."

"Man, you probably put it there yourself but forgot about it. Didn't you spend an entire day at a gun shop researching all kinds of weapons?"

Pilgrim sped north in the direction of Lake Worth. "Yeah, possibly."

"Maybe when they showed you a variety of ammunition, you forgot about putting an M-16 round into your pocket without thinking. You can be pretty damn distracted at times, my man."

Calmed but not convinced, Pilgrim continued north, accelerating onto I-95.

"I'm on my way to Jimmy Jeremiah's place; you think I should mention my suspicions to him?"

A long silence caused Pilgrim to repeat the question.

"I heard you the first time," Bobby replied. "You might bring it up as a theoretical question: what would Tony Lester do if he found out you two had taped him? I mean, that Lester guy is old, right? What's the worst he could do?"

Pilgrim stopped at a mini-market and purchased two quarts of ice cream and a pint of whisky. He shifted the bags uncomfortably as he climbed the steps to Jimmy's apartment. If pure sugar wouldn't sweeten his old friend, he decided, maybe fermented sugar would.

He knocked and then tried the doorknob. The door was open so Pilgrim entered, standing on the threshold.

"Jimmy, you home?"

"Yeah, I'm back here in my planetarium," he called. The voice sounded strong; Pilgrim half-expected to see someone on his deathbed.

Relieved, he walked to the patio, stepped beneath a hanging plant in the doorway, and found Jeremiah busy with a brush.

"How do you like your gun cabinet?"

Pilgrim stared at the mahogany and glass rectangle. "Amazing."

"The only problem now is that the display case might distract from the display. We could distress the legs, I guess, scratch it up and put some dents and dings in the wood frame."

"No fucking way."

Jimmy smiled. "That Italian piece of shit Carcano rifle will really look cheap by comparison but maybe that's what I intended all along."

"How are you feeling, Jimmy? You look good."

"I feel alright—a little tired, but that goes with the territory."

"I brought you some ice cream and a pint. No cigs though."

"Thanks. Pour me a drop into a cup of coffee, would you? I made some fresh."

Pilgrim located a pair of clean cups and splashed a drop of whisky into his and a spurt into Jimmy's and then followed with the coffee. The newsman handed the woodworker a cup.

"I noticed you also finished your coffin."

Jimmy grinned. "Looks good, don't it?"

"You planning to rent it out?"

"Maybe turn it into a condo."

"If you put in shelves, I'd buy it as a bookcase."

"Maybe I'll leave it to you in my will, Dan, and I'll be buried at sea."

The reporter laughed. "Did you hang around and get treated at the VA? Joyce said you went AWOL."

"I get the bare minimum of treatment; I'm too far gone anyway."

"That's not what she said."

Jimmy colored. "Well she doesn't know shit."

"Is the VA jerking you around; is that it?"

"The VA does more than enough for me. They are wonderful, overworked people. It's my own goddamn government--the government I shot into office—the president and Congress cutting veteran's benefits! I feel guilty I helped put them there, the bastards! I feel ashamed of my part in their little cost-cutting scheme, at the expense of soldiers and sailors who sacrificed their health so that big shits could make a lot of money for the last forty years. The people who paid me and Manny a few measly bucks have been pimping for one fucking war after another and making billions!"

The sudden outburst stunned Pilgrim. A minute ago the banter felt refreshing.

"I wouldn't mind if they just came right out and said, 'We're really stealing the oil in the Persian Gulf so you can drive your gigantic SUVs.' But they have to stand up there and lie and line their pockets."

Pilgrim nodded. "Was there ever any honesty in any government, Jimmy?"

"Well, this one's more corrupt than most, and every day they seem to get a little worse-- and I feel like it's mostly my own goddamn fault. The day I pulled that trigger, I felt like I was doing the right thing. I knew what I was doing; I volunteered for FTAP. Money had little to do with my decision. I felt like a change of leadership was good, you know, keep America strong. But I watched and listened and learned, and the only ones who got stronger were the ones behind the fucking assassination!"

Pilgrim feared the old man might have a heart attack.

"What do you want me say, Jimmy, that I agree with you? You know I do."

Jimmy returned to brushing a finish on the gun cabinet and the methodical act of applying the finish seemed to calm him down. For almost a minute he worked in silence, the only sound a soft breeze that rattled the blinds.

"Have you started to write anything yet?" he finally said.

By the way the old man said 'anything', the reporter assumed he meant the account of the assassination and his role in it.

"Just a lot of notes. Where do you suggest I begin?"

"You're the writer; you tell me."

"I could begin with your boxing career; lately you seem to be in a pugilistic mood, like you want to punch someone."

Jeremiah scowled, and then grinned slightly. "Yeah, I get that way after a visit to the VA hospital, just thinking about the shit that goes on down there. You know, already ten thousand veterans have died from Gulf War One and here we are in Gulf War Two."

"What'd they die of?"

"Something called Gulf War Syndrome. A witches brew of vaccines, chemicals and depleted uranium poisoning, which I had never heard of before."

"Damn. I always thought we won the war without suffering any losses."

"That's exactly what they wanted you to think, Dan." The old man finished brushing, contemplated the work a moment, and dropped the brush into a jar of water. "That's what they always want you to think."

"Looks great; that cabinet should be in a museum," Pilgrim said.

"Believe it or not, the wood was scrap. Found all the short pieces in a dumpster behind a wood shop."

"The mahogany really glows."

"I'll put another coat on later. Say, how about this for a start? Why not begin the story of the assassination with the abandoned Navy base? Begin the story in the ruins of Richmond, you know, flashbacks?"

Pilgrim considered the idea from a journalistic angle. Maybe Jimmy was right. Instead of beginning with Kennedy or FTAP or the sinister overtones of the Cold War, maybe the whole damn assassination did gain momentum in the weedy ruins of the former CIA headquarters of Richmond?

The old intel pro seemed to read his mind.

"Who-the-hell knows where the idea first began anyway? How it got from the whispered stage to the planning stage to the operational stage? Maybe it blew up like a hurricane and swept over the country in a firestorm, just like the one that hit at Richmond that left everything in ruins."

Chapter 25

Pilgrim returned to his apartment and again sensed someone had been there. He rushed to his bedroom and retrieved the pistol from under his pillow, jerked the receiver back, chambered a round and waited, listening. If they had wanted to kill him, they already could have done so, ten times over, he realized.

Drawer by drawer and cupboard by cupboard he inspected his apartment for anything out of place. He went through all of his clothes. He opened his socks and inspected them; overturned lamps and telephones; sorted through the frozen foods in his freezer. Was his apartment bugged, he wondered? Paranoia left him exhausted.

He kept all his discs and CDs at the office; how secure was that?

According to Bobby Smith, someone was there every night at the newspaper, a handful of people who preferred the nocturnal hours. But anyone could sift through his desk, he realized. Had he noticed anything missing at work, he wondered?

The tape recordings, especially the one of Tony Lester, were stashed in a safe deposit box, following the suggestion of Jimmy Jeremiah. At least he could be thankful for that.

The pistol in his hand made it difficult to search. He laid the weapon by his leg and knelt in the doorway of his closet, examining each shoe for telltale signs of tampering. But what were the telltale signs of tampering? The dry cleaned suits all hung just the way he remembered.

Likewise the shirts and trousers. He went through every pocket of his sport coats and suits, uncertain what he might find there, if anything. He heaved a sigh when nothing appeared and was about to leave when he spied the laundry hamper, behind the outer door.

He overturned the wicker basket and a cylindrical wad of clothing fell on the floor slowly. At the bottom of T-shirts and socks and underwear he recognized the sweatshirt and camouflage trousers he wore on The Covenant more than a week ago. He didn't know why he had kept them, maybe as souvenirs. He shook them and two things fell out immediately: the smelly hat he had worn that day and a plastic, zip-locked bag.

The quizzical look on his face became one of shock and fear. He tore open the bag and licked a finger and inserted it into the powder.

Cocaine.

Death by a thousand cuts or destruction by a thousand threats; what difference did it make? If their intent was simply intimidation, it was working. Once they tired of the game—and this was just a game—he would probably be conveniently dead.

Pilgrim wadded the clothes into a ball with the plastic bag of coke inside. He crept outside with the pistol beneath his shirt, tucked into his waistband. The dumpster nearest his building loomed at the end of the walkway. Instead he hurried two buildings down and pressed the bundle deep into the garbage. Plausible denial; wasn't that what Jeremiah once said about CIA operations? Pilgrim crinkled his nose at the smell. He had certainly bungled this operation; blown his cover and exposed himself worse than Oswald had and there was no denying that.

The following day found Pilgrim in West Palm Beach, not far from Lake Worth. After interviewing a former motorcycle gang member dying of cancer, the reporter drove to the apartment of Jimmy Jeremiah with a bag of oranges. He rang and Jimmy answered. The old fellow looked tired, looked disappointed rather than pleased to see him, Pilgrim thought.

"I was in the neighborhood, doing interviews, and I have a couple questions."

"I got answers if they ain't too tough."

The pair seated themselves across from each other in the cool apartment. Pilgrim clicked his tape recorder and removed a pencil and pad from his shirt pocket.

"If you were trying to keep someone from talking, would you kill them right away or would you first try to scare them?"

"What happened with a lot of the Kennedy witnesses--if their testimony differed from the official version—they were told politely but firmly to keep quiet. Then, if they continued to hold contrary views, as people like Dallas deputy sheriff Roger Craig and school teacher Jean Hill did, they were warned about something happening to their careers or to their health. Some people got the warnings and took the hint. Others, like Roger Craig, never learned to keep their mouth shut and they paid the price."

Pilgrim scribbled a few notes. "Do you know of many people who got killed by someone working for the government, killed in black operations, killed without warning?"

The corners of Jeremiah's eyes crinkled in thought and he nodded.

"Famous people? Just recently? Paul Wellstone comes to mind. Before him, Mel Carnahan and John Kennedy Jr. Once again, the beauty of those operations was they were so well planned and executed. Normal folks think they were unfortunate flying accidents. We call those kind of hits 'assassination by aviation' at The Company. Used to be only foreign leaders, like Panama's Torrijos got killed, but now more and more American political leaders seem to be dying. All those guys I mentioned were very likely killed in sabotaged plane crashes because they were, what's that word for popular-?"

"Charismatic?"

"Yeah, that too, but maybe magnetic is better. They drew people to them and they were independent, they didn't always toe the party line, and so a few of them had to be killed, because they were seen as a threat. Media called them accidental, mid-air plane crashes, according to reports supplied by the National Transportation Safety Board, the NTSB--which is just another government agency and part of our network."

"A bomb in their planes killed them?"

"No, a bomb in the tail disabled the plane just enough that it made the airplane uncontrollable. The crash killed the people." Jeremiah struggled to rise. "Wait right here." He ambled into the kitchen and reached under his sink. When he returned he held a small electronic device. "This is what we used."

Pilgrim's jaw dropped.

"This is a timer and this is Semtex; plastic explosives. This is what brought down that Lockerbie plane; something small like this. Believe me: a lot of plane crashes aren't accidents. It doesn't take a lot. Doesn't matter what eye witnesses say either. People heard and saw an explosion when Kennedy's plane crashed near Nantucket and those FBI divers discovered--before their report was hushed up—they filed a report noting damage consistent with a blast. Didn't matter. NTSB ruled it pilot error."

"What do you intend to do with that?" Pilgrim regained his composure. A war correspondent wouldn't have flinched.

"Blow up a car. Kill someone who fucked up."

The reporter started. "Who?"

The old man grimaced, hands trembling.

"You."

Pilgrim gasped and smiled weakly. "What—why? You're joking, right, Jimmy?"

The old man gazed at him without emotion; so this was how the assassin looked down upon the passing motorcade forty years before, thought Pilgrim with horror. A complete, detached coolness.

"I wish I was. I really wish I was joking."

"Blow up me?" The reporter's expression passed from disbelief to bemusement. "Blow up my car? You can't be serious, can you?"

Jimmy sighed. "I'm sorry. You just couldn't keep your mouth shut, Dan. I shouldn't even be telling you this; you really disappointed me. By the way, I guess you found those little gifts Ramon left in your apartment?"

Pilgrim couldn't answer. The convenient death list came to his mind.

"Ramon could have killed you when you got home with a silenced pistol and who would have known? Like Kennedy, you've made a lot of enemies in your career, Dan. But I talked them out of that idea—I tried to buy you time."

"But why, Jimmy? You and I were working together; we really had something--."

"Lester found out about the tape through those lawyers you spoke to, lawyers who work for your newspaper. Then the word filtered back to me but I denied everything. Plausible denial, and so they believed me. Still they threatened me through my daughter saying, either I take care of the problem—which was you-- or they would take care of my family, which was Joyce. The only one who matters to me now is Joyce."

Pilgrim sniffed, "I could kill you right here, Jimmy; I have a weapon in the car."

"I guess you could; I probably wouldn't resist."

The remark surprised the reporter and he tried another angle. "Are they really that powerful?"

"More than you'll ever know, Dan. Do you remember that TWA plane crash, Flight 800 that went down over Long Island in the summer of 1996? The FBI interviewed over a hundred eyewitnesses—just like at Dealey Plaza—and over ninety-five of them said a surface to air missile struck that jetliner. The CIA made a video of the event from film taken by one of the witnesses, which showed a streak of light overtaking that plane and then a fiery explosion. During the video these words appeared repeatedly onscreen, 'Not A Missile.' A public hearing was scheduled and eye witnesses were going to testify, almost all of them disputing the official government position. Then the FBI and the NTSB--nervous as all hell--forbid this public testimony, claiming it would undermine the CIA's position. The major news media accepted this official, government decision without a word of protest and so when you ask me if 'They' are really that powerful, the answer is yes."

"So forty years later, the killing and cover up continues," Pilgrim sighed. "Mind if I make myself a drink? Maybe I'll get drunk and kill myself on the turnpike and you and your friends won't have to bother."

"Hardly my friends, since I'm under the same death warrant as you." The old face almost smiled. "I'm sorry I got you into this."

"I'm sorry I didn't write that children's book instead. One thing about dying," said the reporter, passing Jeremiah a double whisky he quickly prepared, "You probably get to find out all the answers to all those mysteries that have been puzzling humans since the beginning of time, like that mysterious airplane crash you mentioned."

"Or like who really planned all those three Kennedy hits," Jimmy said. "Father, brother and son."

"Or whether there is a God or not."

"God, I hope not. Anyway, I'm following you into the grave. We'll both know soon enough, won't we Dan?"

The two drank, listening only to the rattle of ice against glass and their thoughts against eternity.

"What will you tell Joyce about me? Anything?"

The question seemed to freeze the old man abruptly and he said nothing.

"How much time do I have left?" Pilgrim asked.

"Not much; I have to meet Lester the day after tomorrow on his boat to finalize everything. And, Dan: don't try to run—we'll just find your brother and kill him."

Chapter 26

For the next two days, Pilgrim took taxis to work and his car sat idle. Perhaps the information Jimmy passed him was false, a terrifying yet effective threat to silence him. He had no intention of finding out, so he left his Toyota parked in the garage, not even checking the car for signs of tampering.

Bobby approached him at work the next morning but he politely pretended to be overwhelmed with story deadlines. In truth he was. All the interviews of old motorcycle riders he compiled had to be catalogued into a coherent whole before he finished that story. A number of business owners called, asking to be interviewed. They explained the historical status of their business, and especially the buildings they occupied, wondering if he might like to do a story like the one he did that saved that cafe. He politely declined all of them. If he could not save himself now, what did he care about saving others?

He began to write a last will and testament while he sat at his computer, but became bogged down by the terminology. He thought of calling the local FBI and quickly decided that would be a waste of time. Plausible denial: Jimmy would deny everything and he'd look like a fool. He thought of writing the taped interview with Tony Lester as a newspaper story and realized Gonzales would never publish it. He thought of fleeing but realized he was probably being watched. He thought of the predicament he found himself in and felt a measure of self-pity, which slowly passed into something resembling anger. Just before noon, Joyce called and invited him to a play, later that evening.

"'The Secret Life of Our Dear Director'," she explained.

"What's it about?" he replied, already certain he would agree to go.

"'The Secret Gay Life of J. Edgar Hoover', but it's not political. More like a play by Oscar Wilde."

Listening to Joyce explain the play, Pilgrim wondered how they could avoid the political undertones, deciding it must be a farce or a satire.

"Afterwards, if you like, you could spend the night at my place," she said into the phone. "The playhouse is just around the corner from me."

"I'll meet you at your place," he said.

"Great! About six thirty would be fine. We'll walk there."

He thought of the protection Joyce would provide: in the company of the assassin's daughter. The playhouse would probably be well lit and possibly packed with other people. Strength in numbers, he thought, and then realized that Lincoln had been shot while enjoying a stage play, and that Oswald had been apprehended while seated in the darkness of a movie theater. Maybe Joyce was setting him up?

"I'll be looking forward to it," he said, suppressing his suspicion. "Are you going to be home or will I have to wait around outside your apartment?"

"Why? Do you think it will rain?"

"It might," he replied.

She laughed. "I'll try to be home but if I'm not, you're not made out of sugar; you won't melt if you get wet."

Joyce hung up and Pilgrim dismissed his doubts as paranoia. He thought of lunch instead, all the while formulating plans for self-preservation. He had brought a couple of sandwiches, which he rarely ever did, and now began to eat there at his desk. Gonzales appeared and gave him a nod of approval before leaving: the dedicated journalist anchored to his desk.

A familiar face passed and then returned.

"You still busy as hell?"

Pilgrim shook his head. Bobby wandered in with a camera in hand and sat down. The camera flashed once and the reporter looked perplexed. Bobby grinned and explained.

"Hope you don't mind; I just wanted to take the last picture on that roll. The rest were of Manny and that stripper. Too bad he never lived to see the pictures."

Pilgrim thought of the others on the roll of film, himself and Jimmy. By the time the film was developed they could all three be dead. Pilgrim affected a cheerful mood unlike the one inside him.

"Gonzales wants you to take a few rolls of old bikers," he said. "Take some pictures of the shiny bikes too. I have phone numbers for a few of the more colorful ones."

"How about just photographs of the bikes? Did any of the old bikers have a motorcycle for sale?"

"Yeah, if you have a spare ten or twenty thousand dollars."

"Is that what they cost?" Bobby smiled and shook his head. "I guess I'll stick to my car after all."

Pilgrim wanted to unburden his problem but decided against it. The fewer people who knew the better. The tapes he made of the three former assassins would languish forever in safe deposit boxes, joining the secret files rumored to exist in FBI and CIA headquarters related to agent Lee Harvey Oswald. Karma comes around and kicks us all in the ass, he thought, with a mocking realization.

"Say, Bobby; do you mind if I keep your pistol for another couple days?"

"You having trouble with some of those old gangstas? You been staring at their ladies, or thinking of stealing one of the bikes?"

Pilgrim forced a laugh. "Nothing so dramatic as that. I just like the reassuring feel of the Beretta in my hand. Mind if I keep it for a while longer?"

The reporter heard the plea in his voice and looked away.

"Sure, Danny, just as long as the cops don't pry it from your cold dead fingers. And remember, there ain't enough bullets in all the guns in all the world to kill all the injustice we have here."

Pilgrim forced a weak laugh. "Spoken like Yoda, or a Jedi Master from the 'hood."

"By the way," Bobby continued, "what are you doing this evening?"

"Going to see a stage play with Joyce."

"You've been seeing her a lot; anything serious I should know about?"

"No." Pilgrim wanted to add a few more details, but what would he have said?

"Okay—What's the play about?"

"FBI director, Hoover. I don't remember the title, something about his secret life."

The photographer pursed his lips. "I tried to apply for the FBI once, me and another guy."

"I can't picture you as a Fed."

"Neither could they. Something in my blackground they didn't like."

"You mean background?"

Bobby shook his head. "Something in the background of my 'black ground', if you get my meaning, sent up a red flag. Maybe I was loitering too close to a Liberty City crime scene as a toddler or they caught me on a surveillance camera down at the schoolyard. Like I said, something in my blackground the Feds didn't like."

The reporter smiled. "Imagine the secret insider information you might have found out from working at The Bureau."

"I imagine they've got quite a few skeletons buried between the files there. Like, how much pressure did Hoover put on his Dallas agents to incriminate Oswald? They took over 25,000 interviews, according to the FBI, but many of their field agents were leaning heavily on the eye witnesses to shade their testimony according to a prearranged script. Gordon Shanklin personally pressured eye witness Jean Hill to change her testimony and when she resisted,

The Guns of Dallas   211

he had two agents stationed outside her house in a car for months after the assassination."

"According to the old man, it gets curiouser and curiouser. Jimmy Jeremiah claims that J. Edgar Hoover applied a lot of pressure from Washington, even sending two supervisors from headquarters down to Dallas to destroy files on Oswald. They even got the Dallas SAC to perjure himself. What were they protecting and why? You know, Jimmy told me that many former Fibbees became CIA men—like his boss, William Harvey, head of ZR-Rifle and Guy Banister, who Jim Garrison fingered as a key man in the conspiracy. Dallas District Attorney, Henry Wade and his sidekick William Alexander, were both former FBI agents. Where did their loyalties lie?"

"Definitely something to think about, not that anyone in power ever will."

Pilgrim grew thoughtful, suddenly realizing that whatever bits and pieces of the conspiracy he had discovered would soon be lost forever. Bad enough he had never taped Manuel Flores except that once. Now all the knowledge he had gained from conversations with Jimmy Jeremiah would be lost too, since very few sessions had been recorded.

"If anything should ever happen to me, Bobby, I hope you continue your—"

The photographer laughed. "What are you talking about? You planning on going back to travelogue journalism? Or did you catch Jimmy Jeremiah's incurable disease?"

The reporter realized the less said the better. Why endanger anyone else at this point? Why endanger his best friend?

When three very important witnesses were scheduled to give testimony before the House Select Committee on Assassinations in 1977, they were eliminated before they could talk. Carlos Prio Soccaras, former Cuban president under Batista, George DeMohrenschildt, Oswald's Dallas mentor and suspected upper echelon CIA operative, and former FBI deputy director William

Sullivan all died suspiciously just days before giving testimony. Gunshots to the head--ruled accidents or suicides.

"Just wanted to see your reaction," Pilgrim said to the photographer with a crooked grin. "I don't know what I was thinking."

Pilgrim knocked twice and pushed the door open and found Joyce humming a song. She stuck her head around the corner of the bathroom, steam issuing from the room, and giggled.

"Either I'm running late or you're early," she said.

"Don't you ever lock your door?" he chided.

Joyce frowned. "I was expecting you. Tell me you're not in a bad mood?"

"No," he replied, chastised. "I just worry about you."

Flattered by his lie, she gave him an affectionate embrace.

"Let me finish dressing and then we'll go."

He locked the door when she turned away and peeked through a curtain but saw nothing suspicious. According to Jimmy Jeremiah's timetable he still had another day to live at least.

Several minutes later, Joyce emerged and he forgot his problem for a minute while he focused on her.

"I love the clothes you wear," he said, "You wear them well, what little there is of them."

She smiled. "Global warming will make a lot of clothes redundant in Florida. I hope you don't mind if I wear sensible shoes? Two blocks is the absolute limit for high heels and the playhouse is four blocks if we walk."

Pilgrim thought of declining but he felt the weight of the Beretta in the pocket of his shorts and was reassured. His self pity had gradually become anger, and then resolve, throughout the day. All his life he had been somewhat of a coward, not only seeking to avoid confrontation but fleeing from the remotest possibility of it. Still, he wondered, would he have the guts to gun someone down? What if he shot a man lingering in the shadows who only happened to be homeless?

"Let's go," he said, finally. "A beautiful evening for a stroll down Las Olas."

"The kind of people watching you can't do in a car, can only be done on foot."

"Or in a dimly lit bar from a corner table," he added.

Ten minutes later, after stopping to gaze into shop windows along the way, Joyce guided a visibly nervous Daniel Pilgrim into the playhouse.

"You're like a Labrador retriever on a leash," she joked. "Difficult to get you to slow down, always hurrying ahead."

"I didn't want us to be late," he said. His eyes shifted from one person to the next like a suspicious border guard.

Inside the theater he chose the seats. The pair he picked were wedged in the balcony with a wall behind him and to his left. Joyce followed, surveyed the commanding view, and sat beside him for a moment. Then she excused herself and Pilgrim shifted the gun to his waistband, fingering the safety. For a minute he wondered how many men had shot off parts of their lower torso in just this same situation. Before Joyce returned he pulled his shirt over his waistband, concealing the weapon.

The play hardly held his attention. 'The Secret Gay Life of Our Dear Director' danced around the truth, never getting close to the really dark secrets of the most powerful and feared man in America. Indeed, the play was a musical, but Joyce seemed to enjoy it.

During the second act, the arrest of Alvin Karpis by Hoover—one of the few arrests ever staged for the diminutive bureaucrat—actually looked as comical as it probably was in real life. The flamboyant G-man, sounding a lot like Jimmy Cagney, ordered Karpis to get out of the parked car and the audience tittered. So much of what the American public knew of J. Edgar Hoover for fifty years was as staged and choreographed as this play, the reporter reflected. What they didn't know was the subterranean truth: the blackmail of suspected, homosexual government workers, to force them to act as informants or else the FBI would expose them, the opening of mail, the wiretaps of public servants and private citizens, the prudish hypocrisy, the enemy smear list of thousands of decent, patriotic Americans, all an elaborate play within a play.

"That was amusing," Joyce said over the applause at the end of the play. "Were you entertained or bored completely; tell me the truth, Dan?"

"Somewhere in between," he said with a smile. He stood and stretched, always aware of the metallic bulge at his midsection. "I thought the fellow who played Clyde Tolson did a good job."

"The love scenes were believable; almost like Oscar Wilde wrote the lines. Do you think Clyde and J. Edgar were lovers for almost forty years?"

Pilgrim shook his head. "I never gave it much thought." He watched the audience with more interest than he had the play, sizing up each man he saw as a threat to his own security, much as Hoover must have done throughout his nearly half-century tenure in Washington DC, reigning through ten presidents, as America's self-styled, "top cop."

Chapter 27

The following day, Pilgrim caught a taxi to a car rental agency and paid cash for a car, leasing a compact for a week. Then he drove to his apartment and entered with gun drawn, safety off, concealed with a shirt folded over his hand. He felt more hunted than hunter but in awhile, a very short while, he intended to reverse that feeling.

Before returning home he picked up a shotgun he had purchased ten days prior. The stock and barrel were shortened, resembling the weapon used by the doomed hero against the android—to little effect--in the movie, *Terminator*. Pilgrim purchased a box of twelve gauge shells, double-00 buckshot, and carried the items to his rental car. He draped a jacket over the weapon and drove home.

Inside he loaded the semi-automatic weapon and placed it in a long flower box, covering the weapon in roses. Next he stepped into his bathroom and spread a pomade of hair coloring on his palms and worked it into his hair. The glow of his sun-bleached hair disappeared into jet black and he gazed at a man he hardly recognized. After scrubbing his palms he glanced at his watch. Nine-fifteen. Would Tony Lester be on his boat at that hour of the morning, he wondered? Hastily he dressed in a white, short-sleeved shirt and tan trousers. He strapped the Beretta to his ankle after checking the clip and the safety. The round eyeglasses gave him a bookish demeanor, the look of a man afraid of confrontation. With a slight flourish he donned a cap he had shoplifted days earlier, the colorful stitching on the peak stating, Beckman's Flowers/We Deliver. Hopefully he would arrive with his delivery sooner than Lester arrived at the boat.

Jimmy Jeremiah parked his car near the slip and emerged. He reached behind his seat and withdrew a pair of rubber sea boots, caught a glimpse of Tony Lester, gave him a little wave and then watched Lester disappear. Jimmy strode over the gangway and hopped aboard. Just as he peered inside, he stopped.

"I think I forgot my coat," he said.

"I got an extra," said Lester. "You're welcome to use it."

"Hold on; let me get mine."

Jeremiah returned to his car and retrieved a Navy peacoat and a tackle box. When he returned both Lester and Ramon greeted him at the rail. He handed the coat to Lester and saw him smile.

"That's not the coat they issued you, was it?" Tony Lester felt the satin inner lining, examined the outer wool and admired the brass buttons.

"No, that one is now a memory in the minds of many long-departed moths. "I got this one at a military surplus store."

"As an old Navy man, I guess you remembered how cold it can get out there on the water, especially late at night."

"Roger that," replied Jeremiah. He noticed Ramon checking the boots and tackle box and looked pained. "Mind if I use the head? I haven't been feeling too well since my last visit to the VA."

Jimmy scurried away before they could answer, leaving the coat draped over the arms of Tony Lester and Ramon checking the insides of the sea boots. Once inside the toilet, Jimmy locked the door. He removed the items he brought and opened a metal, first aid container.

Carefully, he removed all the bandaids from a smaller box and stuck them in his shoes, beneath the foam liners. Inserting the timer he replaced the white bandage box and closed the first aid kit and slipped on his shoes.

Next he pressed the toilet and listened to the flush. Hurriedly he opened the towel cabinet and gazed inside. With a strip of duct tape he attached his weapon to the wall above the door, out of sight, As the water burbled away he quietly closed the cabinet, washed his hands and emerged, drying his hands.

Ramon met him, a slight look of suspicion on his face.

"I feel much better, Ramon, but I wouldn't go in there just yet."

Jimmy's eyes twinkled. He noticed the weapon on Ramon's waist and affected a look of indifference. He raised his arms in mock merriment and turned slowly around.

"Frisk me, amigo; I'm clean," he said.

Ramon patted him down and the gleam of a smile, like the glint of mica in bedrock, shone for a second from the face of the Cuban, a smile returned by the rosy old man. Honor among thieves and keep your gun within reach.

"Okay, Jimmy; what would you like to drink?"

Lester approached. "Before you mix anything, Ramon, could you cut her loose?"

A moment later, The Covenant drew away from the pier. Jimmy looked at his watch and drew a breath. Not even nine in the morning.

He felt alive. Maybe today was his last day on earth. He planned to make the most of it.

The rental pulled up to the security gate and stopped. Pilgrim smiled and leaned from the car, catching the eye of the uniformed guard.

"Flowers for Mr. Lester aboard The Covenant."

The guard checked his list. "Were you expected?"

"These were called in, and I wouldn't know."

The guard looked perplexed for awhile. "The Covenant left about thirty minutes or forty minutes ago. We don't have a freezer here that you could store the flowers in, sorry."

"The boat's gone?—Damn." Pilgrim felt genuine disappointment. "I told Beckman to call and verify. Do you have a business card, by the way?"

The guard drew a card from his vest pocket and wrote the phone number and handed it to the reporter. "Call here and I can check, but I don't think Mr. Lester will be back today. He left with a guest—I have his name here—a man named Daniel Jeremiah."

Pilgrim frowned. "I'll try again later today."

He pulled around the shack and waved to the guard and drove toward home. Would he have pulled the trigger, he wondered? He could almost feel the thorns as he buried his hand beneath the bouquet; he could almost feel the flow of blood, picture the rise of the cold steel, imagine the look of surprise on the face of Tony Lester as the roses fell away; he could almost hear the click of the safety, feel the kick of the shotgun, hear the blast and the amazing, instantaneous death of Tony Lester.

No, he would not await death, even if it meant coming to meet it, Pilgrim thought. He felt drained, nonetheless. Still he intended to return even if it meant staking out the boat and accosting Lester on the way to his car.

Pilgrim thought of that exact moment, the killing of an old killer. After he was caught with blood all over his clothes--perhaps by that very guard at the gate--he would, no doubt, stand trial. An attorney seeking a "cause celebre" would take his case and his face would be plastered in all the newspapers under the headline: *Florida Reporter Slays Alleged Kennedy Assassin.* As a murderer he would sell more stories than he ever had as a journalist. Of course he would have to do some time, maybe ten years or twenty years behind bars. In prison—for the cold-blooded murder of Tony Lester--he would have all the time in the world to write the true story of the assassination of John Kennedy, all the time that he didn't seem to have now. Pilgrim stifled a laugh. The book would sell at the expense of his freedom. Probably even become the bestseller he longed to write.

But only if he killed Tony Lester before he killed him.

The Covenant cruised past Biscayne Bay heading for Key Largo and Jimmy enjoyed the breeze from the flying bridge. Tony Lester joined him there and pointed to the skyline of Miami.

"She sure has grown a lot since we first arrived, huh, Jimmy?"

"I usually don't get this far south with my boat," he replied.

"How is The Big Lie? Isn't that her name?"

Jimmy looked embarrassed. "Not running very well; I've neglected her lately."

"If you'd like an immediate cash loan—long term, no interest—I could help you out. Say, twenty thousand dollars? You wouldn't believe how profitable we've been lately."

"Drug running?"

Lester smiled but his eyes revealed the cunning of a fox.

"We prefer to call it 'world trade'. I like to think that I'm doing my small part, that I'm contributing to the economy of South Florida, helping build the skyline of Miami."

"Keeping America strong?"

Tony chuckled at his friend. "You disapprove?"

"No, not at all, Tony; I make no judgments one way or the other. Wasn't that how we were trained in The Company? Not to make judgments, not to see the little picture or the big picture, never to ask why, never to let our human emotions—compassion, morality, whatever—effect our mission in the CIA. In fact, I almost envy your success."

Lester warmed to the compliment. "You could still join us, uh, after you took care of that little problem you seemed to have caused."

"Daniel Pilgrim? He'll be dead within twenty four hours. Anyway, I'm too far gone physically to partner up with your enterprise, but thanks for the offer."

"He fooled you, Jimmy—Young Mr. Pilgrim; I'm surprised. You must have lost your touch. But the bad blood between Pilgrim and a few rogue elements of the local police give us a perfect cover. Everyone knows he rubbed some people the wrong way."

Jimmy fell silent for a moment, inhaling the sea air. A line of pelicans skimmed the surface of the water, flying on a parallel course with their boat.

"Too bad that bank, BCCI, went out of business," Jimmy finally said. "One less laundry on the block, huh, Tony?"

Lester shook his head and smiled, baring perfect teeth. "Lose one laundry, gain a whole chain of Laundromats, James. The wonderful thing about the CIA is the mutual arrangement with so many international banks. I never realized it before but almost all the heads of our company, the CIA, were major Wall Street bankers or had close ties to the biggest banks after they left the Central Intelligence Agency. Clark Clifford, former Secretary of Defense, helped form The Company in 1947 and later got BCCI a license to operate in the US. His profession after politics: Wall Street lawyer and banker. Same with John Foster and Allen Dulles, former director of the CIA--the so-called designers of the CIA in 1947—they modeled The Company as much on the Nazi Gestapo as the OSS, bringing over some top Nazi agents from Germany before the war ended. The Dulles brothers were also partners in one of the most powerful Wall Street law firms, Sullivan & Cromwell. Same with Bill Casey--CIA director under Ronald Reagan--who was also a Wall Street lawyer and stockbroker. Same for John Deutch, another CIA director now with Citigroup, and Buzzy Krongard, formerly of Bankers Trust and Nora Slatkin on Citibank: all former CIA but also lawyers or bankers. You catch my drift?"

Jimmy Jeremiah nodded. "They get to use all the secrets they learned at The Company for huge profits? All that insider information, right?"

"The best of all possible business schools, the CIA. And I'm out here like a big fish in a small pond-" Lester laughed and spun the wheel of The Covenant to avoid a chunk of driftwood. "—and the rest of the sheep on the shore, who have to slave for a living, are like that piece of driftwood back there, drifting with the current. Most of them not even aware there is a current, content in their shabby little lives. And goddamn, man, WE are the current!"

Jimmy forced a laugh. "So tell me how exactly you run drugs?"

"Not run drugs. Facilitate the movement of product, or coordinate the shipment and delivery. You almost have to learn a completely new language, James."

The Covenant moved southward at a steady ten knots in the swells. Jimmy felt a little light headed more than queasy. He scanned the horizon to the east before his gaze focused on the Zodiac liferaft secured above the tophouse. Then he spoke.

"Do we have to cruise out in the middle of the ocean in the middle of the day to facilitate a shipment," Jimmy asked, "Do you have to expose your position to the Coast Guard and the DEA?"

"Not at all. We're a sport fishing boat."

Jimmy turned and, sure enough, Ramon had arranged a couple of poles in the outriggers.

"So, whoever you're meeting won't be until after dark?" Jimmy questioned. "Am I correct?"

"On the backside of Big Pine Key in the witching hours of the morning. Another fishing boat. Far from prying eyes."

"I'd love to take the wheel," Jimmy said with enthusiasm. "We're ahead of schedule, right?"

Tony Lester checked his watch, looked at his instruments. Actual speed according to his GPS indicated only nine knots. He pushed the throttle forward and heard the engine accelerate, indicating twelve hundred revolutions per minute. Then he stepped aside from the mahogany wheel.

Jimmy swung the course to the port, angling south-southeast-ward gradually. Tony Lester looked quizzical.

"You taking us to the Bahamas, James?" he said with a smile.

Jimmy shook his head, turned and watched the foamy wake form a gentle curve before he spoke.

"Just putting her on a more gentle course, angling into the waves."

Lester nodded. "The swells making your stomach queasy?"

"Roger. I figured since were ahead of schedule we could angle out, get away from all the small boat traffic and those tankers hugging the shore, and then angle back."

"Good plan; leave it to you Navy men," remarked Lester.

Ramon swung up the steps and studied the course change. The Cuban immediately began conversing with Lester in low, animated tones of Spanish, almost as if arguing a case. The millionaire held a rigid arm at right angles, demonstrating the former course and the swells. Ramon nodded reluctantly and then returned below.

"Ramon's a worrier," said Lester. "Always sees the ulterior motives. To be honest with you, James, he doesn't trust you."

"Not much I can do about that."

"He wanted to remove Daniel Pilgrim the day after our lawyers called about that unfortunate tape. Actually, Ramon wanted to remove you too."

The expression on Jeremiah's face didn't change. He glanced at the compass before turning to Lester.

"You trained him well, Tony. By the way, I'll get that tape and any copies he's made."

"Good. Anyway, Ramon's my best man for domestic, covert operations. Ramon's former Delta Force; a complete killing machine, just like his father was in Vietnam and Mexico City."

"'Dead eyes', wasn't that what we called them? No life behind the eyes." Jimmy smiled faintly. "The best sort of sniper to have is a man with cold, dead eyes."

"Just like we were in Dallas," Lester said.

"You ever get back to Dallas?" Jimmy gently swung the wheel another few degrees to port. "I hear the plaza hasn't changed much."

"No reason. What was Kennedy but one more piece in the puzzle? Granted a bigger piece but no more important than, say, those Mexico City students we popped in 1968."

"Yeah, you're probably right. I never heard about that part of your career."

Tony Lester leaned over the console. "A number of The Company's best mechanics were loaned to the Mexican government just before the 1968 Summer Olympics was held in Mexico City. We even got to bring our own guns into the country without a customs inspection, that's how untouchable we were. Anyway, about eight thousand student protestors had gathered in some downtown plaza to protest what they called the lack of democracy in Mexico, just ten days before the Olympics."

Lester laughed and Jimmy glanced aside.

"Lack of democracy," Lester snorted. "Meanwhile we had over 350 guns trained on those unsuspecting students in the square down below. The snipers were Mexican government Special Forces mainly--called the Falcons--but there were some freelancers among them, like myself. We occupied every rooftop and upper story window around that square."

"Then what happened?" Jimmy said.

"What-the-hell, we opened fire on those pricks, that's what happened. I don't remember whether Luis Echeverria--who was head of state security--or president Diaz actually gave the order. I was firing from an apartment building that actually belonged to one of Echeverria's relatives. It was like Dealey Plaza multiplied by several hundred times. We must have fired over a thousand rounds of ammo between us."

At the wheel, Jeremiah focused on the distant horizon and double-checked the radar. They were almost ten miles off shore with a speed of fifteen knots. No other boats were visible far to the west; Miami appeared as a silvery rim of rectangular pickets.

Jimmy chuckled. "So what happened to all the bodies?"

"All hell broke loose. Students screaming and stampeding every which way. Wounded being dragged out of the square by their friends. After the massacre, the police cordoned off the square and picked up the dead--must have been several hundred—and their bodies just disappeared."

Lester looked thoughtful for a second. "They just don't have the same respect for the dead that we have here in the States, Jimmy."

"Yeah," Jimmy replied, "What do you expect from a bunch of wetback Mexicans?"

Lester roared with laughter and clapped him on the back.

"You feel like lunch? I can have my personal wetback fix us something. Put her on auto-pilot for a moment and let's go below."

The smile of contentment on Jimmy's face faded when he saw the metal first aid container opened on the table. The interior box of bandaids also lay open and the detonator beside it. Ramon glared from the galley and Tony Lester heaved a great sigh of sadness. The steward handed him a drink and he passed it to Jimmy.

"Ramon wants to kill you right here and now, Jimmy. Can't say I really blame him."

Jimmy gazed deliberately at the assembled items before speaking.

"If you notice, there's no explosive substance so what good would a detonator do? Anyway, paranoia is his stock in trade, didn't you just tell me that?"

Ramon cursed him in Spanish and Lester waved him silent.

"But why try to hide the timer?"

"Remember how I rushed to relieve myself when I came aboard? I didn't want to drop the contraption in the toilet," Jimmy explained.

Lester shook his head and Ramon drew his gun. "Lame excuse."

Jimmy shrugged.

"My better judgment says kill you right here and now," Tony began, "But on second thought I believe Ramon will accompany you tomorrow. He'll go directly to your daughter's gallery and if he hasn't heard from you in a certain time, reporting a successful operation against the unfortunate Mr. Pilgrim, then your daughter will be killed. Understand?"

"You call the shots."

"Just like in Dallas," said Lester. "Ramon: I believe we shall have some lunch now. You are hungry, aren't you James?"

"May I wash?" Pilgrim extended his hands.

"Use the galley sink."

The old Navy man grinned. "You want me to piss in it too?"

"Use the head, then!" Lester growled.

Ramon scooped ice cubes into a pair of glasses and held a bottle of gin aloft, pouring slow and steady as the boat wallowed on auto-pilot. Jimmy stepped to the head, entered, and then locked the door to the toilet before turning the faucet to full. The sound of water splashing into the sink disguised the click of the wall cabinet. Extending his arm as far upward as he could reach, Jeremiah felt the gun and wrenched it free. In seconds he checked the clip, tightened the silencer and slipped the weapon alongside his ankle, snugly inside a sock, drawing the trouser cuff down. Before he shut the faucet he splashed water onto his face and hair, dribbling some onto his shirt collar. With a towel in hand he stepped outside to face the pair.

"Have you got another shirt, Tony?" he said, removing the outer garment. He watched the eyes of Ramon stare at his waistband, as Jeremiah knew he would when he removed the shirt. "I'm afraid I got a little sick in there."

"Ramon? Please get him another."

The steward left and Lester flashed his former old comrade a look of cool detachment, the sort of expression an Iraqi executioner usually reserved for Saddam's enemies. He pressed a tray of food towards him and Jeremiah wondered whether it might not be his last meal.

Ramon returned as silently as a shadow with a clean shirt. Jeremiah stood and slipped it on, fumbling with the buttons. His eyes met Ramon's but saw no spark there, no sign of recognition, aside from an overt wariness. What had Tony called him earlier--A complete killing machine?

"I don't know that I have much appetite left," Jimmy said, almost apologetically.

Lester ignored him. Turning his attention to his steward he said,

"Ramon put us back on course for Big Pine Key."

Jeremiah thought of Joyce alone with Ramon. Likely she would be killed too, maybe after closing hours and made to look like a robbery. Maybe not even that. Jeremiah remembered reading about the death of that intern linked to president Clinton--Mary Mahoney--gunned down in that Georgetown Starbucks, execution-style. Mary Mahoney had been shot in the head five times with a silenced pistol, gunned down with two other coworkers and nothing taken: an execution having all the trademarks of an ordered hit. Jeremiah felt the boat swing westward. Tomorrow the same sort of execution probably awaited his only daughter, Joyce Virden, by the same sort of thugs. And the only suspect ever found would be a patsy, just as the one found in the Mahoney case.

Jimmy pondered his probable fate if he failed. The following day, alone in his Lake Worth apartment after killing Daniel Pilgrim, Jimmy Virden, formerly known by his code name "Jeremiah" long ago in Dallas, would die of an apparent heart attack. The obituary would be short--who would even help write it with his daughter gone?—and no connection would be made between the three deaths.

Jeremiah glanced at his watch and saw the grim mask of justice and the reflected glare of Tony Lester smirking at him over the edge of the timepiece. Karma comes around and kicks us all in the ass at last. Jimmy raised his glass.

"To your health and mine, Tony," he said. Lester raised his glass and, from the corner of his eye, Jeremiah watched Ramon at the wheel.

The two glasses clinked and the predator's glare glanced across the swirl of ice and the smell of alcohol. The shot sounded the same instant Jeremiah slammed his glass onto the surface of the table, and Ramon turned briefly before tending the wheel. Below the table Jeremiah held the silencer-equipped pistol only inches from Tony's waist. The steward couldn't see the expression of shock but in the next instant he heard the groan, the gasp, and recognized the fate of his boss. Ramon reached for his weapon as Lester slumped to the floor, but the first shot caught him just as he turned, and the second hit the steward before he fell to the floor.

Jimmy Jeremiah rose and stepped around the table. Tony Lester, still alive, held his mid-section but didn't move. Ramon, with a bullet in his hip and one in the chest, struggled to raise his Glock automatic. Jimmy stepped on his gun hand, breaking the finger at the trigger, then placed a towel over the face of the steward and fired once more. Brain matter stained the fabric red and Ramon lay still. Jimmy turned to face his former friend.

"You want another drink before you die, Tony?"

The face moved and Jeremiah heard a whisper. "Very kind of you, James."

Before he stepped into the galley, Jimmy Jeremiah drew the throttle back and checked the radar. Still almost eight miles off shore, he noticed. He turned the ignition key and listened to the silence, letting the boat drift into the gentle sway of the swells, aware the current was running offshore. When he returned from the galley with a pair of drinks, he realized Lester was dead.

He seated himself and nibbled from the tray. The last respectful meal. He drank slowly, sipping the drink as the day ebbed away. The sun angled lower and the next time Jeremiah checked his watch it was already past four o'clock on a warm winter afternoon.

Rising, he retrieved his peacoat and slit the shoulder pads. Tearing aside the fabric he removed flattened packages of plastic explosive. He found the hatch to the engine room and went below, timer and Semtex in hand. He molded the fourteen ounces—just a fragment of the estimated 40,000 tons stockpiled around the world--into a donut shape and placed it around a stanchion supporting a bulkhead wall. With the engine off he could hear the marine radio above him. In another hour or two, darkness would shroud the boat and it would drift, just another fishing boat engaged in deep sea night fishing. He attached the detonator and returned to the galley. After gathering every floatation device carrying the name of the boat into pile, he doused them with lighter fluid. When the boat blew up they would fell from the sky like so many glowing embers. Next he found the storage locker and removed two spare anchors. He found a spool of poly line and dragged the bodies to the stern and attached an anchor to each, winding several fathoms around each corpse. If any pieces remained floating after the explosion, Jeremiah reasoned, seabirds and fish would probably devour them.

He took a moment to rest and, for some reason, thought of those Mexican students peacefully protesting in the city square, massacred and then buried in unmarked graves by the police. No, there was not much justice in the world—never had been--but maybe the score could be evened sometimes. Not often and never equally, but maybe a little.

He lit a cigarette and then tossed the rest on Tony Lester's lap. Your last cigarette, he said to himself. Then he laughed aloud, the sharpness of the sound pleasing him. Yes, Jimmy Jeremiah was dying but it wouldn't be today, not killed by fellow employees of The Company. They could all go to hell and he'd meet them halfway.

He looked at his watch and sprinted to the gangway leading to the tophouse. He struggled with the liferaft, overjoyed to see the raft carried no registration or boat name. With a line doubled around a block, he lowered the raft and its ten horsepower outboard engine slowly to the deck. After watching the sun sink somewhere over the Everglades--the reflection dappling the water like pieces of pirate gold--Jeremiah launched the ten foot inflatable with a grunt and tied it off.

"Ensign Virden," he said aloud. "Stand by to abandon ship."

Jimmy tossed his torn peacoat into the raft and scattered water jugs into the craft. He grabbed the binoculars and a chart from the upper wheelhouse, located a small compass from a drawer in the galley, and slipped a spare flashlight into his pocket. Mindful of hunger, he pulled packages of food and fruit, boxes of crackers and candy, from cabinets in the galley. He sought a stuff bag for the food and, not finding any in the galley, he wandered into Lester's stateroom. A nylon gym bag lay beside the bed and Jeremiah hoisted it, surprised at the weight. Unzipping it, he upturned and disgorged the contents on the bed. The look of surprise—packets of crisp hundred dollar bills cascading from the upturned bag— left him motionless for a minute beside the bed.

Almost reverently he flipped through a single packet, attempting to estimate the total amount of currency by multiplication.

Jeremiah, never good at math, mused at the complexity of the sum and what, if anything, he should do with the money. For almost a minute he stared at the mound of hundred dollar bills, making mental calculations; debating whether to keep all the money—a couple million maybe--stash it in the raft and motor away?

The beauty of a successful black operation was to make things look exactly opposite of what really happened. Kill the president by committee; make it seem like a random act by a lone gunman. Jeremiah now heaped armfuls of money and carried the packets up to the bridge where he torn open the paper bands and scattered them all over the enclosed cabin. When The Covenant blew up like a volcano, the surrounding sea would be speckled with thousands of floating hundred dollar bills. The first Coast Guard helicopter on the scene would report an oil slick and a flotilla of money, apparently from a drug deal gone bad. News copters and a fleet of pleasure boats would rush to the scene and the feeding frenzy of conjecture would only assist in his getaway.

Jimmy chuckled to himself. Those US Army soldiers in Iraq who stumbled on that 900 million dollars after the conquest of Baghdad, and tried to hide it all, should have immediately dumped all but a few million into the Tigris and buried the rest in the garden of that villa. Four individual stashes with GPS co-ordinates. The Aladdin's carpet of currency slowly floating down the river would have inspired mass confusion and outright lunacy. Had they told their superior officers they assumed the money was counterfeit—and the simple act of tossing the stuff in the river was evidence enough--they would have been home free. A million each, tax free.

Jimmy gathered a dozen packets and returned them to the nylon bag. Then he tossed the foodstuffs on top and zipped the bag closed.

Just before entering the raft, he remembered a spare, five gallon plastic jug of gasoline he intended to bring, retrieved the jug and stowed it and the bag in the bow of the raft. Now he was almost ready.

Jeremiah dashed below and checked the timer, reset it for thirty minutes, and then started the outboard on the raft. He took one last look around from the stern of the drifting cruiser, rescued his tackle box and sea boots in addition to an expensive fishing pole belonging to Tony Lester. Sad to destroy such a fine boat but there wasn't much he could do. Just as he stepped aboard the raft he remembered the EPIRB. High atop the mast, the electronic position indicating radio beacon device--water activated when a vessel sank--would immediately send out a pulse to the Coast Guard. In thirty minutes a rescue copter would be circling the wreck site.

Climbing the mast, Jeremiah opened the container and removed the EPIRB. After the boat sank, with the device safely silent and stowed in the raft, only an oil slick and a paper trail of dead presidents afloat on the Gulf Stream would indicate the last position of the assassin's palatial yacht. Maybe in a week or two, investigators would trace the missing boat to the exclusive marina. By then, Jimmy Jeremiah would be long gone.

From five miles away, the explosion resembled a blowout at an offshore oil platform. A thousand gallons of diesel fuel ignited in an enormous fireball, the sound reaching his ears seconds after the sight of the flame. The column rose against the twilight violet of the sky, terrible and beautiful all at once, as destruction usually is.

Jeremiah motored beyond Key Largo, a mile off shore, cocooned in the warmth of his peacoat. He continued in the fading light, the outboard propelling the light watercraft over calm seas at a speed he estimated as fifteen knots. The night was clear and the seas glossy.

He had everything he needed now; he was self sufficient. Even a new plan had formulated in his mind--audacious, flawed perhaps--but ingenious if he could carry it through.

The money lay at his feet, stuffed below the food in the nylon bag. Of course it wasn't enough, but if he had been greedier he might not have left any money behind. If he had any regrets at all—aside from destroying The Covenant—it was that he wouldn't be able to see the dumbfounded expressions on the faces of the first people on the scene. As they stared hungrily at all that money floating free with the current.

Chapter 28

Daniel Pilgrim returned to the Sun Satellite and slumped before his computer. Should he compose a final column he wondered, perhaps a thoughtful essay or colorful rant that would be remembered long after he was dead and gone? Just as he had chosen a subject, Bobby Smith sauntered into his space as the reporter's fingers hovered above the keyboard.

"Dan, I want you to meet someone interesting. David Mooney, this here is Daniel Pilgrim, the reporter I've been telling you about."

The old fellow collapsed with a wheeze and waved a hand. Mooney daubed his forehead with a handkerchief he extracted from a pocket with considerable effort. Pilgrim waited while the overweight elderly man caught his breath, but Smith continued.

"Mr. Mooney was Naval Intelligence. He says Oswald was ONI when he went to Russia."

"That's right," Mooney said. "How else could a common marine get out of his enlistment so easily and then defect to a Communist country? Not only that, he got back into the USA easier than you or I can drive through Miami traffic during rush hour traffic."

"Did you know Lee Harvey Oswald?" Pilgrim asked.

"I knew of him. I never saw a file on him—they were all destroyed I'm sure—but I heard talk when I was stationed at Norfolk in '64. Seems the Navy once had a program that sent false defectors—actual Navymen—into Russia to gather information or spread disinformation. Oswald wasn't just some slacker—is that the word they use today?"

Bobby nodded and then addressed Pilgrim in a half whisper, "I was thinking that maybe if you wrote how Kennedy and Oswald both served in Navy Intelligence you could entitle one of your historical columns, 'Secret Navy Spy Kills Navy Hero In Crime Of The Century'."

Mooney continued. "Then a month ago I'm in the local VFW club, swapping war stories, and an old marine who had been stationed with Oswald at El Toro—that's in California—he says to me he knew Oswald was crypto—that's a spy term—because he was constantly being briefed just before he defected to Russia. He also tells me when Oswald was in jail, the day before he died, he tried to call someone in ONI who lived in North Carolina."

Pilgrim began taking notes. "Interesting story if true," he said.

"I didn't think anything of it back then. In 1964 we trusted our government and so if the government said Oswald acted alone, he must have acted alone. Then I got to thinking, with all the lies the government is telling me nowadays, why wouldn't they have lied back then? I'm sixty years of age and the daily lies from Washington DC seem to get worse. Or maybe I'm just getting old."

"I don't think you're imagining anything, Mr. Mooney,"

Pilgrim leaned forward with pencil poised. "May we quote you, sir? Can I use your real name?"

"Sure, quote me all you want; what can anyone do to me now? I'm just surprised anyone your age cares anymore what happened forty years ago?"

"It ain't only people our age," Bobby replied. "Not even the fault of most news reporters; we don't make policy. The entire corporate-owned and controlled media don't give a damn about Dallas. Shit, they don't even care what's happening now."

"You mean they suppress the truth?"

Pilgrim shook his head. "Not suppress, so much as ignore the truth. Let's just say the media likes to dance around with the truth without making the commitment."

Mooney laughed, a raspy crackle ending with a cough. "Sort of like the girls we met in the USO."

"Would you like a glass of water, Mr. Mooney?" Pilgrim offered.

Mooney nodded and rose with an assist from the photographer.

"Actually I'd like to use your restroom," he said. After he left, the pair of newsmen continued.

"Too bad everything he said was hearsay," Pilgrim observed.

"I'd use some of his quotes, if I was writing the story."

"I'm almost tempted to write about the FTAP assassins in Dallas or the Tony Lester confession but Gonzales would fire me for sure."

Bobby shook his head with restrained glee. "You know Gonzales goes on vacation for two weeks starting tomorrow, don't you? That's right; he left Miller in charge as editor--Metro, Opinion, the whole works--for two entire weeks."

"Felipe never said a word to me."

"Why should he? So, what say we take Jack Miller out for a few drinks tonight and soften him up? I see not one but two major features—Friday and Sunday—on the truth behind the Kennedy assassination, with additional photographs and captions by the newspaper's film expert, Bobby Smith, who breaks down and explains the entire sequence of events of that fateful day using seldom seen photographs and text by Pulitzer nominated reporter, Dan Pilgrim. What do you say about that?"

Pilgrim looked thoughtful. "I've already written a few thousand words; I could expand that to five or ten thousand. I could also profile all the major suspects—Dulles, Nixon, Hoover, Hunt, Murchison, General Walker and Lyndon Johnson—and outline their considerable motives, and then touch on Oswald's connections to the CIA, FBI, and Navy Intelligence. As David Mooney just said: 'What can anyone do to me now?'"

"Fire you, but what-the-fuck, it's only a job."

The reporter laughed but thought of his probable death instead. Then an idea struck him.

"Maybe I shouldn't tell you this, Bobby, but there's a death threat against me. Not like the others in the past: vague, angry phone calls or letters. The word I got from Jimmy Jeremiah is I'm dead. If true then why not mention all the other suspicious deaths connected to the Kennedy murder and cover up—and include my own death threat?"

"Damn! You're not just making up that last part for drama?"

Pilgrim shook his head. "Wish I was."

"Well, once the death threat gets put into print and everyone reads it, that's sort of like a life insurance policy, which I would recommend you getting also."

While the revelation sunk in and Bobby sobered to the fact, the phone rang and Pilgrim picked it up, relieved to hear the familiar voice on the other end of the line.

"Dan, I got a strange message on my machine here at the gallery from my father."

"When did he call?"

"Eight this morning, but I didn't open the gallery until noon and only just now checked my phone messages."

"What did he say?"

"He said: Don't hang around the gallery but find you. Then he says to tell you to drive out to the area where you both camped—something about scaffolds—and pick him up tomorrow afternoon. Does that make any sense?"

Pilgrim grabbed a pen and pad and wrote the instructions while Joyce continued.

"Then he tells me not to hang around the gallery but close the place up for a week and go visit my Boston friend who lives in Boca Raton. He also says if for some reason he doesn't show up in a week to call the DEA and give them the name of a boat—something called The Covenant. I'm worried, Dan."

The reporter surprised himself by the calm tone he adopted. Perhaps imminent death gives a man an inner reserve of serenity.

"I know exactly where he wants to meet but I can't figure out how he intends to get there." Pilgrim pictured the yacht in his mind, unable to see any connection with the exclusive marina and an overgrown peninsula of land. "I'll meet you at your apartment; lock your doors."

The reporter clipped the holster onto his belt and then checked the clip of the Beretta, reassured by the metallic snap that locked the clip into place. Earlier he had placed the roses, undoubtedly wilted in the heat, and the concealed shotgun in the trunk of his rental car. All the way over to Joyce's he watched for suspicious vehicles in his rearview mirror. The possibility of being followed, the feeling of paranoia like symptoms of a tropical fever he once had, might remain with him forever, he thought bleakly, only dissipating with his death—which could occur that very day or the next. Which was worse: the fatal disease or the death that followed it? He shifted uncomfortably in his seat.

"I'm already packed," she said when he arrived. "The tone of my father's voice got me very frightened."

"Do you want me to drive you to Boca?"

She stood aside as he entered warily.

"Do you know what's going?" she said. "Has something happened to my father; do you think he may be wandering around lost somewhere?"

Pilgrim shrugged. "Did he sound lost or confused?"

"No, his voice sounded firm, almost resolute. Here, you can listen for yourself."

They played the phone recorder Joyce had brought from work, while standing in the kitchen.

"Tell Dan to meet me where we camped earlier; tell him the place where we found the scaffolds and shell cases. I'll meet him there tomorrow afternoon. And Joyce, honey, get out of the shop, go stay with that Boston girlfriend of yours in Boca for a week until I get back....and...I love you, always."

Joyce stared at the tape. "He has never said that to me before, 'I love you always.'"

"But like you said, he doesn't sound lost or confused," Pilgrim reassured. "Listen Joyce, I swung over to a marina where a friend of your father's keeps a boat and the guy at the gate said he went out overnight to do some fishing. I have no idea why he left that message but he's probably catching fish and getting a sunburn right about now."

Joyce's expression wavered between a weak smile and a grimace of embarrassment. She shook her head, hair falling over her brow, evidently unsure what to believe. Pilgrim embraced her and she enclosed him hoping to draw strength from his conviction.

"I'm glad he likes you," she said. "I'm glad my father relies on you."

Pilgrim pursed his lips. Likes me well enough to want to kill me, he thought.

"I'd feel safer at your place, Dan," she said softly. "We could put milk bottles by the door like Audrey Hepburn did in that movie where she was blind."

Pilgrim grinned. "Wait Until Dark; that was the name of the movie. Where would we find milk bottles? Anybody make those anymore?"

She pushed the gun on his waist aside, shaking her head. The reporter wondered if tonight might be his last night; wondered what was happening on the boat, whether Jimmy Jeremiah was luring him to the woods, purposely to kill him there and bury his body in a shallow grave. Should he bring Joyce as insurance, or better yet, bring Bobby with the shotgun? Was he riding into an ambush like the one that killed Kennedy?

They drove to his apartment and he parked two blocks away, wedging his car beneath a massive strangler fig overspreading the street. He had always found something sinister about the tree, the strangler fig that begins life as a delicate wisp, a dangling vine, and then envelops the host tree, strangles it and becomes a massive pillar in the tropical forest.

He removed the flower box from the trunk, the roses now altogether wilted, removed the shotgun in one swift movement, ignoring the gasp from Joyce, and tossed the cardboard box back into the trunk and slammed the lid. Walking to his apartment with the weapon under his arm, Pilgrim shook his head at the montage of imagery, snippets of *High Noon* and *The Road Warrior* flitting through his mind.

"Would someone mind telling me what-in-the-world is going on?"

Joyce said once inside his apartment.

"I wish I could," he said. The reporter laid the shotgun on a shelf and placed the pistol above the refrigerator. Should he tell her the whole story, he debated?

"If you can't tell me because you're protecting some source, I respect that, but must we remain locked up here in your apartment like embattled hostages?"

Pilgrim thought a moment and then made a phone call. A minute later he hung up and turned to Joyce.

"Okay, if bright lights and crowds are preferable, I agreed to meet Bobby and an editor from the paper at Isabelle's near Las Olas. Feel better?"

"Do we have to bring all your guns?"

"No, we can leave the shotgun home. Anyway it might upset the waitress if she sees it on the table."

"Oswald owned a Minox camera, had it among the property the Dallas police confiscated," Bobby Smith explained from a table in Isabelle's, surrounded by a few newsmen Pilgrim recognized. The animated face of the photographer swept over his audience and then lingered for a moment on Daniel Pilgrim and Joyce Virden.

"The FBI appropriated everything and then later--conveniently--couldn't account for the expensive spy camera and who knows where it is today." Bobby drew a breath before continuing. "How did Oswald manage to buy that expensive, imported camera, one not available to the public at the time, on a salary of $1.25 an hour while supporting two kids and a wife?"

Cromwell, an assistant editor of Lifestyle section, spoke. "Speaking of cameras, did you know memorabilia once owned by Lee Harvey Oswald is worth more today than stuff once belonging to JFK?"

Bobby vaulted forward and retrieved a chair for Joyce, without skipping a word.

"That Minox wasn't memorabilia but important evidence that the FBI covered up. Were you aware a double spy named Dusko Popov, possibly the inspiration for fictional James Bond, tried to warn J. Edgar Hoover about the Pearl Harbor invasion back in 1941, briefed him about microdot film--the product of Minox spy cameras--and Hoover ignored his warnings a month before the attack? Oswald, either an FBI informant or CIA operative, or both, was the ultimate enigma. He may have warned the FBI but Hoover preferred to cover things up instead of investigate. What was he hiding? Besides a closet full of women's clothes?"

The crowd laughed and chairs shuffled around the table. A familiar face turned to Pilgrim.

"I'm Jack Miller, editor while Felipe Gonzales is gone. He left me in charge and Smith invited me and the guys to happy hour to celebrate. "

"Doesn't he ever shut up?"

Miller smiled and shook his head. "He's quite a storyteller. Lot's of stuff I never knew about before, like that spy camera. Bobby seems to eat and sleep conspiracy theories these days. He told me about your Dallas trip. Bobby wants me to okay a retrospective look at the assassination for next weekend's edition of the paper."

The Guns of Dallas

The reporter affected an air of nonchalance. "Couple thousand words okay? Maybe an interview with an eyewitness or two?'

"Sure. We could fill two inner pages and offer you a column above the fold for Sunday. Smith said you had some shocking new insider stuff--some interview you made at the risk of your life?"

Joyce rolled her eyes. "Is that what all the guns are about?"

Miller looked shaken. "Guns?'

"Just a precaution against a death threat."

"You bring my Beretta?" Bobby injected. "That shirt covers your holster I noticed."

"Is it serious?" Miller asked.

"I take it serious," Pilgrim assured the editor, shifting the hem of his shirt and exposing the butt of the automatic. "I double-locked my doors but somebody already broke into my house twice. Just for talking to some old man who may have been a part of the Kennedy assassination. Forty years later the power of the conspiracy continues."

Miller said, "Put that in your piece; those exact words. Preface the lead with that phrase. You see, my father, who was killed in Vietnam in 1970, wrote my mother angry letters before he died. I reread them all recently, read them sequentially. He said if Kennedy hadn't gotten killed they wouldn't all be in the mess they were. Now my father's name is chiseled on the Black Wall. I was six years old at the time."

The photographer and reporter exchanged a look. A window of opportunity had opened; very few major newspapers would carry anything more than a sketch about the slain president next weekend on the fortieth anniversary of his death. They were accorded a rare opportunity seldom given to newsmen anymore: freedom of the press. In the coming years few editors would care about the assassination, fewer see the connection, how the repercussions of that single event still reverberated in a thousand different ways.

"You have to realize the hate that was emanating out of Washington DC at the time," the photographer continued. Like a preacher at a pulpit he had drawn the attention of those closest to their table. "Just like the hate today; it starts with government hate, which begets more hate. 'Two minutes of government hate' Orwell called it. When Clyde Tolson, number two man in the FBI, said at a conference in 1968, 'I hope someone shoots and kills the son of a bitch,' he was talking about Robert Kennedy. Six weeks later, after winning the California primary on the way to winning the presidency and defeating Hoover's buddy Richard Nixon, someone conveniently killed Kennedy."

"Conveniently killed by a lone gunman," a listener added.

"The official government theory, as always," Bobby nodded. "But why wasn't this fellow Clyde Tolson at least questioned for his remark? Wasn't that an act of treason for a so-called law enforcement, government official to sanction the murder of another government official, especially a presidential candidate who was also once his former superior? Shouldn't Tolson have been arrested?"

A bystander snickered. "Who would have arrested him? Senator Hale Boggs compared the FBI to the Gestapo in a speech on the Senate floor and less than a year later Boggs disappeared, supposedly in a plane crash--according to the FBI."

"Amen brother," Bobby sighed, "Who is gonna watch the watchdogs when they get rabid with power? You do know--don't you—that the most powerful man in America, J. Edgar Hoover, was in Dallas, Texas the night before the assassination, at a party with Nixon and Johnson—the next two presidents in line?"

Gasps and guffaws of disbelief followed this remark, as the reporter knew it would. Pilgrim continued to listen half-heartedly as Bobby enthralled a handful of new converts with details of a conspiracy that occurred before most of them were born, colorful details about the assassination suppressed or distorted for so long that most of the facts had become relegated to mythology. Truth was stranger than fiction, the reporter knew, but Pilgrim scarcely heard the vivid accounting and the barrage of questions from the listeners. Instead he glanced aside and wondered what the future held. Joyce seemed to be thinking the exact same thing. Sadly, he might not have the opportunity to put down on paper all he had learned in the last several weeks. A man is given certain gifts; no guarantee he'll ever be able to use them. The more he thought of his predicament, the more he determined to bring Joyce along. Not to endanger her or protect himself, but to force Jimmy to confront this final bit of truth he had been avoiding.

"When you go tomorrow to pick up my father," Joyce said firmly, "I'm going along with you."

Pilgrim was just about to agree when someone pointed to the television above the bar. A commotion followed, all eyes diverted to the footage being beamed live from a rescue scene. The bartender turned the sound up and even Bobby Smith fell silent.

"...Reports indicate the boat may have exploded. The Coast Guard says they have found bits of wreckage floating on the water burnt beyond recognition but no survivors and no bodies. No indication of the name of the boat at this time but a large quantity of money has also been reportedly recovered; reportedly large denomination bills—but this is just a rumor--drifting with the wreckage. The reports have not been substantiated—"

Customers along the bar whooped and cheered. Joyce caught her breath and Pilgrim instantly thought of The Covenant, recalling the detonator and the plastic explosive Jimmy had shown him. The news commentator continued to string sentences together while one man at the bar hurried away with a cell phone pressed to his ear.

"—and authorities say drugs may be involved. The channel eleven news copter is now on the scene and as you can see by the powerful lights on the surface of the water little remains of the boat--if indeed it was a boat. Witnesses say they saw a powerful flash; one fisherman several miles away said he saw a flash about thirty minutes after sundown. Another fisherman said he heard a boom and thought it must have been a jet plane. Do we have anything, Mitch, from the scene of the missing boat? Do we know if it was a boat? Could it have been an airplane? Has terrorism been ruled out?"

The sudden buzz of whispers, at the mention of the word "terrorism," hushed the rowdy crowd closest to the TV. The reporters exchanged a knowing glance and almost the entire group finished their drinks with a swallow. A few tossed bills upon the table and scurried away, hastening back to their offices at the newspaper building, and

Bobby Smith rose and reached for his wallet.

"Nothing like money and terrorism to mobilize the troops," he said with a gleam. "And most of the time the two are closely connected."

Chapter 29

Pilgrim awoke early, rose and slipped out of bed without making a sound. He gathered his clothes, turned once to appraise the topography of the female form beneath the sheet, and realized he loved her, the daughter of the assassin. Love, the exquisite torturer, which chooses us as much as we choose it, presented him now with a quandary.

He tried not to think of his problem, side-stepping the subject in his mind as men normally do. Instead he retrieved the Beretta on the table beside the bed. At the door he heaved a sigh and removed the empty soda cans stacked precariously in a pyramid, a pathetic attempt to lend a sense of security to the bedroom. He realized all a determined assassin need do was force his way in and shoot them both with silenced weapons. All over the world good men had died in just such circumstances and their deaths ruled "suicides".

The first light of a new day shone on a world of possibility, however dim. He gazed at the decorations of optimism, the posters and scenes of American greatness, with a skeptical eye. What did the veneer of greatness matter when a desiccated carcass rotted below the surface?

Before they left the restaurant last night, Pilgrim heard a newscaster remark the CIA had helped smuggle an estimated twenty-two tons of cocaine into Florida almost a decade ago despite the Drug Enforcement Agency's attempt to stop them. A DEA agent interviewed on television thought the sunken boat—name still unknown—had been smuggling drugs due to the enormous amount of money drifting on the surface. So much money that a flotilla of scavengers made investigation impossible.

The depth and breadth of corruption seemed to surprise no one at the restaurant watching the television; not a single person seemed shocked or disgusted. Jimmy Jeremiah hinted at the corruption months ago, Pilgrim recalled, when he made the allusion to penguins standing on an iceberg, unable to see beneath the surface of things where ninety percent of the deep, dark mystery lay. We stand on the back of an enormously powerful enigma, he said, threatening to topple us without warning. Iceberg was Jeremiah's metaphor; Pilgrim saw things differently. A year ago a spate of local corruption had seemed earth-shaking to the reporter; now the entire planet seemed bound by invisible filaments of evil, numbering in the millions, of such tensile strength that God himself might not sever them all.

After Joyce awoke they drank coffee in the sunny corner of his apartment facing the ocean and his mood lightened. A breeze crept in and lingered a moment from a window overlooking a file of trees. The medley of notes from a mockingbird reminded him that nature ordered an arrangement separate from men, no less ruthless and territorial, but melodic, almost poetic or inspirational, without the rapacious greed or deceit posing as virtue peculiar to men. Pilgrim recalled what Mark Twain had observed, Man was the only animal that blushed, or needed to--and the reporter chuckled.

"What's so funny?" Joyce asked. "Share it with me."

"What if you found out your father was a great hero, but his heroism might embarrass him?"

"I'd prefer not to know then."

"What if you found out he was an idealistic inventor but his discoveries now endangered millions?"

"Like Einstein?"

"Yes. Or what if you found out he was a great villain, but had won a promotion and medal for bravery?"

Joyce laughed. "You and your 'what ifs.' There's nothing I need to know about my father now except his whereabouts. But tell me something—anything--about yourself?"

Pilgrim placed the coffee cups in the sink, considering the question in silence. He gathered a few items—water, fruit, candy bars—and tossed them into a bag before fingering his keys.

"I'm not avoiding your question," he said. "But my biography is filled with boring details. I'm trying to invent something that sounds plausible but sheds a positive light on me."

"You're being modest."

He thought a bit as they walked to the car, sweeping his eyes around for anything suspicious. A jacket he carried concealed the shotgun and he laid the bundle behind his seat. Before he entered the car he knelt before the hood and examined a hair he affixed there, undisturbed still, and then knelt and examined each wheel well in turn. Satisfied, he turned the ignition key.

"Every year for the past four, I've written stories that have pissed people off, resulting in verbal or written threats. Death threats, occasionally, have been the response to some of those stories but, far more frequently, gratitude from readers. I should tell you right now I'm not a hero, not a man of action, not fearless, but all I've ever had in my arsenal is words for weapons. And although I feel exposed at times--like now—I feel powerful because corrupt people fear me. I threaten them worse than if I held a gun."

Joyce looked amused--and more than a little impressed.

Pilgrim noticed the effect. "But I have to confess, I am afraid of snakes but not spiders, sharks but not alligators, and burly men who might want to punch me in the nose."

She laughed and they drove south through the diminished traffic until he turned onto the I-95 freeway for the Keys.

Jimmy Jeremiah stretched in the hammock he had strung between two trees and folded the book he had been reading across his thigh. The peaceful forest, site of the former para-military training base, murmured with only the wind and infrequent birdsong. The previous midnight he had rafted to the peninsula and beached the Zodiac, securing the craft to mangroves. There he slept until the sun pinpricked his eyeballs with slivers of light and he arose, surprisingly refreshed and limber.

He thought of Ramon and Tony without feeling the slightest remorse. Indeed the only regret he felt was for the boat, an abiding shame for destroying a perfectly elegant yacht. Before he turned to his book again, Jimmy wondered what, if anything, had been found floating at the wreck site. Had The Covenant sunk without belching anything incriminating to the surface? A monogrammed towel? coffee cup? Life ring? Forty years ago, in the Texas School Book Depository, Manny had ejected each spent shell—as all the teams had been briefed—and the spotter recovered the evidence. But they had purposely left the weapon behind on the sixth floor as ordered. Dallas police and sheriff's deputies found the rifle wedged between some boxes and heralded the discovery, as the planners knew they would. But the alleged "murder weapon" that officer Seymour Weitzman and Roger Craig found—the 7.65 Mauser—did not match the empty shell cases the authorities discovered by the window. Thus the weapon was switched for another and earlier accounts of finding a German rifle were denied by everyone, except the two, conscientious Dallas police officers who initially found the Mauser. In every black operation, no matter how well planned, small things were always overlooked. While no one could tie him to that Kennedy crime in Dallas or to this one, Jimmy still wondered if he might have made some insignificant yet fatal error.

Otherwise the day passed pleasantly. A small plane droned overhead but Jimmy had pulled the raft into the mangroves, concealing it completely. The sea was as mute and inscrutable as a forgotten grave and the forest sheltered him like a devoted ally. He sipped the spring water he brought from the boat and nibbled crackers stacked like salted coins on his chest and read of the demise of the American Republic, a demise he had helped hasten along. In a world of shadows, life was best enjoyed in the shade, on the sidelines. He hadn't much life left but he pledged not to waste one moment more in service of the state. The pistol and silencer and fully loaded clip lay nearby; he had no intention of going gently into the good night.

Pilgrim slowed and turned onto the rutted lane leading west into the scrub forest. He halted at a pool partially filled with water and edged the car around, hoping the road ahead was no worse. Joyce seemed to be enjoying the ride, gazing at the tannin-laced pools, grassy swampland and islands of vegetation. Black buzzards floated on warm thermals and cumulo-nimbus clouds opened like gargantuan orchids. Pilgrim glanced at his watch--just past three o'clock—and realized he was early by the old man's instructions.

"Was it this muddy when you two drove back here before?" Joyce said. Every pool he splashed through threatened to stall the car. The reporter could feel the wheels spin before catching, the car swerving forward to dry ground at the last moment.

"It hadn't rained for awhile."

"How much farther?" she asked.

"Maybe five or six miles. Maybe less."

Pilgrim shifted into second and felt the grasp of branches sliding across the top of the car. He noticed no one had passed this way since the last rain. How long ago was that he wondered? They passed the roadside trash dump and he saw Joyce scrunch her nose. A deer dashed from the brush, scampered across the lane and disappeared after two strides into the opposite thicket.

"Watch for turtles," she said half seriously.

"I'm not afraid of them, but I am afraid of that turtle pond up ahead."

He slowed to a stop at the edge of the water and put the car in neutral before stepping out. The other side of the pool appeared twenty yards away and the muddy water might have been inches or feet for what little he could see. He removed his shoes and waded to the middle and the water approached his knees. Looking back from where they had come he saw a wide, tree-shaded spot along the road. He backed the car there and opened the trunk before turning the ignition.

"Now what?" she said.

"I guess I'll walk to where we camped, only a few miles more, I'd say four at the most."

She thought a moment, clearly concerned but trying not to show it. "Yes, otherwise how would my father know we're here?"

"I could yell for him but I think my voice only carries so far. Don't worry; I can't get lost if I follow the road."

They embraced at the car hastily and he started off, armed with the shotgun. The pistol he left with Joyce and showed her how to snap the safety off, while warning her to keep the Beretta holstered otherwise. He carried a jacket and two pints of water. At the pool he removed his shoes, looked back once and waved before hastening on.

For almost two miles he walked, inwardly debating every foot of that distance why he needed to carry the shotgun. To kill Jimmy Jeremiah or not to kill him, that was the gist of his inner debate. Could he do it? Would he do it, if necessary? At last, having grown weary--neither having proved the folly or wisdom of bringing the weapon—he fastened on the idea that he might need the shotgun for a signaling device if he got lost.

He surprised himself by recognizing, once he passed it, the faint corridor that had been a road forty plus years ago. Like an Indian scout he bent at the waist and noticed the faint tread marks of his tires, not entirely effaced by the rain, in the compressed limestone soil. He clicked the safety of the shotgun and started forward, eyes alert for movement.

When he had gone some distance, weapon sweeping across the radius of overgrown road, a voice from the trees startled him.

"You hunting rabbits with that cannon, or plan on shooting me?"

Pilgrim turned and noticed the recumbent form of the old man relaxing in the hammock. Jimmy Jeremiah held a paperback propped on his chest and his tone carried a slight annoyance. Pilgrim studied the title of the book, *Farewell America*, and noticed the pistol inches from his right hand. Quickly Pilgrim lowered the twelve gauge shotgun.

"What's the news from the outside world?"

Like Stanley encountering Livingston for the first time, Pilgrim approached with a gleam in his eye.

"A boat blew up; I was afraid you were dead. Joyce was worried—I left her at the car about three miles back—and the Coast Guard is searching for bodies amongst hundreds of people looking for money on the water. No one's saying how much money has been recovered, for fear of confiscation I guess, but the estimate is in the tens of thousands, maybe even millions of dollars. You have anything to do with that?"

"Might have. Any word about the name of that boat?"

"Nope. Nor any bodies recovered."

"That's too bad." Jeremiah turned another page. "Could have been The Covenant, for all we know."

"I guess we'll have to wait for the Coast Guard to tell us."

"Might be a long wait."

Pilgrim shifted. "Joyce is back at the car. We couldn't get the car through."

"You tell her anything about me?"

"No—I never found the right words."

"I do appreciate that, Dan, don't think I don't"

"Thanks. Nice out here, miles from nowhere." Pilgrim sat down in the shade and uncapped a pint of water. "Have you just been reading or just relaxing, doing a little exploring?"

"Counting my blessings, among other things?"

"What's in the bag?"

"Blessings that I counted," said the old man. "Also curses, if a person ain't too careful."

Pilgrim didn't ask, although he was curious about the contract on his head, but he didn't ask about that either. The old man seemed to be in a reflective mood, and the reporter chose not to spoil it. Finally Jeremiah spoke again.

"I also brought me a book, I always intended to read. Written by a team of French intelligence boys right after we popped the president. They pieced it all together pretty exactly. Lucky for us the book was banned here in the States for thirty years."

Pilgrim drained the rest of the pint, content to listen.

"The power and influence of the conspiracy surprises even me, and I'm one of the conspirators." Jimmy laughed softly before continuing.

"I no longer believe in the institutions of America."

"None of them?"

Jimmy smiled. "Well, maybe the Red Cross."

The reporter rubbed his jaw. He hadn't bothered to shave, half convinced he might be caught in a shoot out and killed anyway. For that reason he felt immeasurably happy, alive, even if the country was going to hell at the speed of a few short generations.

"As God is my witness, I'm sorry I ever served those fuckers now entrenched in power," Jimmy continued. "I guess after reading the viewpoint of these guys—the French CIA—the murder and cover up wasn't a patriotic act, not that I ever thought it was, but a goddamn coup!"

"Welcome back to humanity, I guess."

"You hungry?" Jimmy swung his legs down. "That's good food there. Try those crackers; Tony Lester wouldn't want them to go to waste."

The reporter caught the faintest hint of a smile from the weathered face. Pilgrim helped the old man down and together they gathered the gear and walked out.

Chapter 30

Alive again, each day a reprieve now, Pilgrim arrived early at work. Immediately he began writing the retrospective account of the Kennedy assassination, surrounded by a feeling of calm, however false, and a sense of mission. Jeremiah assured him during the walk back to the car the danger hadn't passed but had only transformed. He cautioned the reporter not to speak to anyone about what he knew, while shocking him with the full details of the disappearance of The Covenant. The deaths of Tony Lester and Ramon would not solve their problem permanently, Jeremiah said; too many intelligent men with a vested interest would unravel the mystery in time. Then he showed Pilgrim the money—a fraction of what was aboard the boat—nearly $120,000 in hundred dollar bills at the bottom of the gym bag he carried.

"Once again, don't mention a word to anyone," Jeremiah said, "And I'll call you in a few days."

The words came quickly now, running into paragraphs and then into quiet accusations in the form of columns. Beneath the title, *Nightmare On Elm, Dark Day In Dealey*, the reporter fashioned an argument for conspiracy while allowing the reader to see each side. Undisturbed for many hours, this is what Pilgrim wrote.

No matter what you might think of the Kennedy Assassination, Whether you believe one man, Lee Harvey

Oswald acted alone or that a conspiracy killed the president, the fact remains that a shift in America's perception of itself occurred soon after November 22, 1963. A subtle mistrust of the government began to fester, compounded eventually by dissent over the war in Vietnam, disgust over Watergate and the plethora of abuses that followed. The repercussions of that grim day in Dallas reverberate even today; the imperial designs, deceptions and cover ups culminating in a thinly disguised resource war in the Persian Gulf, trumpeted as liberation, mimicking the deceptions leading to the Vietnam War. The repercussions ricochet ceaselessly around the world, around America, rebounding from the rifle shots first heard in Dealey Plaza forty years ago.

A thousand days after his controversial election to president, an election assisted by rumored payoffs to Chicago gangsters, charismatic John Fitzgerald Kennedy and his photogenic wife, Jackie, arrived in Dallas, part of a brisk, four city swing that would also take them to Houston, Ft. Worth and San Antonio. A string of limousines awaited the presidential entourage at Love Field for a motorcade through the streets of the city. With the protective bubble top removed from Kennedy's Lincoln, with the removal of secret servicemen from the running board of his car, the motorcade would be almost a leisurely photo opportunity for the president and his wife before he addressed a group at the Trade Mart. Texas governor John Connelly and his wife, Nellie, would ride with the Kennedys that day, while Vice President Lyndon Johnson followed two cars behind. Altogether they would ride off at high noon, not only into history but into a puzzle missing several pieces, a mystery that increases rather than diminishes with time.

The Texas School Book Depository, seven stories tall, loomed a block from the original parade route along Main, but sometime at the last moment, according to conspiracy theorists, the parade route was changed. Ostensibly, the detour down Houston and then Elm Street was coordinated by two Secret Service agents, Winston Lawson and Forrest Sorrels, early in November, but the Texas trip was planned months earlier. Although the motorcade map on the front page of the Dallas Morning News didn't show the turn onto Houston or Elm, a brief description inside the paper described it.

Perhaps more ominous than the series of tight turns was the headline of the DMN the day Kennedy arrived: "Storm of Political Controversy Swirls Around Kennedy" and "Nixon Predicts JFK May Drop Johnson." Earlier, on November 9, 1963, Nixon had remarked that Kennedy's "extravagant campaign promises" were largely responsible for the racial crises simmering throughout urban America. The divisiveness of race hatred and federally mandated integration was a powder keg for the Democrats, and potentially pivotal issue in the elections. Nixon, also in Dallas that weekend, boasted to reporters that he hadn't needed Secret Service protection or a bullet-proof bubble when he traveled, a boast that may have induced Kennedy to dispense with his security. Even more ominous, a full page in the Dallas Morning News carried a column bordered in funereal black, paid for by the John Birch Society, sarcastically welcoming the President and criticizing his policies toward Cuba in no uncertain terms.

At 12:28 PM the motorcade approached Houston Street and Elm—a cul-de-sac for a killing if ever one existed---with Lyndon Johnson visibly nervous two cars behind the President's Lincoln, according to witnesses. Some researchers claim the motorcade route was actually implemented by Dallas mayor, Earle Cabell, brother of general Charles Cabell, recently deposed Deputy Director of the CIA, who, like his boss, Allen Dulles and fellow CIA heavyweight, Dick Bissell, had been acrimoniously fired only months before the assassination by the very man riding in the open limousine.

Kennedy's three ton Lincoln motored down Main, slowed at Houston and turned north, drove another block and slowed to a crawl at Elm. The severe angle at Dealey Plaza from Houston to Elm required the ponderous car to slow even further and swing around the 120 degree turn at six miles per hour. The vehicle had hardly accelerated past the Texas School Book Depository when a sound—backfire? burst tire? firecracker?—resounded, scattering pigeons from the rooftops. Kennedy looked radiant, tousled hair swirling in the gentle breeze, sunlight capturing the easy smile, and people in the crowd waved or snapped pictures.

Jean Hill, closest eyewitness to the president and co-author of "The Last Dissenting Witness," claims she heard four to six shots and saw a man run from the TSBD and a shooter flee from the picket fence above the Grassy Knoll. Dallas policeman, J.B. Marshall, astride a motorcycle at the right rear of the President's car, said, "When that head shot hit Kennedy, I was sure it was coming from the right front because of the direction the blood flew. It looked to me like at least two people were firing from a forward position, and I thought there might be as many as six in all." Abe Zapruder, clothing manufacturer with an office in the nearby Dal-Tex building, aimed his Bell & Howell 8mm movie camera from atop a pedestal near the Grassy Knoll and filmed the motorcade as it crawled past Jean Hill. Although Abe suffered from severe vertigo, his secretary steadied him while he recorded, without pause or hesitation, the 19 seconds that changed America.

Curiously, the Zapruder film began a journey of its own that day. After being duplicated into three copies that evening, however, the Zapruder tape would not be publicly shown on television for a dozen more years. Except for a brief airing in New Orleans at the famous conspiracy trial of Clay Shaw—basis for the movie *JFK*--brought by District Attorney Jim Garrison, the public would rely only on memory and the statements of witnesses for details of the JFK assassination. The film and all rights were purchased by Henry Luce of Life magazine for a reported $200,000 in 1963. Returned to the Zapruder family years later—for the token sum of one dollar—the film is estimated to have generated almost $10 million in income for those privileged to own it.

Following the first shot, which all sides seem to agree somehow missed the open limousine and the President altogether, Oswald—or a confederate--wounded Kennedy with his next bullet. According to proponents of the Warren Report, Oswald chambered a second shot from the concealment of the sniper's lair on the sixth floor and wounded both Kennedy and Connelly with the pristine bullet—or so called "magic bullet" to detractors—which was found on a stretcher in nearly pristine shape at Parkland Hospital, where the two wounded men were taken.

The third shot (or fourth or fifth?), the traumatic and fatal head shot to Kennedy--captured vividly on the Zapruder tape--occurred as the limousine slowed to a crawl. Many witnesses testified the Lincoln stopped altogether, as the Secret Service driver turned twice to look at the stricken President, a serious breach of security in a city surrounded by tall buildings, open windows and thinly veiled threats. This last shot, the kill shot, which either rocketed JFK's head back according to those who believe a shot or shots originated from the Grassy Knoll, or thrust him forward and then wrenched him back, according to a new theory by Nobel prize scientist Louis Alvarez, which corroborated the Warren Commission. The only bullet retrieved—the pristine or "magic bullet"—matched the caliber of the rifle reportedly found on the sixth floor of the TSBD.

Called the "humanitarian rifle" by the Italian soldiers issued it, because it never intentionally hurt anyone, the Mannlicher-Carcano had a poor reputation for combat. The Mannlicher-Carcano cost Oswald $12 and the 4x scope another $7. A former member of the House Select Committee on Assassinations' firearm panel and an expert marksman, Monty Lutz, declared during a mock Oswald trial in 1986 that no one had ever duplicated Oswald's alleged shooting expertise. Likewise in a test held earlier, in 1967 by CBS, closely duplicating the Warren Commission version of Oswald marksmanship, not one of the eleven marksmen scored two out of three hits on their first attempts. Seven of these top riflemen failed on all of their attempts. Oswald, hardly the steadiest individual or most proficient marksman, according to all who knew him, had only one attempt with his war rickety surplus rifle and his first shot inexplicably missed!

Allegedly, Oswald had attempted an earlier assassination in Dallas with this same rifle. General Edwin Walker, a decorated war hero and outspoken critic of Kennedy, a fiery orator and member of the radical John Birch Society and a segregationist who was arrested for blocking federally mandated integration in Mississippi, had apparently angered Oswald, according to author Gerald Posner in *Case Closed*. In April 1963, Lee Harvey Oswald reportedly took a shot at the general with his Italian war-surplus rifle. On that April evening, Oswald aimed across Walker's lawn at the general, seated inside his home, but the bullet shattered a window and missed him instead. Which begs the question: If Oswald couldn't hit a stationary target from less than a hundred feet of level ground, how could he have hit a moving target—Kennedy—from over twice that distance, while shooting from fix floors above? Even more puzzling:

Why had Oswald tried to assassinate a prominent Right wing figure—Walker—a man with a violent grudge against Kennedy and then, six months later assassinate Kennedy, who was vilified by all factions of the Right?

Instead of Oswald, could powerful members of these diverse and loosely connected factions—who most benefited by Kennedy's death--have coalesced into a unified entity with one secret goal in mind: To get rid of Kennedy? Could members of the ultra rich Right, oilmen and entrepreneurs, together with hostile elements of the CIA and harassed Mafia dons (who were then aligned in an effort to rid Cuba of Castro), allied themselves with virulent racists who blamed Kennedy for forced integration and unrest, together with violent, anti-Communist Cubans have toppled Kennedy in a bloody coup using professional hitmen and disguised the killing as the work of an angry ideologue? Using fear and the threat of retribution, plus a compliant media and Congress, the answer is yes.

Former CIA Colonel Fletcher Prouty said, "It is possible now to reconstruct the scenario of that day and, with new information, to show why the murder of JFK may properly be called the 'Crime of the Century.' If we the people of the United States do not demand its resolution...it will doom a third century of democratic government in this country." Yet if a convincing story with the official, government stamp of approval, a story of an embittered, lone assassin and defector—Lee Harvey Oswald—satisfied the media and most of the public in 1963, then the dissent should have died. Right?

Lyndon Johnson took office and handpicked a panel of seven men, including former CIA head Allen Dulles and Hoover's personal FBI informant on the panel, Gerald Ford, to sweep the heresy under the rug and bury it under enormous paperwork. The result satisfied those in power that Osald acted alone. Anyone who disagreed with the

official version and tried to shed some light on the subject-
--like Jean Hill, Mark Lane, Jim Garrison or former CIA
insider, Fletcher Prouty—would be branded by the media as
ambitious crackpots espousing wacko conspiracy theories.

But did Oswald really act alone? Forty years later fewer
than 20% of Americans think so. "Almost anyone who
has taken the time to do any reading and thinking about
the crime knows by now that John Kennedy was killed
not by a lone assassin," says CIA insider Prouty. "This is
a game for the biggest stake of all—absolute control of
the government of the United States of America; and with
control of this government, control of the world. And
yet the real crime underlying all of this has not even been
identified, stated and charged. The real criminals still walk
the streets, run their corporations, control their banks,
and pull strings throughout their political and financial
machines." Conspiracy Anyone?

Daniel Pilgrim finished typing and then added a postscript at
the bottom of the lead: Tomorrow in the Sun Satellite: Interview
With The Kennedy Assassins: An Exclusive Report and the
Shocking Truth Behind the Conspiracy.

Pilgrim knew that thousands of copies of the newspaper would
already be printed and on the street—the ponderous early weekend
edition—by the time Friday's edition went on sale, and no way in
hell the shadowy powers could keep the truth from spreading like a
virulent plague after that. By then the shit would really hit the fan,
as Jimmy Jeremiah had already advised him.

Chapter 31

"Tell me how this sounds," Bobby Smith said before reading from the first column he had ever written. "I titled it: Gulf Stream Gold Rush Leaves Boaters Flush."

Pilgrim stared at the photographs Smith had taken to accompany the story. One water level picture showed a hundred-dollar bill adrift while a boater with a net poised to retrieve it.

"How did you take this picture?"

Smith smiled proudly. "I was right there in the water, eye level. Sharks and all!"

Pilgrim arched an eyebrow. "You get any money?"

"That bill in the photograph you're looking at. Most of the money got scooped up early; early birds got the worm."

Pilgrim tried to sound interested. "Okay, Bobby, read me what you wrote."

Bobby began, his voice conveying the excitement he felt. "The currency drifted northwest into the rising sun. At daybreak of the first day, the fleet numbered well over fifty boats but by noon that number had easily doubled. In what might have been the ultimate money-laundering operation, untold millions of dollars--in newly minted hundred dollar bills--drifted toward England with the Gulf Stream, cleansed by the current. Dead men may tell no tales but for the ill-fated crew of sixty foot yacht called The Covenant—Anthony Lester, 67, Ramon Montez, 31, and Daniel Jeremiah, 65—the profitable pleasure cruise would prove to be their last."

"I like that phrase—'profitable pleasure cruise would prove to be their last.' Good use of alliteration. And Jimmy Jeremiah will be pleased to know you've officially killed him off."

Smith beamed. "You like the title or does it sound too tabloid?"

"The New Yorkers living here in South Florida may enjoy it—they're used to tabloid headlines. Don't change something you wrote even if they ask; that's my motto."

Gonzales passed and gave Pilgrim a look of elevated disdain. No, not exactly disdain but distance; he simple gazed upon him from a great distance, as if Pilgrim were already gone. Felipe wasn't very happy having to rush back hurriedly from his vacation, the reporter realized. Thus when Pilgrim arrived at work this morning, having received the curt phone message notifying him of his termination the night before, he began emptying his desk hurriedly, avoiding the sympathetic advances of his fellow newsmen. Now he gloried in the moment—fired!—and defiantly examined each item as if a fragment of the Holy Grail.

"No—perhaps I've advised you wrong just now, Bobby. Make the changes. Don't make waves. To get along, go along; what's good for the company is good for you. Take a bullet for the story—always the story—but just the basic facts; don't dig too deep and never ask the tough questions."

Bobby frowned. "Now you're talking out your ass 'cause your mouth got more sense. I know you better than that, Dan Pilgrim."

"You're right. Just my bitterness getting the better of me."

"I'm sorry to see you go, but a man's gotta pick and choose his fights selectively. For awhile there I let my passion get the better of my good sense. This conspiracy and that one; I can't fight every injustice and neither can you."

Pilgrim tossed some floppy disks into the trash after staring at the titles. "True, but I'm all fought out before I even got started and so are you. I don't blame Gonzales; he warned me earlier and now he's under fire too from the owner and publisher."

Bobby sighed. "Some things are too hot to handle, even forty years later. Like nuclear waste."

"Yeah," Pilgrim replied. "Like Kennedy."

"So tell me again what you plan on doing?"

"I've saved some money and I've always wanted to freelance. Pitch story ideas to magazines and then go research them, historical stuff."

"I almost envy you," said Smith.

The reporter looked sheepish. "And I've always wanted to write a children's book. I feel there's one in me waiting to be written."

"Might as well get in touch with your inner child; we adults don't seem to have ourselves together."

Even at the last moment a man might change, whether for better or worse. Some men left jobs, some left homes, some even left spouses; Jimmy Jeremiah left boats and then he left countries.

"I traded for her even up!" he shouted from the deck of the sailboat. "How do you like the name?"

The sailboat known as The New Life rode calmly on the water like a self-assured duck. While still secured to the wharf, she appeared ready to bolt and fly away. Aware of the admiration Jimmy raised the mainsail and an enormous red cross appeared boldly against the white canvas.

"What happened to The Big Lie?" Pilgrim asked.

"Come aboard, both of you, and I'll tell you all about it," the old man replied, his voice hinting at intrigue and adventure.

Joyce leapt aboard and Pilgrim followed. The cabin of the 48 foot sloop widened once inside and the headroom surprised the reporter. Almost with envy he appraised the sailboat, some part of him inwardly desiring to sail away from everything the shore represented.

"Take a seat, swabbies, and I'll spin you a yarn."

Joyce slid into the banquette, her admiring gaze everywhere. This was the father she remembered from her early youth, the confident, clever and good-natured man who had died or become dormant almost two decades ago.

"I didn't know you sailed," Pilgrim remarked once seated. Several charts lay open on the table but the reporter hardly recognized the coastal features, many of them Spanish.

"Hell, I'm an old Navy man! I can read a compass, set a course, shoot the sun or plot a course by the stars—well, maybe not that—and feel for shoals with my eyeballs, chart and fathometer."

"What happened to your cabin cruiser?" Joyce said. "You loved that boat."

The old grin of the leprechaun appeared, an expression Pilgrim had seen once or twice before, most recently in the forest.

"I traded The Big Lie for something more environmentally friendly. Where I'm going there might not always be expensive fuel available."

"And where is that?" Pilgrim said. "The moon?"

"Might as well be; I'm heading for Cuba."

The old man looked pleased by the reaction to his words. He lifted a chart slightly, as an archivist handles rare or delicate parchment.

"I plan on going back to where it all began for me. You know they allow small boaters to land in Cuba now, right where Hemingway kept his boat."

"But what about your treatment, Dad?"

"I already thought of that. They have some of the best doctors in the Caribbean right there in Cuba," Sensing his daughter's concern, Jimmy softened. "I'll be fine, Joy, I really will. The VA said I was coming right along. From Cuba I plan on making regular stops all throughout the Gulf of Mexico—Honduras, Costa Rica, Panama."

"You think anyone's still looking for you?" Pilgrim remarked, aware that he had broached a sensitive issue, unsure if the old man had spoken with his daughter. One thing Pilgrim knew, he would never reveal what he discovered about a man named Jeremiah and his direct effect on history. The interview that got him fired from the newspaper identified the trio of hired guns who killed Kennedy forty years ago only by vague code words. Still the story had caused a firestorm and, although no other newspapers had reprinted either of his Kennedy columns, they apparently got him fired.

"Looking for me? That old fellow, Jeremiah, died but The Company might still be looking for him," Jimmy replied to the reporter.

"Who died?" Joyce wondered. "The former owner of this sailboat?"

"No, the former owner of the other boat died, the owner of The Big Lie. I was only speaking—what's the word you newsmen use, Dan?—I was only speaking metaphorically. Now I've been reborn as a saltwater sailor."

The pair of listeners laughed.

"What's with the red cross?" Pilgrim said. "You a pirate for a charity organization?"

"Nothing of the kind, but it might keep real pirates from boarding my ship. Joshua Slocum, when he circled the globe, had to deal with pirates and if I was poor I might be a pirate too."

"Looks very decorative," Joyce added.

"And since I've saved some money over time," Jimmy gave the reporter a knowing look, "I hope to purchase medical supplies in more prosperous ports and sail them to remote locations and donate them to clinics."

"You could apply for status as a charitable organization," Pilgrim said with a grin. "Maybe get hired by the State Department as a good will ambassador."

"Dan has a very good idea, dad; then we might know where you are exactly. I wouldn't worry so much."

"Dan should come with me if he's so worried. You both should."

The reporter glanced at the assassin's daughter. He had never been to sea although he lived almost his entire life right next to the water. Pilgrim considered the remark, searching the face of the old man to see if he spoke in jest or seriously. The leprechaun's grin again contrasted with the look of confusion he saw on the face of Joyce. Her glance fell to a chart and she lifted an edge.

"Punta: Does that means port or point in Spanish?" she asked.

Jeremiah fastened his eyes on the face of his young friend--the former Pulitzer Prize-nominated reporter—before turning to his daughter. Then he gently explained.

"It means a point we reach where we need to choose one side or the other. We sail by charts and navigation, careful not to get in danger but if we do, we rely on God, a good ship and true friends to get us safely through."

The smile on Joyce's face and the serious way she studied the chart indicated she had made her decision. For Pilgrim the choice was easy, he realized it had been made for him months ago. You chart your life by the daily decisions you make, by the moral bulwarks you choose to defend or surrender, whether the choice seems right or wrong in retrospect hardly matters at the moment.

Jimmy "Jeremiah" Virden would be dead in a month but none of them knew that now, nor would it have changed their decision. The freedom of the ocean beckoned and the burdens and bondage of land were about to be left behind.

Afterword

Forty years ago they killed Kennedy. Now one of them finally talks. Much of the story you have just read is true. The historical record verifies most if not all of what Jimmy Jeremiah has to say. Indeed, the confessed assassin, "Jeremiah," is himself based on an actual person of about the same age, 65, who contacted me after two of my JFK-related columns appeared on the internet. He had read both of them--*A Return To The Scene of The Crime* and *Nightmare On Elm/ Dark Day In Dealey*--and wanted to add to my limited knowledge. Jeremiah claimed to have once worked with the CIA and referred to himself by a similar cryptonym to the one I've given him in the book. His role was not so pivotal as that of my character but his knowledge appeared acute, repeatedly requesting that I look up information on the Internet to verify whatever claim he made that I may have found incredible. Like myself, he also lived here in Florida, in the rundown area of Lake Worth that I described in the novel. I met him on a few occasions and found him friendly in paranoid way. Whether or not his "confession" was true or a complete fabrication, I cannot say. Like the anti-hero of this book, the fellow who inspired "Jeremiah" is dead, as are so many of the other pivotal players of the assassination.

Many of the books written in the last forty years about the JFK assassination were mentioned in *The Guns of Dallas*. Among the best are *Farewell America*, by James Hepburn, the complete text available on the internet (after being banned for several years in the US), and *Rush To Judgment*, by attorney Mark Lane. This was the first widely read book to refute the Warren Commission Report. The following year, William Manchester's *Death of A President* topped the best selling list for non-fiction and appeared to refute the conspiracy theorists. Since then, however, a wide range of dissenting opinion has appeared. Indeed, Jean Hill wrote *The Last Dissenting Witness*, her autobiographical revelation of how the FBI hierarchy handles an uncooperative witness. CIA liaison, Colonel Fletcher Prouty sought to understand who benefited most by the removal of JFK from office with his highly recommended book, *JFK: The CIA, Vietnam and The Plot to Assassinate John F. Kennedy*. Josiah Thompson wrote *Six Seconds in Dallas*, also an excellent critique, and even a former US Marine sniper, Craig Roberts, penned a criticism of the official government report with his *Kill Zone: A Sniper Looks at Dealey Plaza*.

The most recent blockbuster, *Case Closed*, by Gerald Posner, written in support of the WC findings, appeared immediately after the immensely popular movie, *"JFK,"* itself based on the book, *On The Trail of The Assassins*, by District Attorney, Jim Garrison and *Crossfire*, by Jim Marrs. And of course, there is Seymour Hersh's revelatory *The Dark Side of Camelot*, and Sylvia Meagher's difficult to find, *Accessories After The Fact*. Incidentally, the timeline mentioned by Jimmy Jeremiah, of the APB radio announcements, at 12:45, 12:48 and 12:55 PM by the Dallas police, for a suspect fitting Lee Harvey Oswald's description, just fifteen minutes after shots were fired and long before the rifle was found on the sixth floor (allegedly belonging to Oswald), was excerpted from the condensed Warren Commission Report published by the New York Times in 1964. Rush to judgment indeed.

About The Author

Freelance reporter, Douglas Herman, has been published in a wide variety of periodicals, large and small, from National Fisherman to The Washington Post, from the Kodiak Daily Mirror to Al Jazeerah. As a regular writer for www.strike-the-root.com, his Internet essays explore topics too sensitive or sensational for the mainstream media to handle. Born in Howell, Michigan, he served the USAF in Texas. Presently he divides his time between Kodiak, Alaska and the Banana Republic of South Florida.

Printed in the United States
84447LV00002B/213/A